CRIMEUCOPIA

A LOAD OF BALLS

A Murderous Ink Press Anthology

✶✶✶✶✶✶✶✶✶✶✶✶✶✶✶✶✶✶✶✶✶✶✶✶✶✶✶✶✶✶

CRIMEUCOPIA
A LOAD OF BALLS

First published by Murderous Ink Press
Crowland, LINCOLNSHIRE, England
www.murderousinkpress.co.uk
Editorial Copyright © Murderous Ink Press 2025
Cover treatment and lettering © Willie Chob-Chob 2025
All rights are retained by the respective authors & artists on publication
Paperback Edition ISBN: 9781909498686
eBook Edition ISBN: 9781909498693

The rights of the named individuals to be identified as the authors of these works has been asserted in accordance with section 77 and 78 of the Copyright, Designs and Patents Act, 1988

All rights reserved. No part of this publication may be reproduced, stored in or introduced into a retrieval system, or transmitted in any form, or by any means (electronic, mechanical, photocopying or otherwise) without the prior written permission of both the author(s) and the publisher. Any person who does any unauthorised act in relation to this publication may be liable to criminal prosecution and civil claims for damages.

Every effort has been made to obtain the necessary permissions with reference to copyright material, both illustrative and quoted. We apologise for any omissions in this respect and will be pleased to make the appropriate acknowledgements in further editions.

No generative artificial intelligence (AI) was used in any aspect of the creation of this work. Without in any way limiting the author's [and publisher's] exclusive rights under copyright, any use of this publication to "train" generative artificial intelligence (AI) technologies to generate text is expressly prohibited. The author (and publisher) reserves all rights to license uses of this work for generative AI training and development of machine learning language models.

This book and its contents are works of fiction. Names, characters, places and incidents are either a product of the authors' imagination or are used fictitiously. Any resemblance to actual people living or dead, events, locations and/or their contents, is entirely coincidental.

Acknowledgements

To those writers and artists who helped make this anthology what it is, I can only say a heartfelt Thank You!

And to Den, as always.

Contents

A Short Third Leg on the Square…	vii
The Purple Figurine Murders — Arthur Vidro	1
Thank God for the Nineteenth Hole — Dave Dempster	13
Nothing Personal — Diana Parrilla	19
Rules of the Game — John M. Floyd	33
Death in the Dugout — Jesse Aaron	39
Rochwal's Blue Balls — John B. Elliott	59
Side Pocket Bank Shot — William Kitcher	73
Never Bet Against Death — J. F. Benedetto	81
You May Already Be a Winner — Nikki Knight	105
Major League Collectibles — Mark James McDonough	117
The Baby Lawyer — Paul R. Paradise	125
The Perfect Game — Robert Petyo	133
Dust in the Field — S. B. Watson	139
Be Careful What You Wish For — Wendy Harrison	159
The Center is Your Friend — Kai Lovelace	171
Golf Widow — Diane A. Hadac	185
Par None — Wil A. Emerson	193
Fancy Car Lover — Ed Teja	201
Ballbreaker — Harris Coverley	221
The Usual Unusual Suspects	237

TNC

The Next Chapter Presents...

Poetry, Fiction & Creative Nonfiction Night

7:00pm ~ 8:30pm in The Back Room

Looking for a spot to share your writing with an audience? Join The Next Chapter for our monthly poetry, fiction & creative nonfiction night! There will be a few writers reading their work aloud each night.

Work read aloud will be limited to 7 minutes per reader except for that night's featured reader who will have 15 minutes. Please keep that in mind when curating your submission!

Each session will be hosted on the last Wednesday of every month. Mark your calendars!

Interested in joining? We are looking for new writers to present their work.

Please note that filling out the application does not guarantee a spot as a presenter, but you can always re-apply!

Those accepted will be notified and subsequently asked to submit an author bio and the work they plan to read.

204 New York Avenue Huntington, NY 11743 ~ (631) 482-5008
thenextchapterli.com ~ info@thenextchapterli.com
Follow us on Instagram at @thenextchapterli

A Short Third Leg on the Square...
(An Editorial of Sorts)

Play Ball! Or, in this case, Balls. When we put the call out we didn't expect so many to step up to the plate. And while none (that we know of, that is) have previously appeared in any swimsuit edition of a particular Sports magazine, the 19 players here all have tales designed to serve you a slurve of a plotline, with clues as devious as a full-on wormburner from a regular swinging pin-seeker.

So, while Casey works out which end of the bat is which, we let *Arthur Vidro* punt the pigskin, and kick off this collection with *The Purple Figurine Murders*.

Meanwhile, tee-ing one straight down the fairway, *Dave Dempster* explains why we should *Thank God for the Nineteenth Hole*, before *Diana Parrilla* lets us know that there's more to basketball than just shooting hoops, although she assures us it's *Nothing Personal*.

John M. Floyd shows why we should all know the *Rules of the Game*, before *Jesse Aaron* explains to the Umpire why there's been a *Death in the Dugout*.

And from baseballs to *Rochwal's Blue Balls* as *John B. Elliott* boots a story that is guaranteed to soccer you in with its ingenuity.

Nearby in a local bar, *William Kitcher* racks 'em up and demonstrates a neat *Side Pocket Bank Shot*, without sending the cue ball totally off the rails — and *J. F. Benedetto* leads us into the half time break by offering up some sound advice in regard to the game of *Ts'u-chü* in that you should *Never Bet Against Death*.

During the interval, while you indulge in beer and snacks—*Nikki Knight* suggests that Lottery balls may offer up a better result than laying off a side bet, and who knows—*You May Already Be a Winner*....

Proving that you cannot make an omelette without using yeggs, *Mark James McDonough* explains how you can 'acquire' some of the best *Major League Collectables*, before *Paul R. Paradise* lets us know just how lucrative counterfeit basketball merchandise can be. Luckily *The Baby Lawyer* is on hand to sort things out by slam dunking the perpetrators.

Meanwhile in the bowling alley, *Robert Petyo* sets us up for *The Perfect Game*—though he assures us that no Turkeys, Badgers or Sparrows were harmed in the process.

And as the departing marching band's sousaphonic notes echo into silence, *S. B. Watson* lets us know just how dry it can get, by mentioning that there's *Dust in the Field*, while *Wendy Harrison* takes us over to Track & Field country—though as she says, you need to *Be Careful What You Wish For*.

Kai Lovelace counters that, in the pool hall of Life, *The Center is Your Friend*, before we head back to the golf course, as we let *Diane A. Hadac* tell you about a *Golf Widow*, and *Wil A. Emerson* assure us that no turtles were armed in the writing of her *Par None*.

Ed Teja supplies the transport via his *Fancy Car Lover*, and we finally pull up to *Harris Coverley*, back here in good old Blighty, who not only racks and stacks, but lets us know that his *Ballbreaker* has never had an albino in the subway since he started taking the game seriously…

So, as with all of these anthologies, we hope you find something that you can immediately roll with, as well as something that takes you over your Mid-Court Line, and slam dunks you into a completely new No Charge Zone.

Because, in the home team locker room spirit of our *Murderous Ink Press* motto:

You never know what you like until you make a play for it.

The Purple Figurine Murders
Arthur Vidro

The man in the bed stared at me stupidly, perhaps because of blurred vision, constant headaches, and senses dulled by painkillers.

"We've got you dead to rights," I advised him. "You are the Purple Figurine Murderer. You are in a hospital but whenever you are well enough we will take you to headquarters for processing and arraignment. I am here to take your statement." I didn't tell him the doctors doubted he would leave the hospital alive. I advised him of his rights.

Eschewing a lawyer's presence, he agreed to talk. His voice was a frequently broken whisper.

"Sure…got me. I'm the one. Who are you…how did you…figure it out?"

I thought back to the start of the case…

* * *

The first killing hadn't aroused much public interest. A seventy-year-old black woman who used a cane had been stabbed to death in an alley. Because her handbag was taken, we assumed it was a robbery that turned violent. But later we learned her bag had been lifted after the fact by a pair of winos. The murder weapon was not recovered. Beside the victim was a thumb-sized piece of purple plastic that resembled an astronaut. Whether it was normal alley debris, or something dropped by the victim or killer, we didn't know. So much for the death of Ms. Jamie Marshall.

A fortnight later in his one-bedroom apartment, the next victim surprised an intruder. This tenant was sixty years old and built like a bulldog. We figured he made the mistake of tackling the intruder instead of calling for help. Perhaps the victim, a chap named Winston Troy, would have won the fight if it had been fair. But the knife made the fight unfair. The killer claimed his second victim. Beside the corpse was a piece of purple plastic resembling a soldier.

The coroner alerted us to the similarity of wounds in the two victims. It was likely they had been killed by the same weapon.

Would he strike a third time? If so, where? Minneapolis is a big city. The two victims didn't seem to have anything in common. One black, one white. Lived in different neighborhoods. Different ages. Different heights. Different genders. Different everything.

But the brightest detective on my force, Trudi Harrov, saw a possible pattern.

"They were both killed on Tuesdays," she said. "Maybe the next one will be on a Tuesday too. Also, Victim One was seventy years old, Victim Two was sixty. So it could be the next victim will be fifty."

I shook my head. "I can't tell the public that all fifty-year-olds should stay locked in at home every Tuesday. We don't have enough information to act. Let's focus on the plastic figurines."

Ten days later Harrov's hypothesis was disproved. The third killing took place on a Friday, and the victim's age was seventy-three. Early that morning, retrieving a newspaper from outside her secluded side door, Veronica Rayy was stabbed. Clad in a bathrobe and slippers and without makeup, she had stepped out, coffee cup in hand. Beside her body we found the broken cup with a few drops of coffee still inside. Next to the cup was a rubber band, which probably had held the newspaper together. Now the pages of print littered the lawn.

She had stepped outside without locking up, but the house had not been disturbed. No attempt at burglary or sexual assault.

Neighbors, who hadn't heard anything, said yes, this was Ronnie's usual way to bring in the paper. And Ronnie never wore jewelry for that task, so nothing of value could have been stolen off the body. At first we didn't think this killing was connected with the prior two. Until a gust of wind shoved a sheet of newspaper, revealing underneath a lump of purple plastic shaped like a pirate.

Harrov and I and the others kept trying to find a common denominator among the victims. They were all listed in the phone book, but so was the vast majority of the city's residents. They were all adults. They were all registered voters. They all had driver's licenses. They all lived alone. But they didn't seem to have any common friends or enemies or activities. They didn't frequent the same restaurants. They didn't use the same dry cleaner or laundromat. They didn't share a common bank or pharmacy. They attended different churches. Chats with friends elicited that they didn't even watch the same television shows.

We didn't have a line on the plastic figurines. No marking to indicate place of manufacture or sale. Typical cheap plastic, like what comes from the overseas factories every day.

Harrov tried to tie the victims' backgrounds to the purple figurines. Yes, it was true Mr. Troy had been a soldier in the army. But Ms. Marshall had no connection, past or present, to NASA or any other space program. As for Ms. Rayy, Ronnie—that's what her neighbors and friends called her—had clearly never been a pirate.

Harrov discovered another point in common. All three victims shared the same Zip Code. Was that the link? "Maybe," she said, eyes sparkling, "the victims all have post office boxes! Better yet, in numerical order! No wonder we couldn't connect them!" We visited the post office branch and learned Winston Troy had rented a box. But neither of the other victims had one.

"Back to the drawing board," Harrov sighed.

By now the coroner's office had confirmed the same knife—likely a large switchblade—had been used in all three murders.

While we waited for another victim to surface, we checked with the Board of Elections. The victims included one Democrat, one Republican, and one member of the Green Party.

I asked Harrov to focus her team on the figurines themselves. They made the rounds, in case the trinkets had been sold locally, but nobody stocked purple figurines.

The fourth killing shocked us, and outraged the public. A diminutive fourteen-year-old known to her family as Little Frieda (her mom was Big Frieda) had been stabbed on a quiet trail in Kenwood Park. Her body was discovered by joggers. Beside the body was a bicycle confirmed by the Cox family as Frieda's. Leaning against a tire was a purple figurine that, but for its color, resembled the Jolly Green Giant.

I had Harrov drive to Faribault County, where a fifty-five-foot statue of the giant stands in the small city of Blue Earth. "Maybe," I said, "there's a tourist trap there that sells Green Giant figurines."

That, too, was a dead end. "No purple figurines in Blue Earth," she reported. "One Green Giant expert studied my photo of the figurine and said it's not even the real Jolly Green Giant. He suggested it's some Titan from Greek mythology. Maybe Prometheus or Atlas." She sat down dejectedly. "We're spinning our wheels. The Green Giant was too far-fetched a solution. The figurine wasn't even green. And if it ever was green, now it's purple."

"Say that again," I told her, as a glimmer of an idea came to me.

"If the figurine was ever green, now it's purple. What's the big deal?"

I told Harrov to explore the figurines again, this time examining them to see if they had been created purple or painted purple.

The next day another victim turned up. Edwina White, age sixty-two, a church leader and youth counselor, was found on her front doorstep amid a heap of groceries spilling out of cloth bags. She had apparently done some nighttime shopping. A receipt in one of the bags showed a checkout time stamp of 9:26 p.m. Her porch light was not on, though it worked just fine when we tried it.

"She must have gone out during daylight," I told Harrov, "not turned on the porch light, then when she returned and fumbled with her keys the killer got her. Plenty of bushes in the dark he could have hid behind."

Harrov wasn't so sure. "Maybe the killer—and we don't know for certain it's a man—followed her when she drove home from the supermarket."

"Not likely," I said. "Too easy to be spotted by the victim in her rear-view mirror."

The body hadn't been found until morning. Beside the body was the victim's house keys. There was no evidence the killer had been inside. Also, amid a splatter of broken eggs, was a purple plastic figurine. This one was a construction worker wearing a hard hat. Mrs. White, a widow, lived alone in the Dinkytown section and had a slightly different Zip Code than the previous victims.

Other than all living in the same city, the victims seemed to share only one tenuous connection: they were all Christians. But so was the overwhelming majority of Americans.

The press would have raked us over the coals, except they didn't know the killings were connected. We kept secret the purple figurines and the shared weapon. Still, with homicides up, we were feeling heat, serial killer or not.

The next day we got our first break. Harrov came running into my office from the police lab. "The figurines were all painted purple!" she trilled.

"There's an awful lot of paint sellers in the county," I said. "You'll have to check them all out. It might not be easy but –"

"But it's easier than you think," said Harrov. "The purple came from spray paint. That will make it easier to track." She hustled away to oversee the spray-can tracking.

I wasn't sure this would pan out. The painting could have been done anywhere and anytime. I kept trying to find a connection among the victims.

Two days later another killing. Hildy Walgenberg, age fifty-eight, had been quietly pruning some bushes in her walled-in garden when the killer struck. Beside the pruning shears was a purple plastic figurine. This one wore a mortarboard and gripped a diploma. The victim was a psychiatrist with no known connection to the other victims. Had one of her patients gone over the edge? Another angle to explore. Another dead end.

Harrov reported in. Her team had made the rounds throughout the county and were following up all sales of purple spray paint. Purple was not a popular color for spray paint. Most purchasers were unknown to the sales staff and proprietors, but payment records existed. Still, a few customers had paid cash and would not be traceable. So far, the purchasers who could be traced all had alibis for one or more of the killings.

For the umpteenth time I stared at my typed list of the victims:

Ms. Jamie Marshall, age 70

Mr. Winston Troy, age 60

Ms. Veronica "Ronnie" Rayy, age 73

Frieda Cox, age 14

Mrs. Edwina White, age 62

Dr. Hildy Walgenberg, age 58

By now we had learned the Walgenberg woman was Jewish. So not even Christianity linked the victims.

We were still stumped.

And then Roberta Bryant cracked the case for us.

A skinny co-ed, Roberta Bryant was attending the University of Minnesota on a track scholarship. In the words of her coach, "She's built for distance running." Every morning before dawn she went for a five-mile run through her neighborhood and the surrounding communities, the same route every day. Usually the streets were empty at that hour. But this time a killer had been lying in wait. We found a bunch of cigarette butts the killer had smoked inside a bus stop shelter on Marquette Avenue, where he had waited for his intended victim.

According to Bryant, as she approached the bus stop he had jumped out and blocked her way. At first she hadn't seen the knife—the sunrise had barely begun—but she saw the man and effortlessly detoured around him. As she did, she glimpsed the knife and kicked into a faster pace.

That's when the killer made his mistake. He gave chase.

Drew Glud was fifty-nine, a smoker, and not in great shape. Bryant was twenty, a running specialist, and an athlete in her prime. She had no trouble outpacing the middle-aged man and frequently looked behind her to check on the distance between them.

Then Glud collapsed. His head rammed the cement as he landed. He lay there motionless, an open switchblade knife beside him.

Bryant cautiously approached to check on him. She didn't get too close, in case it was a ruse. But Glud remained motionless and gasped like an asthmatic. Blood spread from his head.

Bryant trotted around him, ready to sprint away if the man stirred. But he didn't. She was wearing a pouch that contained her keys, some emergency money, and a flip phone. She called the police. We summoned the ambulance.

Glud was in the hospital before we got to question him. There was never any doubt as to his identity. The wallet in his pocket contained a photo driver's license, two credit cards, and a library card, all in his name. Surprisingly, he toted a pocket book of anagram puzzles in his jacket pocket. A separate pocket held an open pack of cigarettes, same brand as the butts at the bus stop. Plus a thumb-sized plastic figurine of a purple ballerina.

The coroner would later confirm the large knife found beside the body fit all the stab wounds in the victims. We had the murder weapon and the murderer.

But no motive.

Harrov and her team visited the culprit's house and found much incriminating evidence, including a stash of purple plastic figurines. There was one—and only one—can of spray paint in his garage. The color? Purple.

Meantime, I stayed in the hospital room waiting for a chance to question Glud.

The doctors cautioned me they doubted he would live. The fall had badly damaged his skull, there was internal bleeding building in pressure, plus a broken wrist and some cracked ribs. They did their best to relieve the blood build-up in his cranial cavities, but he was so far gone they didn't bother to put a plaster cast on his wrist; they just put a temporary splint over the area.

And now that he was conscious, he had confessed, followed by his question:

"Who are you … how did you … figure it out?"

This stumped me. We hadn't figured anything out. We had gotten lucky. "My name is Harold Grant," I told him, "and I'm in charge of the police investigation."

The man stiffened, which caused him to wince, but he stared at me, startled. "Coincidence! Or … that how you solved it? Wanted … nail you, too."

I had no idea what he was talking about.

"We would like to know," I said, "why you turned killer."

He closed his eyes. His voice got so faint, I had to lean close in to make out the words. "Whole life wanted … win big one. If they were … league champions … even once … wouldn't have … done it. Guess something … snapped. Got idea at drugstore … Cox girl's father … picked up … medicine for daughter … heard her name … decided go after … namesakes … you would have … cracked case easily … if went after real ones … sometimes had to … play name games … no wonder took … cop with your name … to figure … it out. Just regret … didn't get … all eleven …"

And then his head tilted over. I called the doctors but Glud was dead.

It's good to get a confession (even one unsigned), and great to be spared a trial. But I sat there, only half-satisfied. Too much mystery remained. And no more information was forthcoming, at least not from the killer.

Idly I pulled out my list of the victims and studied it for the umpteenth time. So, there were eleven intended victims, with nothing in common, except somehow they were namesakes.

Still stumped, I returned to headquarters.

I was sitting at my desk in a funk when Harrov came in.

"Case solved," she said, trying to sound merry. "Beyond the knife and the paint and the figurines, we just uncovered a list hidden in a dictionary in Glud's house. It's a list of all the victims he killed, or at least people with similar names, plus a few others he probably was planning to kill. The dead ones have check marks next to them. I brought the list to show you. Why so glum?"

"Because," I growled, "until I understand why these victims were chosen, I'll never consider the case solved. Over, yes, but not solved."

"Yeah," she said, "and we still have to figure out why he bothered with all those plastic purple people."

I sprang forward in my seat. "What! What! Say that again!"

"I said we haven't figured out the reason behind those toy purple people."

"That's it, Harrov! You're a genius!"

She smiled complacently. "Yes, I even belong to Mensa. But what's the importance of what I said?"

"We were always calling them purple figurines, but now you called them people! Not figurines, but people!" I beamed. "That was the key!"

She didn't understand. "Figurines, people, baubles, tchotchkes, what's the difference?"

"All the difference in the world. Hold on to that list. Don't let me see it yet."

I tore a sheet of paper from my notebook and scribbled hastily. When I had finished, I gave it to Harrov. "Does this resemble the list you found in Glud's house?"

She stared in surprise. "Why, yes. How on earth—"

"You're too young to remember," I told her. "But in 1969, 1973, 1974, and 1976 the Viking teams were so good they reached the Super Bowl each following January. And lost all four. Glud was killing people with names similar to the eleven players who were on all four of those teams. He even chose people with ages matching the corresponding uniform numbers. If Bobby Bryant had worn number 47 instead of 20, then whoever Glud chose instead of Roberta would have been forty-seven and possibly wouldn't have evaded him. And we'd still be in the dark."

The list I had handed Harrov was:
Bobby Bryant, cornerback, #20
Fred Cox, kicker, #14
Carl Eller, defensive end, #81
Wally Hilgenberg, linebacker, #58
Paul Krause, safety, #22
Jim Marshall, defensive end, #70
Alan Page, defensive tackle, #88
Mick Tingelhoff, center, #53
Ed White, guard, #62
Roy Winston, linebacker, #60
Ron Yary, tackle, #73

"But why the purple figurines?" she asked.

"The Viking defense was known as The Purple People Eaters. That's why the purple people figurines. Only thing I can't understand is Glud's excitement at hearing my name. Oh, well. If that's the only piece of the puzzle we can't solve, that's not so bad. But it's too bad I couldn't talk to Glud before the killings. They wouldn't have been necessary. I would have explained the Vikes did win the NFL championship—in 1969. They lost in that Super Bowl to the Chiefs, who were champions of the then-rival AFL. While nowadays an NFL championship is equated with a Super Bowl win, it wasn't so for the first four Bowls. But that 1969 Vikings team were the NFL champs. Everyone should have been proud."

Meanwhile, a gleam had entered Harrov's eyes. "Your list," she proclaimed, "contains eleven names. But the list we found in Glud's home has twelve names. When you see the twelfth, you will fully understand."

She handed me the list, in protective and tagged plastic, that had been found in Glud's house.

I eagerly read the list.

The one name I hadn't thought of was there, and it explained the last loose end:

Harold "Bud" Grant, head coach

Thank God for the Nineteenth Hole
Dave Dempster

"Come back, Rufus." He regretted letting him off the lead. When he caught up, the dog had disappeared behind a bush, doing what dogs do, he thought. But with no sign of Rufus a few shouts later, patience was running out. The retired widower enjoyed these early morning walks, especially on a crisp February day, but enough was enough. He was about to grab the mischievous pet when Rufus barked, oddly. He looked closer and saw. Stepping back, and gasping, he reached for his mobile.

The call came in. Another murder. Another chance to redeem himself. Decades earlier, and hardly into his stride, a youthful DS Jim Cooper was really going places in the Norfolk Constabulary. Very promising. Promotion assured. Widely seen as going as far as the dizzy height of Detective Superintendent or perhaps even Assistant Chief Constable. And entrusted with an interview some of his older colleagues would have given an arm and a leg for. A drunken patron in a Norwich pub had been hospitalised after a severe beating. The biker gang thought they had disabled all the security cameras before the police arrived but they had missed one. Footage of the gang leader holding a baseball bat was just what every detective dreamt of.

The gang leader was arrogant enough to start the interview minus the protection of his usual lawyer. He vehemently denied involvement, again and again. He even swore on his mother's grave that he knew nothing of a baseball bat that night. At last, one of Norfolk's biggest drug dealers had no way out. Just end the interview and it's all over.

When the fish is on the line, don't try for more. It's a risk that even experienced cross-examining lawyers can be tempted to take. Perhaps it was over-confidence or merely inexperience. Jim just couldn't stop himself from asking that one last question. "I have footage of you with a baseball bat…" The notion of drug dealers being as thick as two planks is mistaken. The defusing recovery came in a flash, interrupting the questioner. "Oh, yeah. I picked up the bat. Didn't want any scrap to get out of hand, mate."

What a blunder. As it turned out, the police had over-estimated their chances in any event. The pub had been crowded but, perhaps unsurprisingly, no-one saw anything of the 'scrap'. Even the drunk's friends were too frightened to speak up. The Crown Prosecution Service, never a favourite with detectives, considered in their wisdom that there was not enough evidence to pursue any charge at all.

Jim bore the brunt. It turned out to be the end of a promising career. As the years went by Jim's early promise slowly and painfully ebbed away. He had long since accepted that he would never be more than a mere sergeant. They say time heals, but the pain didn't leave completely. Only eight years earlier, Jim's wife had left him for another man. The stressful life of a detective is hardly conducive to marital bliss. Jim had managed to fight his way through the awful divorce jungle and emerge almost intact emotionally. Yet it was that interview debacle from all those years earlier which still haunted him.

Approaching retirement, he longed more than anything for an opportunity to correct the stain on his record. The chance to make amends, to show that, when all was said and done, he was a worthy team member. Some luck would be involved, he knew, but was that too much to ask?

In walked the boss, and the chattering stopped at once. DCI John Sutton was respected but at the same time junior officers were careful not to cross him. "Sorry to call you all in on a Saturday. The pathologist gives the time of death as between seven and nine last night. The body was found in an unusual position. In a mangled heap, really. Rigor mortis had set in but" There was a pause as the boss picked up a postmortem photo from the table beside him. "This shows that some body parts defied gravity. The left arm is the best example, here. See how the left hand sticks up in the air. Which means the man was killed elsewhere. It also means that he was kept in some sort of bag or bundled in some way, before he was dumped here, between two and four this morning."

The boss tapped his fingers on an area map on the whiteboard behind him.

"Two stab wounds into the back did the damage. Both were life-threatening, so this bastard really wanted to kill. There was no sign of a struggle. Seems likely the victim was taken by surprise. It's reasonable to conclude that he knew his attacker. Nothing on the body, so no ID yet, I'm afraid. First things first. Who is the deceased? A well-dressed man in his late forties. Expensive suit and shoes. Bound to be missed quickly. We'll put the word out in the usual ways."

"The second most urgent task is to track down any CCTV and sightings of any vehicle in the vicinity of Muck Lane between 2 and 4 this morning. I know it's isolated but cast the net as far as you need to. There are a few small businesses off Wroxham Road and the same at the other end, near Salhouse Station. If there are no questions, let's reconvene at two."

"Afternoon", began the boss. "We have identified the deceased as Norman O'Sullivan, the jeweller. The media will be all over this. For heaven's sake, don't let out even a whisper. His wife reported him missing this morning. Said he went out last night to a meeting at 7.30 and didn't come home, but I'll let Luke tell you the rest."

DS Luke Taylor explained. "Yes, boss. May be nothing. Grief affects people differently, of course. She claimed she never asks about his business dealings. Didn't quite ring true. She's very attractive and about twenty years younger than the deceased, if you get my drift." A few chuckles went round.

"Thanks, Luke. This is unlikely to have been a robbery gone wrong, because robbers don't usually kill first, and then go to lengths to hide the body, but, as always, we'll keep an open mind. The area around Muck Lane is so remote it's unlikely we'll ever get a lead on the vehicle but thanks for your efforts so far and keep your ears to the ground. We need to focus now on motive. His whole estate goes to his widow, as sole survivor. We need to find out everything about the man and his jewellery business."

Thank God for the Nineteenth Hole

On Monday's lunch break Jim took the short stroll from the office along cobbled streets to The Plough in St. Benedict's Street. Not his favourite pub but he knew who would be there. And there he was, in the beer garden at the rear. A man who had had a hard life, obviously, who had given up on his appearance and who had reached an age where he lived only for quiet and simple pleasures. Jim had a natural empathy, as his own career had hardly met his aspirations.

"Hi, Fred". Fred had been half asleep. "Oh, Jim. How's it going?" They had known each other for as long as Jim could remember. Circumstances had forced Fred a very long time ago into a life of petty crime. He was neither clever nor brutal enough to climb the criminal ladder but he knew everything worth knowing about the dark underbelly of Norwich. Over the years Fred had been helpful.

"Another?" Jim hardly waited for a response. It would be unthinkable for Fred to refuse a free beer.

Hearty thanks when Jim returned with the next round. "How's tricks?"

Usually, Fred would give a long list of his troubles and ailments, but he came across as more cheerful. Jim had to be patient to keep on the right side of his source. That hadn't been easy at times. "Did you hear about that jeweller up Salhouse way?"

"Yeah, bad business". Fred didn't miss much, not that sort of business anyway. Jim slipped a twenty-pound note across the table. No-one was any the wiser. Jim expected the money would go straight down Fred's throat but this was mutual benefit. No question of judgement. "Word is, she's been sleeping around."

"The wife?"

"Yep" A gentle slap on the back concluded the meeting.

DS Ewan Hall got in first at that afternoon's briefing. "A witness at the jewellers saw the wife in what looked like a romantic hug with one of the directors, Matt Johnson. She said she could be wrong, but they seemed far too close. She also noticed the way they look at each other." Beaten to the draw, Jim was dejected but stopped himself from swearing out loud. He offered his two cents' worth. "My source says the wife's been sleeping around." "Thanks, lads. We'll watch this Matt Johnson carefully in the meantime, but I think we should re-interview the Missus first."

Matt Johnson, Matt Johnson, Matt Johnson…. Jim just couldn't place the name. He'd definitely heard it before but where? It really bothered him. He forgot about it, but it kept coming back.

Then on Monday night Jim was watching tv and finishing a beer when he suddenly thought he had it, but then he hadn't. Memories are strange things. Finally, it came to him late that night.

The next morning the barman at his local golf club had an amusing story to tell. "He's an arrogant prick, frankly, but there was a good laugh on Saturday. He's been going on and on about this fancy golf bag rain cover he got from America. Big black plastic contraption. Fits over trolley and clubs, with a flap for access. Kept boasting about it. But on Saturday he forgot his treasured accessory. It pelted down on the last few holes and his mates were in stitches. He didn't take it well, but boy he asked for it." The barman enjoyed the laugh again.

This was Jim's eureka moment, and he really felt it when it hit him. He hurried to his laptop in the car. There it was! Advertised, as the barman had described. When he saw the size of the rain cover Jim knew he was on the right track. Next came a search for cleaners close to Johnson's address in Sprowston.

The first was a waste of time but the second was the break Jim had longed for, *if* his hunch was correct.

"A peculiar request? You bet", replied the Launderette manager. "The guy wanted the *inside* of the thing steam cleaned. I'd to tell him a few times that the soft plastic would be damaged, before he agreed to a normal wash. I had to do a separate run, but he was happy to pay extra. It's at the head of the queue now."

The manager turned his booking page to reveal *the* name and address. In his excitement Jim nearly forgot to photograph the entry on his mobile. The co-operative manager retrieved the large rain cover and set aside the item.

Jim phoned the boss, who did not need much persuading. They had a warrant within hours, the item was rushed to Forensics in Wymondham, and then word was awaited.

There was helpful news. Under pressure, the wife had dissolved in tears and admitted the affair. She was now claiming that the two lovebirds were making merry after the deceased left home, thereby giving both suspects the same alibi.

The deceased's blood and DNA were recovered from the golf bag cover. When faced with the evidence, the wife had little choice but to give a third version—Johnson told her he would only threaten her husband. However suspicious the latest version was, it would probably be enough to save her. On the other hand, Johnson, the real killer, was beyond hope.

Always supportive of teamwork, the boss seldom praises individuals. However, at the end of this investigation he went out of his way to single out Jim for congratulation. Loud applause from the team broke out. Jim was delighted. They didn't know how delighted Jim was.

Nothing Personal
Diana Parrilla

Nicholas paced in front of the line of men, arms crossed behind his back. "I want to see those killer looks, fixed on the hoop, on the basket, and nothing else, dammit!" He stopped abruptly in front of one of the players. "You got that, Serge?"

"Yes, sir," the man replied, eyes skyward, trying not to meet Nicholas's piercing blue gaze.

"I want you to grab that basketball and weigh it in your hands. Feel its heft. Imagine it's a human head, with its fine hairs and rough pores. I want you to sense that fragility and ignore it. Focus only on the hoop, on that ball slicing through it like a knife sinking into the sweet spot of a man's chest."

Nicholas reversed direction, covering the whole lineup. "You following me, Ronny?" he barked, his voice rising as he planted himself in front of the player.

No one knew who would be the unlucky recipient of the spittle flying from his mouth as he spoke with such intensity. Unintentional, they assumed, though with Nicholas's temperament, no one could be sure.

"At my signal, you'll start training. If you do it right—and that remains to be seen—you'll gain precision, hand-eye-mind coordination, reflexes, reaction time, and the cool to perform under pressure."

He positioned himself before them, pulling an oddly perforated pipe with holes on top, like a flute, from the pocket of his black sweatpants with vertical blue stripes that made him look even taller. He put the pipe to his thin lips and blew, producing a shrill sound that signaled the start of training.

The boys broke ranks and scattered. Nicholas's watchful eye never left them, pipe still clenched between his teeth.

"We need to fill Mitch's spot, and I'm only keeping the best. So you'd better sink as many baskets as you can, or you'll be discarded and crushed like skulls on the pavement," he said, his voice too high-pitched for the menacing tone he affected.

The boys were shooting hoops, each with their own ball, trying not to lose focus. But it wasn't easy with Nicholas running his mouth. No, it wasn't coincidence he chose this precise moment to lay it on them. He was testing their nerves of steel, seeing if they had the right stuff.

"Mitch, what a great man, right? Wrong. He bit the dust, and that's a clear sign of his weakness, his incompetence. We're all mortal, you're thinking. Sure, but some more than others. Dying on the job isn't a badge of honor, it's a disgrace. That's why no one from my team's going to his funeral. His soul deserves to be haunted until it learns to be strong, down in hell where it belongs. If we can't hack it here on Earth, what can we expect from the great beyond? To be eaten alive, like Mitch."

Nicholas kept ranting as he weaved between the boys, eyeing their finesse with the ball. "How did Mitch buy it? I'll sum it up: He failed. Got cocky, underestimated his mark. Rookie mistake, my little ones. Doesn't matter if it's a tatted-up mobster with tattoos even on the wings of his nose or a 93-year-old granny with a cat and a parakeet."

He tapped the back of one of the men who couldn't sink a shot to save his life. "Nothing personal, but get out and don't show your face around here again, got it?" His killer instinct was palpable as he stared the poor sap down.

"Y-yes, sir," the guy stammered, scurrying out of the room, his sneakers squeaking against the slick floor.

"As I was saying," Nicholas continued, removing the pipe from his mouth and raising it in the air, his fresh drool dripping towards the synthetic floor. "Mitch had a clear job: take out a dangerous rebel, Fabiana Mildred. A girl with barely any muscle or height. What must he have thought? Easy prey. That's why he never came back. The woman had an arsenal that would put any army to shame and she's sharper than all of you tied around a tree put together."

Nicholas clapped his hands, the pipe caught between his massive, hairy hands. "Enough, stop. I've seen all I need to. Drop your balls."

The halt wasn't because he had made his decision, but because the coin-op basketball machines were flashing that the pre-fed coins were running out. Soon, none of the men would be able to keep playing on the arcade machines.

The cadets backed away from the machines, waiting for Nicholas's verdict.

"The world of professional hits, this extreme sport includes many disciplines: archery, sharpshooting, martial arts, and more. You're the most well-rounded athletes in the world. I don't want anyone less than that on my team. So, as the leader of this organization, I've decided to keep... Serge!" He pointed at the man from before, who now held his hands together and bowed in gratitude.

"The rest of you, beat it. I'm keeping Serge to start his recruit training," Nicholas said, waving his hands like he was fanning away smoke as the others evacuated the room.

"Dear Serge, now I'm going to prepare you for the final assault," he said, grabbing him by the shoulder and pulling him close. Serge could smell his boss-turned-trainer's putrid breath, a mix of nicotine and caffeine. "Bring in Pat Norton!"

The back door swung open, revealing a man with an intimidating stature and shoulders wider than an ironing board. But it was his mean mug that really sent chills down your spine.

"Come in, comrade," Nicholas said, approaching him but not daring to lay a paternal hand on this one's shoulder. "Pat here's fresh from losing a fight, ain't that right, friend? Johnson MacPherson, the most famous boxer in the world, gave you one hell of a beating, I heard. You, so proud, turned to mush. All the bets had you pegged as the winner, yet here you are, tail between your legs and a broken nose."

Nothing Personal

Pat sniffed through his bandaged, blood-stained nose.

"How's it feel to lose all your dignity? To be stepped on like a worm, poisoned like a philosopher, and gutted by your peers?" Nicholas prodded.

"Makes me want to kill someone," Pat growled, his voice rougher than a teenager's after three consecutive nights of partying.

"Exactly! That's the spirit! That's why we recruit athletes here. They've got the qualities and the motivation—that's the most important part. Pat's been with us for a while now, so I think he can help you out, Serge. Go get ready," Nicholas said, pointing to the other room visible through the open doors Pat had left ajar.

"Give him a few punches to test his resistance and get him in the mood, okay?" Nicholas whispered to Pat.

"Sure, boss. How many hits? Should I finish him?"

"Oh no, save all that anger for the job I'll give you later, alright? I'll let you know when you've given the new recruit enough of a beating, okay? Now go." Pat left, leaving the door cracked for Nicholas to supervise the 'training'.

Just then, the main door to the room made a hoarse sound, opening slowly. Nicholas turned to give it his full attention. There stood a bald man with clothes in tatters, bits of jeans hanging pathetically from his bloodied legs. One arm clutched his abdomen, covering a weeping gash, while his right eyebrow sported a wound that would surely leave a mark.

"Mitch? What are you doing here? I thought you weren't coming back, man," Nicholas said.

The man limped into the room, while the sound of muffled punches and Serge's pleas for mercy adorned the background.

"Oh yeah? And why did you think I wouldn't return, huh? You've even found my replacement," Mitch sputtered, spitting blood. "Wait, I know why. Because that job you gave me, yeah, the last one before I was supposed to be promoted to your current position, it almost killed me! You intended for it to kill me! So you could hang onto your job because you knew the director saw something in me that nobody else here has. The rest are mediocre rats, that's why you stand out among them. In the country of the blind, the one-eyed man is king! But here I am!"

He approached menacingly.

"Calm down, it wasn't like that. Just a regular job. I thought you could handle it—you're one of the veterans here," Nicholas said, sweating like he was in a desert sauna, hands up in surrender.

With no one to stop Pat and his killer hook, Serge finally collapsed to the floor.

"Oh look!" Nicholas said, startled by the thud of the body hitting the ring's floor. "Your replacement has been knocked down. There, you can have your job back. All fixed, huh?"

Mitch was so badly hurt he only said, "We'll talk about this, you damn traitor. For now, I'm going to the infirmary."

Nicholas sighed with relief as soon as he saw him leave, but then he felt a sudden jolt. Something clicked in his mind. He spun around to face Pat, who just shrugged under his intense gaze.

"Is he dead?" Nicholas blurted out, alarmed at the sight of Serge's body on the floor.

Pat grimaced, clueless. "Nobody told me to stop."

"Mr. Gardner's calling for you, Nicholas," another man in the training area cut in.

A bit later, Nicholas found himself nervously swallowing in front of his boss, Kevin Gardner. The office walls boasted shelves of wooden basketball trophies, their plaques gleaming. Gardner, a retired pro player, had dreamed up this business. He claimed it kept him sharp, physically and mentally. It also cushioned the transition for athletes, from the wild competitiveness of active play to a quieter life. Here, they could still flex their skills. Different game, same rush.

Gardner toyed with a keychain. A metal basketball, deflated, with a knife piercing it. His eyes never left Nicholas. Nicholas didn't dare look away. Weakness wasn't an option.

"Didn't think you had killing in you, Nicholas."

"Sir—"

"One of our own, I mean."

"An accident. I was just training him."

"Serge wasn't a big loss, but he was one of our new recruits. Young, strong. We need fresh blood too, not just has-beens. Angry kids with broken dreams work just as well. But I'm not just talking about him. There's Mitch too."

"Wasn't me, sir. I gave him a routine job. Didn't know the target would be so tough. I swear."

"See, Nicholas, we don't just kill for cash. Sometimes we protect. One death can prevent a lot of innocent ones. Get it?"

"But sir, usually—"

"Usually we kill for money, period. I know. That's our bread and butter. But sometimes we shield people. Look at this."

Gardner tossed a file. Nicholas caught it, reading aloud.

"Barnaby Lamerick. Ex-basketball player. Retired at 29. Wrist injury."

"Bingo. Can't dribble like before, but he can still aim a gun. More than qualified. Just need to pull him out of his funk. Keep reading." His fingers kept playing with the metal keychain, ice-cold and steady.

"Depression after the injury. Fell into drugs. Mixed up with some bad crowds."

"That's why we'll rescue him. Give him purpose. See? Not all bad, what we do."

"What do you need me for? Make him an offer? Not my usual gig."

"Not quite. He owes more drug money than he can scrape together. His lack of cooperation has put a target on his back. Kill his pursuers, he'll owe us. Big time. He'll join up, and gratitude means he won't ask for much."

"Sounds like you're killing two birds with one stone, sir."

"Sharp kid. Yep. Stuart Court, gang leader, is our real mark. Someone's paying for his head. Detached, of course. It's your job, Nicholas. Prove I can trust you."

"I'll do it, sir."

"Oh, and make peace with Mitch. Clear your name, got it?"

"Of course." He almost bowed, but that would've been weak too.

In the infirmary, a nurse was tending to Mitch's wounds. His screams of pain quickly turned to insults when he spotted Nicholas in the doorway.

"Come on, Mitch. You know I wouldn't do that to you. It was just another job. Now I've got a new one. Rush job. Barely know anything about it."

"Worried, Mr. I-Can-Do-Everything-Better-Than-You?"

"Boss trusts me on this one. If I screw up again, I'm out. You know how people leave our organization."

"Feet first, pal. That's why I suspected you. But now... I'm thinking something else."

The nurse stepped back, bloody bandages in her gloved hands. She didn't leave completely.

"Boss seems real keen on recruiting young blood lately, as if he didn't already have enough active workers on his hands. Meanwhile, veterans like us? Seems he wants us gone. What if it's on purpose? A restructuring. Purging the old guard without telling us. Thought about that? Your little case? Could be a trap. I don't trust anyone here anymore, man." Mitch raised an eyebrow at the nurse. "What's up, Dory? Topic interest you?"

"Sorry, didn't mean to eavesdrop. It's just... I've noticed more agents coming in lately. Injuries are normal in this job, but the work seems tougher these days."

"All our age?" Nicholas asked, worry creeping in.

"Yeah, all significant age. Most here are at least forty, but around your age—fifty, sixty—they're coming in most. Young ones seem to manage fine."

"See?"

"But Mitch, it's always been like this. Veterans know more, but we can slip up too. It happens to everyone. I don't think it's a conspiracy.

It's normal. This job... it's just how it is. We're not office workers. We were all athletes. I was a soccer player, second division. Then a coach. Didn't succeed. Started hanging out in bars where they whispered about these kinds of jobs. I tell you, I got hurt at first too. But I was used to it. After all, it's not worse than after a match. You're hurt, physically and mentally, almost every time."

"Whatever, man. Your call. But don't say I didn't warn you when you come back in a body bag." Mitch's scratched palms rose to his face, a clear sign of alarm.

"I have to do it, Mitch. I have to complete this job. If I don't, he'll kill me anyway by kicking me out."

"What if it's a trap? Isn't it better to run? I might, you know."

Nicholas had made his decision. One he still weighed as he climbed the metal stairs to the floor of the abandoned, crumbling building. Guitar case slung over his shoulder. There, he carefully set up his sniper rifle, shielded by falling chunks of ruin. In his crosshairs: his target, bouncing a basketball on an empty court. The tall, mustached, athletic guy ran back and forth. Pretending someone was trying to steal the ball, dodging with graceful skill.

In a fleeting moment of stillness, Nicholas held his breath and pulled the trigger. "Nothing personal, mate," he murmured, lining up his shot on Court's head. The man fell silently, the sound muted by the silencer, distance, and the urban background noise. He landed on the grassy ground, where soon his lifeblood would drain away, marking the spot where he would meet his end.

Nicholas smiled to himself as he began to pack up his rifle. But then he saw someone he recognized instantly: dark skin and silky obsidian curls. Unmistakable. Barnaby, the recruit he was supposed to save by eliminating Court. Something he had done mere seconds ago.

He could have called it a day and walked away, but he decided to stick around for another minute. That extra time gave him a front-row seat to something totally unexpected.

A sound of metal cutting through air, then Barnaby fell. Just meters from the second corpse, joining the list of the dead.

"No, no! Boss! Nicholas here! They've killed Barnaby!"

"You saw it happen?"

"Yes, but it wasn't Court! I just took him out."

"Agent, you didn't kill him yourself?"

"No! I mean, yes, I killed Court, but not Barnaby!"

"But they were both killed at the same time?"

"I know it sounds crazy, but it wasn't me. There must be another sniper in the area or something. I didn't do it!"

An uncomfortable silence stretched on, too long for Nicholas's liking.

"Find out who killed Barnaby, agent. Or I'll start thinking thoughts I don't want to entertain."

"No, don't think anything! I'm innocent! But how am I supposed to know who did it? If he was into drugs, it could be any of his underground enemies! What do you want me to do?"

But no one answered. Now he was the prime suspect—the only one with a sniper rifle in the vicinity at the time, and the only one with a motive: if Barnaby had lived, he might have taken Nicholas's job. Unsure of how to proceed, he called Mitch right after hanging up with his boss.

"I think you were right," he said, almost sobbing. "They killed the new recruit right in front of me. Now I'm the prime suspect. But why would the boss kill his own recruit just to frame me and get rid of me?"

"He told you it's his recruit, but do you really believe him? It could be anyone. Maybe someone even ordered the hit on that one too—he just didn't tell you. He gave you half the job to set you up and frame you. I don't know, man. I wouldn't trust it. Run now while you can. Or if you've got the balls, go to the boss's place. See if you can find something to incriminate him. Maybe we can go to the cops, make a deal."

"You're crazy. That would incriminate us."

"I know, but how else do you leave a company like this? I'd rather do time than die. We might get out, and if we give info on the boss, maybe they'll offer better conditions or something."

"This isn't insurance. What better conditions? We'd get the death penalty!"

"Don't exaggerate. Look, I gotta go. Think about it, man."

The call ended, but Nicholas's mind raced on. From his vantage point, he clearly saw Barnaby on the left side of the court, in the lane that would have led him right under the hoop. Ironically, he had died near something symbolic of his profession. Jokes aside, the bullet's trajectory he witnessed came from the right. This made him consider possible shooter locations.

Far from being a rookie, Nicholas quickly visualized the bullet's imaginary line. The shooter's position had to be somewhere high and relatively close. Looking around, he observed several buildings surrounding the basketball court. One in particular, a sleek office building, seemed to have a clear line of sight.

He sprinted toward the location, eyes locked on the towering structure. If someone had taken a shot from up there, they would still be making their descent like a player coming off a fast break. Moving as fast as his physical condition allowed, he soon planted himself at the building's street-level entrance. Only suited office workers were coming out one after another, cigarettes ready or talking on phones. None carried anything that could hide a weapon.

"I'm wasting my time," Nicholas muttered, ready to pivot and head back. But a sudden ruckus at reception caught his attention. Security guards were restraining a man clutching golf clubs and sporting an unmistakably bright red nose.

"Where are you coming from, sir? You don't work here. Police just reported two deaths in a nearby yard. Where were you?"

Police cars were already surrounding the area, alerted by gunshots and neighborhood uproar.

"I'm coming from the bar, up there."

"There's no bar here, sir, especially not upstairs. Did you sneak in through the service elevator? Check his bag!"

The men found a sniper rifle among the golf clubs. "Police, we've got the killer of those victims outside. Repeat, possible suspect."

"Let me go! It's my job, okay?"

"What do you mean, your job?"

"Yeah, I'm a hitman. Freelance. They called me to kill some Court guy. Said he'd be in that yard around this time. Though they called later to cancel 'cause they said something about missing references. I did it anyway to show I'm a pro!"

"Are you drunk? Who hired you? You confirm killing this Court?" The guard was radioing the police on scene. Nicholas watched with the crowd of nosy neighbors outside.

"Yeah, I shot when Court arrived where they told me. He had black, curly hair," said the man, eyes as red as his nose.

"Suspect admitted killing a Court, with curly black hair," the guard spoke into the radio.

"Yes, Court is one of the identified victims, but the curly-haired one is another subject named Barnaby, also identified," the radio voice responded.

"You killed two?"

"No, just Court, the curly-haired one."

"Seems he killed both, doesn't appear sober," the guard confirmed.

Police entered and took him away in cuffs. "Both deaths seem to have happened in quick succession. We're taking the suspect in."

Nicholas watched as they hauled away the wannabe hitman. The guy would likely take the fall for Barnaby's death, whom he had mistaken for Court, already dead when this man took aim. He would probably be pinned for Court's murder too—Nicholas's handiwork. Whoever contacted him to kill Court was likely the same person who later called Gardner. But how could Nicholas explain this to his boss? Would he even believe him?

In a desperate move, Nicholas decided to break into Gardner's house. If he found anything incriminating, maybe he could use it against him when they talked. Even if it was a useless defense, he had to try.

The unexpected decor was a brawny guard standing at the door, sunglasses on and an earpiece with a cable as thick as a judo belt.

"Hi, I work for Gardner. He asked me to pick something up from his house. Bit of a mess," Nicholas lied.

The man looked him up and down, touching his ear, apparently listening.

"Look, I don't want to say anything, but I work for Gardner. I'm in the game. Don't make this a full-court press, or we'll have problems." Nicholas was so terrified the words tumbled out, playing a role he didn't even fully grasp. He felt like a fly staring down an elephant hidden behind dark sunglasses.

The guard bolted down the stairs, jumped into a black car, and sped off.

"Huh, guess I really intimidated him," Nicholas muttered, forcing the door with an X-ray and the pick he always carried for work. Soon he was inside. The house was luxurious but nothing extraordinary. Too many bright windows—he had imagined someone like Nicholas would avoid windows for obvious reasons. He spotted his target with the swift precision of a hawk: a laptop on the bedroom desk. He turned it on, and the password prompt appeared before he could even start guessing.

He typed in his name, just to try. Nothing. "Basketball, too obvious, but he's not that bright." Bingo, he was in. The open email tab was the first thing he checked.

An email in the list was from someone named Nadia Gordon: "There's a mole in your organization. Interpol's on your tail. If this splashes back on me, you'll regret it."

Nicholas clicked on the name to see her profile. "Nadia Gordon, corrupt federal cop. Ordered the hit on a coworker who uncovered her double game. Pays well and on time. Has good dribbling skills both on the court and—"

"Ugh, too much info. Focus, Nicholas," he muttered to himself. "A mole? Did Mitch finally decide to sell us out?"

His phone vibrated silently with an incoming call. "Hello?"

"It's Dory, the nurse. Are you okay? Where are you? I'm home watching the news. They're saying Interpol's dismantled a criminal organization of former athletes, especially basketball players, led by Mr. Gardner. They're combing the area. What happened?"

"News to me, Dory. I don't know anything either. I'm not there right now, but I'm starting to connect the dots. Gardner's guard must have found out and that's why he bolted before getting caught up in it. I'll do the same. Thanks for the heads up. Take care and stay out of it."

Nicholas, already stepping onto the street, tuned into the radio for updates. "Erick Houston, the former basketball star from two decades ago, has been detained by authorities but is expected to receive leniency due to the valuable information he's provided about the hitman organization he's been involved with for over a decade. The tipping point came when his boss, another disgraced athlete from the same era, began reshuffling their ranks using the same ruthless tactics that propelled his criminal enterprise."

The broadcast was interrupted by another call. "Nicholas? It's Gardner. This is my only call. Can you go to my house and take care of things with my family? You know what I mean. They're holding me at the police station. Please, listen, I didn't do any of what they're accusing me of. If I came down hard, it's because I got a tip that Interpol was after us. I was trying to flush out a mole, not restructuring anything. You'll see I'm telling the truth if you go to my house."

Curious that Nicholas had just come from there. He knew Gardner wasn't referring to his family, as he wasn't married, and his relatives didn't live with him. He was asking him to destroy evidence, the same evidence that could incriminate Nicholas himself. "Apparently Erick was the mole, sir."

"No, the mole spread rumors about my supposed restructuring to have my own team, like Erick, gather evidence against me and rat me out."

"Sir, you need to hang up," another voice was heard in the background before the line went dead.

Nicholas's fingers did all the work, dialing a number they knew by heart.

"Mitch? You were the mole, weren't you? Where are you?"

"What are you talking about? I'm heading to the office. I was going to skip town, but Dory said the boss called me in for a good offer. Could be another trap from the boss, but it's not like I have enough money to just up and leave, you know?"

"Dory? Didn't she tell you Interpol's taken over the place? Haven't you seen the news? And Dory was supposed to be at home watching TV."

"Haven't seen anything, I'm driving. But it's her shift at the infirmary. Why would Dory be at home?"

"You weren't the mole? Spreading rumors about our boss wanting to get rid of us?"

"What mole? Dory told me all that stuff. Said other injured veterans mentioned it during their infirmary visits."

"Shit, she didn't call to check on me, but to find out where I am. Listen, run. They're after us. Dory must be there with the police, trying to locate those of us who aren't at headquarters!"

"Negative," a female voice came from behind Nicholas.

Dory, without her usual bun and white cap but still wearing gloves—black now instead of white—was there, gun aimed at Nicholas.

"Hands where I can see them. And sorry, it's nothing personal."

Rules of the Game
John M. Floyd

Sheriff Lucy Valentine parked her cruiser in the driveway of her childhood home and sat there a moment, adrift in memories, before spotting her mother Fran kneeling in the flower garden. Lucy reported in to her dispatcher, climbed out of the car, and called a greeting. As she approached, the streaks of mud on Fran's face reminded Lucy of war paint, but she decided it might be best not to point that out.

"I need your advice, Mother," she said instead.

Frances Valentine wiped dirt from her forehead with an even dirtier glove, which didn't do a lot of good. "Say that one more time."

Lucy heaved a sigh. "I need your advice."

"I like the sound of that. What do I get in return?"

She studied her mother's garden and lawn for a moment. "Yard work?"

"I can handle the yard and garden, myself."

"What, then?"

"I'll let you know." Fran grinned, rose to her feet, and brushed off the knees of her jeans. "Let's hear the story."

It took five minutes. According to Lucy, the teenaged daughter of one of her friends at City Hall had accused a local high school baseball player, Kevin Bassett, of stealing and pawning the wristwatch her parents had given her for her seventeenth birthday. Not only had the daughter, Brittany Douglas, identified the thief, so had the owner of a local pawnshop. Bottom line was, Brittany wanted Kevin arrested and charged, and to either return her watch or pay her the equivalent in cash—which was no small sum.

Fran shrugged. "So arrest him."

Sheriff Valentine let out another breath. "There's a problem."

"What problem?"

"I just found out Brittany and Kevin have been dating for some time," she said. "They broke up the night before the incident. And Kevin's family's wealthy—his mother's one of the Memphis Remingtons and his dad owns two movie theaters and a skating rink up in Tupelo. Why would Kevin need—or want—to steal a girl's wristwatch? Or her purse, I guess, because the watch was inside it." Lucy shook her head. "The whole thing sounds funky, to me."

"So you think your friend's daughter might be stretching the truth a little."

Lucy said, with a twinge of sadness, "Yes. I do. But I have no proof of that."

Fran took off her gloves and tucked them into a back pocket. "What did Brittany see, exactly?"

"She says she'd just parked her car in the lot beside our baseball field right after the game two weeks ago, when our team played Starkville High. It was a cool night, and while the teams were leaving the field, Britt left her purse on her car's hood and leaned back inside to get her coat. When she looked up again, Kevin Bassett was standing there, going through her purse. He saw her looking at him, dropped the purse quick, and ran off."

"Wait a minute. This Brittany—is she a senior or a junior?"

"Senior. Why?"

Fran frowned. "If she's a senior, and this was a home game, I have to wonder—"

"Wonder what?"

"Why she didn't go to the game. I know I'm old, Lucy, but I also know that senior girls usually like to show up at the games, and that has nothing to do with whether they like sports."

"Well, in this case, she doesn't like baseball *or* the games *or* showing up at the field. Said she'd rather go someplace else, or just stay home. Anyhow, on that night—she'd just broken up with one of the players, remember—she told her mom she just drove over to the ballpark to meet a girlfriend there. They were gonna go to a movie afterward."

"Hmm. And she's sure it was Kevin who grabbed her purse?"

"Positive," Lucy said. "There's not a lot of light in that parking lot, but she says it was him all right. He was still in uniform, she said—dark jersey, with his name printed on it."

"She didn't yell at him or chase after him, or call the police?"

"Said she was too shocked. Plus, she didn't know anything was missing from her purse until later."

A silence passed as Fran gave that some thought. A little post-office truck eased up to Fran's curb fifty feet away, and the man inside dropped what looked like bills and couple of letters into her mailbox, waved to Lucy and Fran, and continued down the street. Fran waved back.

"Anyone else see this happen?" she asked.

"Nope. Brit's friend wasn't there yet."

Fran studied her muddy trowel. "Why was Brittany's watch in her purse and not on her wrist?"

"Does it matter?"

"It might. You want my help, or not?"

"Okay, okay," Lucy said. "She told me it didn't go with her outfit that night."

"And what made you check the pawnshops?"

"Just a hunch. As it turned out, Eddie Taylor—you know Eddie, he runs the shop on East Main—remembered buying the watch, and identified Kevin Bassett as the seller from a picture I showed him in the yearbook. Kevin was wearing sunglasses and a baseball cap the whole time he was in the store, Eddie told me, but he recognized him."

"You said it's been two weeks," Fran said. "Why'd Brittany wait so long to report the theft?"

"Her brother Jack's a ballplayer too, and about Kevin's size—when she told Jack about it, she apparently had to talk him out of confronting Kevin and taking matters into his own hands."

"In other words, whipping his ass."

"In other more accurate words, yes. And getting himself into trouble for doing it."

Another silence dragged by. The sheriff heard crows cawing in the stand of pines beyond Fran's garden.

"So what do you think?" Lucy asked.

Fran hesitated, as if making up her mind. Thoughtfully she said, "I think you should ask Brittany's brother to put on dark glasses and a cap and have the pawnshop owner take a look at *him*."

The sheriff blinked. "What? You mean … you figure she set the whole thing up?"

"It makes sense, and I think it's possible. That way, she pins this on her ex-boyfriend *and* gets the money for her 'stolen' watch. If Kevin's the one who broke off their relationship—and I bet he was, right?"

"Right," Lucy said.

"Well, if he was"—Fran shook her head—"young ladies can be mean and vengeful creatures, Luce, when they've been wronged."

Lucy thought that over. "I don't know, Mother. What I need is a firm *reason* not to arrest him."

Fran took off her gloves and was quiet for a minute. Finally she grinned, and turned to look her daughter in the eye.

"You have that, already," she said.

"What?"

"Brittany was lying to you," Fran said, "when she described what happened that night. My guess is, Kevin Bassett is innocent."

"Why?"

Fran's smile widened. "I never played ball—but I know the rules."

Lucy threw up her hands. "What rules?"

One of Fran's neighbors, jogging along the sidewalk on the other side of the street, grinned at them and waved back. Lucy ignored her. "Tell me," she said. "How, exactly, is Kevin innocent?"

"Because Brittany couldn't have seen him in a dark jersey when he left the field that night."

"She *what*? Why?"

"*Because*," Fran said again, and paused as if waiting for a drumroll, "in high school baseball, the home team typically wears white. Only the visiting team wears colored uniforms."

Her daughter stared at her, speechless.

"Your mouth's hanging open," she said.

Lucy shut it, opened it again, and whispered, "You're right."

"Of course I'm right."

"Brittany was lying."

"Sounds that way, to me."

Still pondering this, Lucy turned to walk back to her car. Then she stopped and looked back at her mother. "What do you want in return?"

Fran chuckled as she pulled her gloves on. "My hands are dirty," she said, pointing to the street. "Bring me my mail."

Death in the Dugout
Jesse Aaron

Detective Weepy Willy Williamson hitched up his pants, wiped a trail of sweat from his wide brow, and smoothed down his few remaining wisps of thinning brown hair. He hated the heat. It made his skin itch and his stomach turn sour. His gun, handcuffs, and radio felt like heavy rocks sewn into his pants. They tugged his belt down and he could feel them dig into the sweaty skin of his waist.

As he exited the tunnel and stepped out onto the empty baseball field the stadium felt cavernous and massive. The center field wall felt like it was in another state. He squinted myopically to try and see the numbers on the left field wall, but he did not need to read them. He already had the stadium dimensions memorized.

There was only one thing in the world Willy loved more than his prized action figure collection, and that was this baseball team. He followed every player, every game, and every twist of fate that his team experienced with his very soul. Standing on the field he felt a silent chill run through his body. He mentally checked off an item from his lifetime bucket list.

This was his second catch of the day, and the last crime scene was still rattling around in his brain. It was a family dispute that ended with a dead wife, a crippled husband, and two children that would probably never be able to forget what they had seen.

Willy closed his eyes and breathed in deeply. He smelled the grass and the slightly sour odor of spilled beer, and these smells brought him back to the moment and helped him to clear the fog of despair that had settled in his mind from his last job. He looked up and around one last time. For some reason, the colors always seemed to scream at this stadium. It was as if every sight, sound, and smell was amplified to beautiful levels any time he was at the ballpark.

Now that he had walked on the field of his favorite team, he felt slightly more complete. His list of life accomplishments was short, but at least he could confidently check one box. His only lament was that this moment had to be soiled by the homicide.

He reminded himself sullenly that he had a job to do, and that job was to untangle the violent destruction of another human being. The victim had nothing left but the justice Willy might be able to deliver, and his shoulders sagged with the weight of this task. He turned around and looked at the dugout, and he could see the yellow tape flutter in the breeze as the last of the crime scene unit Detectives sauntered off into the same tunnel he just exited from.

There, crumpled up on the floor of the dugout was the body of the team mascot. The mascot, a baseball player in the team uniform with a large baseball for a head, was laying on his back. As he neared the body and stood silently on the top of the dugout steps, he could see a huge dent on the right side of the mascot's gigantic empty baseball head. Next to the dented costume head lay the body of a young man.

The head wound and the dent on the costume head were both on the right side, which meant the blow had come from the left. Willy deduced the killer was most likely a lefty. The victim's blonde hair was matted with sticky red stains, and his dark eyes stared straight up to the sky. His mouth was open, and he looked shocked, as if he was asking in a desperate scream "why?"

Willy approached one of the uniforms that was posted at the edge of the tape.

"Williamson, from the squad. What do you have on this so far?"

The uniform looked Willy up and down and leaned on the railing as he removed his hat and wiped the sweat from his forehead and neck.

"Someone brained the mascot with a baseball bat. Looks like it was done right through the costume head on the right side. You're here kind of late. Crime scene already dusted the bat-they left it in a paper bag next to the D.O.A. and I'm guarding the scene until the evidence guy comes and bags and tags everything. My partner and I were the first on the scene. We are assigned to the stadium detail. Security called it in.

Ground's crew guy found the body, then he let Security know. Nobody heard anything or saw it happen, but we know the mascot was alive fifteen minutes before the body was found-he stopped by our office just before we got the call. Most of the team is not here this early on an off day and the stadium is practically empty down on the field level. Only guys around are three of the players, and they are being held with the grounds crew guy in the locker room. My partner is with them until you can do your interviews. Go down the back of the tunnel. Follow the black "locker room" sign, it will take you right there."

Willy glanced down at the body again and let this information sink in.

"I'm late to the scene because this is my second catch of the day. My partner is still cleaning up the last one. There was no one else available. Are there any cameras in the dugout or the tunnel? Any footage?"

The uniform shook his head slowly.

"Naw, they don't allow cameras on the field level, you know the cheating scandal and all of that, don't want anyone stealing the signs."

Willy silently nodded. He would have to double check this, but he knew the uniform was probably right. Willy marveled at how routine this seemed to the uniform. Just being here made him dizzy. This cop was assigned to the stadium detail, so to him being in the dugout was routine.

Willy had to check his excitement at being so close to the players and inside this sacred place. He had a job to do. He quickly forced himself back into work mode by looking down at the body to remind himself what this was.

"Okay, any witnesses we might of missed or obvious suspects so far?"

"Naw, only the grounds crew guy that found him. Like I said, there were three players in the locker room and they are still there. Zeus was there, and the Exterminator too, and that big catcher, what's his name again?"

"Minelli. Tony Minelli. Hit .296 last year with 23 home runs."

The uniform smirked at Willy as he put his hat back on.

"Oh you're a fan huh? Well, that will wear off once you talk to these guys."

Suddenly the uniform straightened up. He rolled his eyes as he walked off quickly.

Willy looked towards the tunnel. Approaching him was a small and wiry man wearing a very expensive suit and a gold watch. The man glared at Willy with his muddy brown eyes as if he was coming to attack him, and for a moment Willy unconsciously began to reach for his gun. He stopped himself as he realized this man must work here.

When the man got to within a few feet of Willy he stopped and glared at him like he was a piece of used toilet paper, and Willy suddenly recognized the man as the team owner's son. The son, whose name was Stuart, had a known reputation as a controlling meddler, and was probably the second most hated man in the city. The most hated was Stuart's father, the team owner, for reasons too numerous and painful to the fan base for Willy to even remember at that moment.

Stuart was barely 5'6, and he had dark slicked back hair and a long thin nose. He resembled a hunting dog, and by his quick and sharp movements Willy felt like the man might explode with tension.

"Well Detective? Do you have any suspects?"

Willy noticed that Stuart seemed to be ignoring the body. It seemed odd, as most people would have stared, but from his cold and arrogant reputation this did not surprise Willy.

Willy combed his thinning hair nervously. He knew he had to be careful. This man could probably get him transferred to a precinct far away from his home with one phone call. He was able to balance the fear of this man's political power with his hunger for the truth. While he recognized Stuart's power, he was also aware of his relentless desire to solve anything unknown.

Willy was the type of person that could never wait until the end of a good mystery book. He always skipped to the end halfway through. He was driven to find the solution and this burning force was what made Willy a good detective, and in volatile situations like this it also protected him.

"Well sir, we are working on it. I just got here, I have some witnesses to talk to and we need to see what happens with the Crime Scene. By the way, can you tell me how you found about this? How did you get notified?"

"I was on a Zoom call for the last hour or so before this happened. Right after the call Security called me, and I had them call you."

Willy scratched the back of his hand and could see a small drop of blood ooze out from his most recent patch of psoriasis.

"They found a body and they called you first? Is that normal protocol?"

Stuart looked slightly surprised, and even though he was shorter than Willy he seemed to sneer down at him with his response.

"I don't know why these idiots did it that way, but they did. *Are you going to do your job and find the person that did this, or do I have to call downtown?*"

Willy sighed and rubbed his hands together. He pulled out his pad and his pen.

"I'm getting started right now. How can I reach you if I need to?"

Stuart pointed to a red phone in the dugout.

"Any red phone, dial 666-that's my personal line. I'll be in my office. I've got a lot of work to do. And by the way-you need to talk to that grounds crew guy. I hear from my people he had some kind of beef with the mascot."

With that, Stuart turned around quickly and went back down the ramp. Willy was relieved to see him go. Willy gathered himself and leaned down to the body. It was clear the victim had been bludgeoned to death. Next to his body was the murder weapon in a paper bag. Willy gently lifted the edge of the bag with his pen, and he could see that inside the bag was a blood-stained baseball bat.

Willy let the bag lower back down, and after putting on his hyper-allergenic gloves he examined the body. He could not find any other wounds and it was obvious the baseball bat had done the job. He got the victim's contact information from the uniform and the made his way down the tunnel. Willy quickly realized that this case was going to be complicated. Too many people had access to the dugout to rely on the physical evidence alone, but the stadium employed an army of workers, and it was as big as some small towns.

Someone somewhere had seen something, and this thought caused Willy's blood to course through his veins in a sudden rush. He could feel the little man inside him who was always hungry for more information come to life. He was on the trail, and now obsessed with collecting all the information he needed to solve the case.

Willy walked down the tunnel and followed the sign to the locker room. He felt as if he was walking into a sacred and unknowable place. Willy immediately felt the blessed coolness of the air-conditioning wash over him as entered this baseball shrine.

The grounds crew man was seated by the trainer's table with his head hanging over his knees, and Zeus and the Exterminator were speaking softly to each other by their lockers. The Catcher, Minelli, was not to be seen. Willy nodded to the uniform guarding the possible suspects.

"Williamson, from the squad. Where's Minelli?"

The uniform nodded back and pointed to the exit.

"We had to let him go home. He got here after the body was found, so the patrol Sergeant said there was no way he could be a suspect. His arrival time was corroborated by several of the Security team. Minelli's lawyer called and screamed so they had to let him go. Here's the pedigree information on these three."

The uniform handed Willy a sheet of paper with the information for the three possible suspects. Willy was slightly disappointed because he was not going to be able to meet Minelli.

"Alright, take the grounds crew guy and the Exterminator into the detail office and hold them there until I call you on the radio. Go to six and wait for my call. I need to interview Zeus."

The uniform nodded and escorted the other two suspects to his office, which was located somewhere in the labyrinth of the stadium. Willy approached Zeus and was immediately in awe. Zeus stood up to shake his hand and Willy felt like a small child. Zeus towered over him, and with his massive frame and gray beard and long salt and pepper hair Willy thought he might be talking to some type of Greek God. His hand covered Willy's like a gigantic heavy catcher's mitt.

Zeus, (whose real name was Samuel Lockstone) was given that nickname early on in his career. He was 31 and his shoulder length hair and beard had gone gray in his late twenties. He could throw 102, and his slider was known to be impossibly filthy.

He had the look, stature, and presence of a hero, and it made Willy wince as he knew this was going to be a difficult interview. He was speaking with a man who was immortalized in plastic on his display shelf at home. He gulped and his first words croaked out like those of an adolescent boy, and Willy unconsciously blushed.

"Hello, I'm Detective Williamson. I need to speak with you for a little bit, if you don't mind. Do you prefer to go by Zeus or Samuel?"

Just saying his name gave Willy chills. Zeus nodded and leaned forward with concern.

"Zeus is fine Detective, and I'm here to offer anything I can to help."

Willy tried to straighten up so that his head was a little closer to Zeus, but even with his back stretched he still felt like Zeus was towering over him. Everything about Zeus was massive. His head looked like it was made of heavy stone, and his body was as wide as a door. His thigh looked as wide as Willy's mid-section, and the longer Willy was in his presence the smaller he felt. They both sat down, and Willy began the interview.

"So, how long did you know the victim, the mascot? His first name was Tom, right?"

Zeus leaned back a little, but Willy could see he was still tense.

"Yeah, Tommy. I didn't know him really well, but he was always nice off the field. He seemed like a good kid. We used to talk about books. We both liked to read a lot, and there were not too many other guys I could discuss books with in the club house."

"Did you ever have any arguments with him? I know he used to give it to you pretty good on the field. There was also some chatter on social media that you had some kind of an altercation off the field a couple of weeks ago."

Zeus let a small smile creep onto his lips.

"Oh that? No, we always got along. That stuff on the field, that's the show. Half of it was choreographed by me and Tommy during practice. The other stuff you heard about on social media was just nonsense some blogger made up. He was really a good kid, and I'm, well, I'm going to…."

Suddenly Zeus began to shake and for a moment Willy felt a stab of fear as he thought Zeus might be getting ready to hit him. Then Willy realized it was the beginning of a sob. Willy could see Zeus shake and shudder and then he was wracked by sobs and was openly weeping into his hands. Willy pulled out a couple of tissues and gave them to Zeus who accepted them quickly. He wiped his eyes and after a few more seconds of sobbing he wiped his nose and looked back up at Willy.

"I'm sorry Detective. I just really liked that kid, and for him to get it like this, well it's just not fair. Geez, I don't know how I'm going to pitch tomorrow. I've got to call up my sports psychologist. He can help me get through this."

"it's quite alright. I'm sorry for your loss. Just one more question. I'm sorry to have to ask you this, but can you tell me where you were when it happened?"

Zeus looked up at Willy and without any hesitation or trepidation he gave a confident and calm answer.

"Sure, I understand you have a job to do. I was in the tub soaking my arm. None of the trainers were there, I was alone, but if you check the memory on the tub controls you can see when it was run, and the tub water will probably still be warm, if you want to check."

Willy shook his head.

"No need, you can go for now. Again, I'm sorry for your loss, and have a good game tomorrow. Try to put this out of your head."

Zeus thanked Willy and walked out of the room. Willy waited and when he knew Zeus was safely away, he walked over to the next room and felt the water in the tub. It was as Zeus said, still warm, and when he checked the memory on the controls it showed a forty-five-minute session had just been run.

Willy ran through the facts and for now was satisfied that Zeus had no part in this. He had the strength to commit the physical act, but Willy could sense he did not have the rage or malice to hurt the mascot. He would have to corroborate the relationship with some of the coaches, but currently he did not look like a serious suspect. Willy mentally turned over the card with Zeus on it for now. He called the uniform on the radio and told him to send the Exterminator in.

Willy looked over the pedigree information for his next interview. Thomas Dewey, A.K.A. the Exterminator. He was one of the best pitchers the game had ever seen. He was twenty-nine and his arm seemed to be aging in reverse.

Unlike most pitchers, the Exterminator seemed to throw harder the older he became. His fastball, which started out in the mid-nineties was now clocked at an average speed of 98, and often came in at over 100. His secondary pitches had so much movement that some of the hitters swore it was invisible. Willy felt that he was in the presence of a legend as Thomas walked in and nodded as he sat quietly in front of Willy.

Much like Zeus Thomas was a massive human being but he was leaner, and his arms seemed longer than any Willy had ever seen. Thomas had a shock of brown hair that fell loosely over his forehead, and as he sat down the clean lines of his face seemed to gleam. His eyes were a dark brown and Willy immediately noticed that Thomas was uncomfortable. He looked down at his feet and continuously moved his leg up and down as they spoke. Willy noticed that his left hand had some bruising on the knuckles. Thomas was a left-handed pitcher. Willy filed this fact to the side for now, but it might be useful later.

"So, Thomas, or do you prefer your nickname, the Exterminator?"

Thomas spoke in a soft and slow ramble.

"Thomas is fine."

Willy had to lean forward to hear all the words.

"So, Thomas, you know what happened earlier in the dugout?"

Thomas nodded and said nothing. He stared down at the top of his size 14 sneakers. Willy was not sure how to read this. He knew from his media presence that Thomas was very quiet and focused, but he seemed more introverted than Willy could have imagined. Was his reluctance to look at him a sign of guilt? Willy had seen it before, but he had to be sure. He would let the questions draw out the truth.

"So Thomas, how well did you know the victim?"

Thomas finally looked up at Willy, and Willy thought he could see watery tears in the corners of his eyes, but he could not be sure.

"Umm, I knew him for the past two or three years. We weren't friends of anything, but we would see each other every day."

Thomas looked back down at his feet as he finished.

"Okay, and did you get along with him? Ever have any problems with his antics on the field?"

Suddenly, Thomas looked up at Willy with a startled look as if he had just woken up from a horrible dream.

"Wait, you don't think I could have hurt him? I would never, I mean I'm not that type of person. The only thing I think about is throwing and the game. I would never ever…"

"I'm not thinking that Thomas. I just need to try and make sure and figure out if you saw anything. Can you tell me about your day today?"

Thomas looked down again for a moment, then straightened up.

"Yes, of course, of course. I got here about two hours ago and began loosening up. I've been throwing most of the morning with the catcher. You can ask him, we were together most of the day, until this horrible thing happened."

"Thank you Thomas, I will speak with him. Where were you when it happened?"

"I was here, in the locker room."

Willy rested his pen against his lower lip and paused.

"Anyone else in here with you or see you in the locker room?"

"Hmm, no, I was here by myself. Tony the catcher left after our session and Zeus was soaking in the tub. Is that bad that nobody saw me?"

"No probably not, but I just need to know where everybody was when it happened. One more question. How did you hurt your hand?"

Thomas hesitated and was about to answer when he raised his eyes and then quickly stood up. Willy looked behind him and could see Stuart had returned and Willy could see he did not look happy. Willy stood up as Stuart walked straight to him and got within inches of his face.

"What the hell are you doing Detective? This is my God damned ace. *Why are you even talking to him?*"

Will took a step back as he could feel spittle hit his face as the rage poured out of Stuart.

"I'm doing my job sir. I have to talk to…."

"No! No you don't! You don't talk to my players without my permission. Thomas, you can go. You are done here!"

Thomas got up quickly and nodded as he left the locker room. Stuart approached him, whispered something in his ear, and then patted him on the back as he walked out. Once Thomas was gone Stuart turned back to face Willy.

"Listen, this is my team, and these are my players. We have a big series that starts tomorrow, and we need a win. So stay the hell away from my damn team! Why don't you talk to the other staffers? I can tell you right now it was not a player. I know my men and I know my team dammit!"

Willy sighed and took a step back.

"Well Stuart, the last time I checked, it was still your father's team, and he gave us permission to talk to anyone we needed to."

Stuart turned a deep shade of red and threw his hands up to the sides of his head.

"*My dad gives me full control of this team! I'm going to have you transferred far away from here before this is over, you son of a bitch!*"

Stuart slammed the closest locker door shut and stormed out.

Willy sighed again and made some notes on his pad about the last interview, and then called the uniform on the radio to let him know to send in the next and final suspect. He now turned over the Exterminator's card in his mind to face him. Thomas had seemed nervous, but Willy did not know if this was his normal personality or if it indicated guilt. Willy felt like he was on the edge of something when Stuart had interrupted them. He was going to have to revisit this interview, even if it meant going above Stuart to his father.

He had no motive, but at this level of the game things were so tense that it was possible for people to forget reason. He needed to talk to some of the other team members to find out more. So far, he had no legitimate suspects, and this worried him. He knew that if he did not solve this case quickly that he might very well find himself back in uniform walking a foot post.

Willy buried this at the back of his brain. There would be plenty of time to worry about this later. Now he had a job to do. Five minutes later the grounds crew man slithered in. His name was Ramon Santos. He was a tall and lean man. The pedigree listed him as aged thirty-two, with a prior arrest for assault eleven years ago.

Willy guessed he was over six feet tall. He had dark skin with a short goatee and a jet-black crew cut. He looked strong enough to have been capable of killing the mascot. There was something very smooth and quick about this man's movements.

He sat down and locked eyes with Willy.

"What can I do to help Detective?"

"Hello Ramon. I need to ask you some questions about the mascot. First, how long did you know him?"

Ramon stroked his short and small beard as he stared at the floor for a moment before he answered. It was an odd reaction to a simple question.

"Hmm, about a year, I guess. That's when I joined the grounds crew."

"Okay, did you get along with the mascot, any problems or anything you ever fought about?"

This time Ramon did not hesitate.

"Absolutely not. We hardly interacted with each other. I would see him on the field and pass him in the training room. I think we only exchanged greetings."

"Okay, can you tell me where you were when he was assaulted today?"

"Yes, sure, I was in the grounds crew lounge, its down the third base line."

Willy tapped his pen on his knee and paused.

"Anyone see you there? Any witnesses that can verify that information?"

Ramon gulped and began to look worried.

"Umm, no, but that's where I was. Ask Security, I passed one of them in the hall on my way in today."

"Okay, I will ask. How did you come to find the body?

"I was checking the infield grass, and I saw something on the ground in the dugout. I came over to check it out and found the body. Then I called Security."

Willy nodded.

"Okay, there will probably be more questions, but I think that about wraps it up for now."

Ramon looked relieved and stood up quickly. Willy stood up as Ramon began to leave.

"Oh, one more thing Ramon. Your arrest, for assault, what was that about?"

Ramon's entire face fell so drastically it looked like the goatee was going to drip down his chin.

"I knew that was going to come up. It was a bar fight, over a girl, it was a long time ago. Some drunk grabbed my girl so I laid him out. "

Willy let that sink in.

"Okay, one last question. Are you a righty or a lefty?"

Ramon tensed up again and his back seemed to straighten into a tall letter I.

"Lefty, why? Jesus, you don't think that I...."

Willy shook his head.

"No Ramon. But I have to ask. We will talk more later. For now, please go back to the lounge and wait with the officer."

Ramon leaned into Willy and looked down.

"Listen, Detective, you did not hear this from me, but word around the club house was that the mascot was about to be fired. Apparently he had some kind of issue with the owner's son. And if you met him, you know how he is."

Willy raised his eyebrows in interest.

"Yes, I met him, quite a character. What type of issue?"

Ramon leaned in close enough that Willy could smell his cologne. It smelled like sweet warm licorice.

"Word is that it is something involving the mascot's girl. That's all I know and if anyone asks I'll swear it did not come from me, but there is a dead kid out there, so you deserve to know. Besides, that rich daddy's boy has this coming, the way he pushes everyone around."

As Ramon said this, Willy could see his fists tighten into to two solid balls of bottled-up rage and resentment. The goatee crawled back up Ramon's chin as he snarled.

"That son of a bitch is ruining this team!"

Willy patted Ramon on the shoulder to try and absorb some of the venomous hate he could see leaking out of Ramon's body. Now was not the time to lose control of a witness. Ramon's apparent disdain for Stuart was interesting, but Willy wanted to have more ammunition to use in his next interview with Ramon before he dug into the relationship.

"Thank you Ramon, that will be a big help. I'll talk with you soon. Right now, you need to go back to the lounge."

Ramon quickly walked off. His movements were silent, smooth, and fast, like a snake moving through a puddle of oil. Willy sat back down and turned over Ramon's card on the table in his mind. Was Ramon his main suspect? He might have been lying about Stuart to deflect guilt from himself. There was something off about him. Was there a legitimate reason to look at Stuart, the owner's son? It was at least worth exploring. Willy knew he needed to watch the video for the Zoom call that Stuart claimed he participated in.

The only problem was that Stuart would never cooperate. It was time for a call to Stuart's father, the owner of the team. Willy had to play this carefully. It was a delicate squeeze play, and one step to early or too late could blow the whole thing and result in Willy back on a foot post forty miles from his house. He felt a sudden stabbing pain behind his eyes which told him a migraine had arrived. He sighed and got to work.

* * *

Two hours later Willy sat at his desk at the station house as he watched the footage of Stuart's Zoom call. It had taken four phone calls to finally get through to the team's owner, and Willy had to fight the urge to ask him about the team and why he had made so many illogical trades and acquisitions. Willy wanted to scream at the team's owner that he was putting the city and the fans through Hell.

Instead, Willy had reminded himself he had a job to do, and so he had calmly reasoned and pleaded with the owner that he needed to view the video of Stuart's Zoom meeting. He explained that it would be necessary to clear Stuart, and that without this key piece of the puzzle he would not be able to move on with the investigation.

The owner finally agreed, and Willy had the video. He had watched it three times and thus far there seemed to be nothing there. It was an hour-long call which more than covered the approximate time of the murder, and Stuart spoke at the beginning of the call and at the end. Throughout the video Willy could see Stuart moving around.

Willy was about to quit and refocus on Ramon and Thomas. He rewound it to the beginning one more time, and then noticed about fifteen minutes into the video there was a small glitch on Stuart's image. The image blacked out and then came back. It was only for a second, but Willy rewound the video and watched it frame by frame and it was clear there was a momentary fade out and then a quick fade back in.

Willy replayed the video again, then zoomed in on the desk. Before Stuart's video went to black there was a red stapler on his desk. After the fade back in the stapler was gone. Willy stopped the video and watched it one more time to confirm it.

While he had been waiting for the video to arrive, he had done a little research online. He quickly learned that there was a social media personality that had created a video loop of himself so that it would appear as if he was in a Zoom call. In reality, the other participants were watching a clever and detailed pre-recorded video loop. The social media personality also demonstrated how he had created recorded canned responses that could be triggered by certain words or phrases.

Willy leaned back and scratched his hands. He was having another psoriasis flare up, but he ignored it. He was fascinated and locked in on the possibility that Stuart had run a fake video during the Zoom call. If that was true, then Stuart had created an alibi with a phony Zoom presence. He needed to confirm the fade out with the guys in the tech. unit, but it had promise. He needed to get in touch with the owner immediately. He had to interview the Exterminator again.

An hour later Thomas sat in front of him in the interview room, and out of his uniform he looked more like a tall and gangly teenager who had grown too fast than a professional baseball player.

"Thomas, thank you for coming in. I really needed to talk to you. It seemed as if you were about to tell me something that was bothering you before we were interrupted in the locker room earlier today."

Thomas was tapping his leg up and down quickly, and a small bead of sweat jogged slowly down the side of his head, like a runner covering his daily route.

"Yeah, I guess, I mean, I guess there is something…."

Willy leaned in.

"Yes, please, go ahead."

"Well, the thing is, I know I was not supposed to say anything, but I saw the owner's son walk by the locker room right around the time this happened. He was in a hurry, and his hands were jammed in his pants pockets."

Willy tried to remember what kind of pants Stuart had been wearing. He leaned back and ran through the afternoon in his mind, and he was able to picture Stuart's dark grey slacks. It was a clear image, and Willy could almost feel the smooth wool of the grey material in his hands.

"What color were his pants? Do you remember?"

"Umm, yeah, they were tan Khakis."

"Are you sure?"

"Yes, I'm sure."

Willy paused. This meant Stuart had most likely changed his clothes. If his hands were in his pockets on a hot day like today, he was probably trying to hide something.

"Ok, thank you, that is good, very good. Did you hear about anything going on between the mascot and the owner's son? Did they have some kind of an issue going on?"

Thomas leaned in a little.

"Yeah, word in the clubhouse was that there was something going on between the owner's son and the mascot, maybe girl trouble or something."

Willy nodded and tried to appear calm, but inside he was jumping up and down. This was a big piece of the puzzle, and with this information he almost had a clear picture of the entire image. He was closing in on the truth, or at least as much of it as any Detective ever got.

Willy asked Thomas a few more questions and then headed back to the stadium. On his way he received a call on his cell phone that the Crime Scene unit had found some partial prints on the murder weapon.

When he arrived, he was informed by Security that Stuart was still working. As the Security man led him into Stuart's office, he quickly learned that the room was empty. Willy left word with the Security team to contact him immediately if Stuart appeared.

As he was leaving, he decided to make one last check on the crime scene and the locker room. Another Security man dropped him off at an entrance that led him to the field through the left field wall. As he walked out into the expanse of the stadium and the fading sunlight, he could see a figure standing by second base. Although he could not clearly see the person's face from the outfield Willy already knew who it was. He yelled,

"Stuart! We need to talk!"

Stuart looked up at Willy and then made a mad dash towards right field. Now it was a race to the wall. If Willy beat him there, Stuart would have no place to go. If he lost the race, Stuart would escape over the low wall and into the bowels of the stadium.

Willy pumped his arms up and down and squinted, focusing every inch of his being on running. He let go of every thought and just felt the muscles moving his legs. It was pure physical action, and after all of today's tedious procedures, it felt like he had ripped free of the large wet blanket that was the routine of an investigation.

He easily beat Stuart to the wall, but just as he was about to get close enough to grab him Stuart changed direction and made a turn towards the infield and the dugout. Willy was running with so much force he had to slide into the right field wall to stop himself, costing him precious seconds and widening the gap between them.

Stuart beat him easily to the tunnel next to the dugout, but just as he was about to keep going into the depths of the stadium he stopped and froze. Willy could see a large shadow moving towards them from the tunnel, like a large black swirl of animated smoke. He could not see the face that drove the shadow. The delay had allowed him to close the distance, and he was now standing less than twenty feet from Stuart.

Stuart backed up and ran into the dugout. He glanced behind him at the opposite dugout exit, but both he and Willy knew he would never make it. Willy was too close. Stuart crept back slowly, tensed and ready for battle, like a feral cat out of options and ready to fight.

Stuart looked up for anything he could use as a weapon and grabbed a bat from the bat rack. He stood in the shadow of the dying sun as it covered him like a deep and dark translucent blanket. He glared at Willy with rage and pure fury.

"You had to pry! You had to get in the middle of this! Well, now you are going to pay!"

Stuart walked slowly towards Willy with the bat in his left hand. Willy could see Stuart's hand was gripping the bat so tightly the knuckles on his hand were red. Without any thought he quickly drew his gun and leveled it at Stuart's chest.

"Drop the bat Stuart! Don't make me do this!"

Stuart snarled and lunged at Willy, swinging the bat wildly. Willy had his finger on the trigger, but he hesitated, and this gave Stuart enough time to close in and knock the gun from his hand. Willy tried to move in and grab the bat, but Stuart swung it wildly and landed a blow to the side of Willy's arm. Willy felt an explosion of pain in his elbow and fell backwards, knocked to the ground.

Stuart moved in and stood over him and prepared to swing the bat down onto Willy's head. Willy could see the writing on the bat and could plainly read the inscribed words "*Authentic Zeus Thunderbolt*" as the bat began the arc down to his head.

He closed his eyes and waited, and then heard a large grunt and the sound of a body slapping onto concrete.

When he opened his eyes, Zeus was straddling Stuart, looking down at him while he was holding his bat menacingly.

"This is *my* bat. Nobody touches the Thunderbolt without my permission."

Willy slowly picked himself up and winced. He could feel his elbow swelling up and he thought it was probably broken, but he ignored the pain as he walked over to Stuart and handcuffed him.

"Stuart, you are under arrest for the murder of the team mascot."

Zeus helped him raise Stuart from the ground and smiled. As Willy led Stuart away Zeus waved and bowed to him.

A week later Willy sat at his desk as he completed the last of the paperwork on Stuart's arrest. The case had been all over the papers, and there would still be months of depositions and court appearances. He rubbed his elbow under the sling and felt a jolt of pain. It was badly bruised and there was hairline fracture, but fortunately it was not broken. He had been lucky as it was not his writing or typing hand. He was still able to peck out his reports on his computer, so against the protest of his Sergeant he had immediately returned to work.

The crime scene unit had verified that Stuart's prints were on the bat. Willy later learned that Stuart had utilized his own in-house I.T. Department to create a phony Zoom video to make it appear he was in the call when all the other participants were watching was a recording.

Willy shook his head as he read over his report. How could someone with so much money and so much power over his beloved team be so stupid? Willy later learned from the dead mascot's girlfriend that Stuart had become romantically involved with her.

The mascot had discovered his girlfriend was cheating on him with Stuart. Stuart was married, so the mascot's plan was to blackmail Stuart with the information about the affair. He was going to use this information to keep his job and for a hefty cash payout. Stuart could have simply gone to the police with the blackmail request, but instead he killed the mascot in a frantic rage.

Willy's phone rang and he answered with his good hand.

"Squad, Williamson, how can I help you?"

"Detective, it's Zeus, I'm just calling to see how you are doing."

Willy blushed, as he still could not believe that this baseball God had saved his life.

"I'm fine, just a little banged up. How are you doing?"

"Okay, now that I know that you are alright. Just wanted to check on you."

"Yeah, thank you for checking on me. Umm, this is awkward, but, I feel like I owe you a beer, or maybe a few."

"Sure, Detective sure. I'm on the road this week, but when I get back home you are on."

Willy jotted down Zeus's cell number with a shaking hand. He was so happy he wanted to scream to the world that he was friends with Zeus, but he knew no one would believe him. As he leaned back in his chair, he stared at a water stain on the ceiling and mused how it reminded him of the shape of a thunderbolt.

Rochwal's Blue Balls
John B. Elliott

"That much exercise is unhealthy, Rochwal, to get up at five in the morning so you can bat a black rubber ball against the wall with your hand for an hour before work."

"I plan to die young, anyway, Daggett, so it makes no difference."

"It does! Sports are killers, football players beat their brains into early dementia, baseball players have a hard ball crash into them at ninety-three miles per hour, everybody gets ACL and MCL tears and Tommy John surgery—the whole sport apparatus is a boon to orthopedic surgeons: joggers get knee replacements, tendon repairs, new hips, you name it. Our whole country is obsessed with exercise mania, which in itself is obsessive compulsive—and think of all the money being made by manufacturers of equipment and clothing so people can tear their bodies apart with sports and exercise, all the while claiming it's healthy. Think of all the different industries that put people back together again—doctors, physical therapists, orthopedic specialists, brace manufacturers—everyone's making money on this mania. I like Lacrosse, though, especially the team that practices in a park near my house, an all-girl team..."

As usual with Daggett, the starting premise of one of his monologues was forgotten by the time he got to the end, and he concluded his speech with a new subject. This time he didn't drift too far away, but finished with a criticism of school and professional sports which do not provide the opportunities they should to girls and women, especially schools, whose funding for female sports is a mere fraction of the sport's budget, and professional sports, where women are not paid the same as men.

This discussion occurred as they were driving to a destination a few miles beyond the town of Motherly, the scene of an accident involving a truck driver who was an independent hauler carrying the U.S. mail. Rochwal took in the town of Motherly with interest, though Daggett barely noticed—it was merely another small town in a rural area—and soon the accident scene was obvious even in the distance. A white, medium-duty Freightliner truck had skidded off the road, hit a tree and flipped onto its side, looking forlorn in the winter landscape. Daggett came to a halt behind the truck where they met the local sheriff.

"The driver's still in the cab being examined by our local doctor. He fills in as coroner."

They walked to the front of the truck where the doctor was dangling over the fuel tank while he reached into the cab from the driver's side door. Daggett had no intention of trying to balance his oversized belly in the same position, so he and Rochwal walked to where they could see inside the cab through the front window.

"Picalo Andressen is the name of the driver," continued the sheriff. "He's local, everyone knows him, in fact my son and his son pal around together, and only last week his boy was over at my house for Robbie's birthday." The sheriff shook his head and sighed. "I'm going to hate breaking the news to his family and to Robbie. Picalo was a good guy and coached the kids in after-school basketball and baseball."

Daggett refrained from asking if girls were on the afternoon teams. He stared into the window where he saw that Picalo's life ended when his head crashed against the metal frame of the door near the front window. "Probably a broken neck, Rochwal, a pretty quick exit from the woes of living, although not instantly like all those television shows falsely claim for the victim."

"The cargo has been broken into," the sheriff said. "It's obvious since the padlock's cut off."

"We'll look into it and see if we can figure out what's been stolen."

"That won't be easy. I think he runs through several other towns before he picks up here. That's a favor to Motherly so people don't have to rush out early to mail something."

As they walked to the back of the truck to get a general idea of the thefts, Daggett asked Rochwal, "How long do you think this cargo compartment is?"

"I'd say twenty-five or twenty-six feet."

"Yeah, a lot to steal from, but I doubt there was ever a jam-packed load out here in the country, even with the other towns."

"I put the cutoff lock in a plastic bag," the sheriff said, "didn't touch it. Maybe you can get prints."

The cargo door was the roll-up type and was opened three feet. Since the body of the truck was on its side, it was easy to step inside. Rochwal pushed the door open wider so Daggett's immense bulk wouldn't be hindered. They saw a jumble of duffle-sized canvas mail bags and shipping boxes.

"Well, Rochwal, we can't tell what's not here by staring at what is. Let's get this secured with our own lock. We'll have to call out some men to inventory what's here and send the mail on its way. The local P.O.s will have tracking numbers on many of the packages."

They studied the road, and Daggett sized up the situation: "It's straight and no snow on the road, though there's at least six inches of it to the side, but no obvious melting onto the road to create slick ice overnight."

"The tire marks are odd," added the sheriff, "like the front wheels skidded sideways and the marks from the braking wheels are intermittent and twisted."

"Where are you going, Rochwal?"

"Up the road, where else?"

He walked along the road, casting a glance to each side until he came to what he was seeking. Pulling gloves from his coat pocket, he stepped into the snow a distance until he could pick up the object, then worked his way back to Daggett and the sheriff.

"You're obsessed with balls, Rochwal. I suppose you want it for your collection of devious exercise equipment! We're on a case, not a play day!"

"Get me a large bag, will you? I don't want this on the ground."

"Those bags are for evidence!"

"And that's what this is."

Daggett reluctantly opened the trunk of his car, obtained an evidence bag, and held it open for Rochwal to drop the soccer ball into the bag.

"A blue soccer ball!" said the sheriff. "Evidence you think?"

"Could be."

"Oh, Rochwal!" Daggett sighed but said no more.

Rochwal asked: "I think the thief is local—know anything about resident thieves, Sheriff?"

The sheriff looked at Daggett, and they both smiled. "A little," he replied, then he and Daggett burst into laughter. Not knowing their inside joke, Rochwal remained quiet.

"There's three people I think you should investigate: Plum Meredith, Bradford Pearson and Cecil Tagback."

"Well, let's get going, it's cold out here," Daggett said as he walked to his car. Rochwal joined him, and the sheriff in his car led the way.

They interviewed Cecil Tagback first. "I can't say I reckon I stole anything lately, Sheriff, except a stick of gum from the candy shop, go ahead and cuff me."

"Can we look around?" the sheriff replied.

"Sure, search the whole house, but stay out of the garage. Won't let you go in there. No." Tagback twisted his lips in consternation.

The sheriff and the two Postal Inspectors did a quick turn through the house, noting its disorganization and need for a thorough cleaning.

"Wished we hadn't asked," said Daggett.

"What about the garage? What's he hiding there?"

"Nothing but junk," the sheriff replied, "he's pulling our chains." Yet he asked: "What's in your garage, Cecil?"

"Wouldn't likely know. Dead bodies, maybe, or next year's model of the latest electrified automobile. Had my eye on it even before they designed it."

"Thanks, Cecil, you're a big help—as always."

Plum Meredith wasn't home, or they didn't think so until after they returned to their cars and heard her yelling to them from a window. She wasn't dressed, and they had to wait several minutes while she made herself presentable. When she finally appeared at the door, Rochwal noted that though she was no glamour queen, she wouldn't scare anybody on a dark night. She had medium-dark brown hair and a thin body, making him wonder if her thinness had been achieved by drinking rather than eating. Her face was one that may have been cute at one time due to her high cheek bones and dimples. She stood in the doorway with the door positioned slightly in front of her ready to slam it shut—not against the sheriff, who knew her well and had helped her out of jams—but from years of dealing with men she had no interest in. At last, she let them inside to a living room furnished with couches, chairs and end tables purchased thirty years before.

"I work at Christie's, Sheriff, I don't go thieving."

"It was a mail truck, U.S. mail, that's why these gentlemen are with me here, Inspector Daggett and Inspector Rochwal of the Postal Inspection Service."

"Mail truck? Do I look like a stevedore? You've got to be kidding me! It's all I can do to get in my car and drive somewhere."

"What are you, Plum, five feet?" Daggett asked.

"Five one if I haven't shrunk in old age, or lost it working too hard at Christie's. So, why are you guys really here?"

"As I said, Plum," the sheriff answered, "we're visiting anyone who has a past that might indicate they could be involved."

"You're never going to let go, are you? It was only—"

"Several times, I know, so don't sing about that one-time youthful mistake."

Plum frowned. "You don't have to embarrass me in front of these gentlemen. I like to think it's in my past."

"So would I. Can we look around?"

"Be my guest, but leave my panties and bras alone," she laughed.

"I'm not hiding a gun in my 'Luxury Underwear' from Amazon."

Rochwal, Daggett and the sheriff looked through the house, finding nothing significant. Her house didn't have a garage, but they looked through the boxes in the carport and a storage shed in the backyard.

"Nothing, gentlemen. Shall we end the tour of Motherly's finest citizens by visiting Bradford Pearson?"

When Pearson answered the door, Rochwal immediately realized the inside joke between Daggett and the sheriff. Pearson was a dwarf, at most four feet five, neither chunky nor thin, with faded red hair and an aging face which looked questioningly at the sheriff.

"What is it? Out for me again for something I didn't do?"

"Mail theft, Bradford, and manslaughter."

"Hah! That's never been my specialty! Those guys behind you, who are they?"

The sheriff laughed. "You know one of them. Can we come in?"

"Might as well." Bradford held the door for them to enter, and as Daggett walked by, he said: "Hello, Fatso."

Daggett chuckled and pulled himself up to appear taller. "Hello, Midget!"

"Don't call me a midget! I ain't a freak in an eighteenth-century carnival! You know damn well you don't call us dwarfs midgets."

"Then don't call me Fatso!"

"But you are!"

"And you are a—"

"Not a midget! Call me by my name, Bradford Pearson!"

"As soon as you stop calling me Fatso."

"Mr. Bradford Pearson, Sir, is even better coming from you, and I'll stop calling you Fatso when you lose that circle of flesh around your belly."

"Then you'll have to live with midget, Midget."

"It actually starts at your chin, doesn't it? Your whole upper body is a beer barrel. Unfortunately, I can't tap it."

"You two can clown around later," Rochwal said impatiently. "Let's get to work."

"Work is my middle name," Bradford assured him. "What is it you guys want?"

Everyone remained standing, since Bradford didn't invite them to sit down. He actually wanted to leave them on the porch, and he would have in warm weather, but he had a dislike of the cold.

"A mail truck was robbed after a crash," Daggett said, "and the driver...well, he wasn't up to preventing the theft."

"Doesn't have anything to do with me, I don't steal things no more."

"You mean you no longer harvest those gift packages and Amazon orders left on the doorsteps?"

"The past is past, Fatso, except your past eating is your future, and I assume from the looks of it, your future will arrive soon. Now, if there's nothing else, have a nice day."

"Puny midget!" Daggett muttered as the sheriff asked Bradford: "Mind if we look around?"

"Don't mind at all if I can see your warrant."

"I expected you'd say that," the sheriff replied, "even if you had nothing to hide."

"I'm always accommodating to the letter of the law, you know that."

"Yes, but I think you read the text in a mirror."

After they left Bradford Pearson, Rochwal and Daggett discussed the robbery with the sheriff, but there wasn't much that hadn't already been said.

"I'll have the truck towed to a safe place after your men unload all the mail," the sheriff assured them, "and I'll send you the autopsy report, though it won't make a difference to your investigation. It's clearly an accident that someone took advantage of, to get something by looting."

Before they left Motherly, Rochwal told Daggett he wanted to visit the sports store he had seen when they passed through on the way to the accident.

"Can't get away without looking at all the ways to harm your body, can you, Rochwal?"

"Nope."

The sporting goods store also acted like those convenience stores located in strip malls or gasoline stations with the usual assortment of hot dogs, milk, candy and other commodities. Daggett was happy because he found a good price on cigarillos and beef jerky. The cigarillo he had chewed since leaving for Motherly was beyond rescue, and he tossed it away to chew on jerky. Of course, he already had more of both items in his pockets, but he never bypassed a good price on any goods.

As Daggett shopped, Rochwal talked with the owner.

"Bradford Pearson? Oh, he comes in all the time, particularly in the summer since he loves fishing, always buying fresh bait or some feathers and such for tying his own flies, but he'll come in during the winter time to daydream a bit or pick up a carton of eggs or milk."

"Visited you recently?"

"Yeah, now that I think of it."

"Buy anything?"

"Only milk, but he spent time in the sports section as he always does."

"What about Cecil Tagback? Or Plum Meredith?"

"Yeah, them two. Came in together, but didn't really buy much after walking all over the goddamn store—a candy bar or something like that."

"You have a camera installed?"

The store owner laughed. "One, but only because I got a state grant, more or less forced on me. It shows the front door and a little of the store."

Rochwal skimmed through what was available, which wasn't much since the store owner only kept a week's worth of video. He found Bradford Pearson mulling about in the sports section, picking things up and putting them down. Of Cecil Tagback and Plum Meredith, he found nothing except a fragment which wasn't erased showing them leaving the store together.

"Do you have soccer balls?"

"Sure do."

The next day in the office Daggett and Rochwal discussed the case.

"Well, Rochwal, what do you think—Plum, Bradford, Cecil, or persons unknown?"

"Don't you know?"

"I might, but I want to hear your idea first."

"Bradford Pearson."

"Bradford? Midget?"

"Definitely."

Daggett's phone rang and he glared at it, but after answering and listening, adding in a chuckle and a few grunts, he hung up and said: "Well, Rochwal, your theory went greyhound, there were absolutely no fingerprints on the blue soccer ball you collected, and none but the driver's on the padlock, so it wasn't Bradford."

"On the contrary, no fingerprints prove my case—it's the dog you didn't hear barking. If that soccer ball had prints, we would know it was in use by someone, maybe a child or several children, but because it's clean, it was used in a crime."

Daggett looked at him, realizing the logic. "And how was it used?"

"Well, the road was straight, no ice, there shouldn't have been an accident. Did you notice the disturbance in the snow on the opposite side of the road across from where I found the ball?"

Daggett puckered and twisted his lips.

"I think the driver swerved to keep from hitting a child chasing after his soccer ball, and that would be so unusual in this weather he wouldn't have time to think, only react. The child, of course, was Bradford Pearson."

"That pygmy puppet? You know, Rochwal, I'm not in favor of name calling and I know I shouldn't call Bradford a midget, but it gets my goat that so much of this 'Politically Correct' stuff is a call to conformity, and what's the difference between society forcing others to speak as a certain group of people want, or forcing people to conform to a particular religion or to fascism or to communism? All of those ideologies want people to have the same thoughts and speech, all are telling others what to believe and what to say, the politically correct group included. The poor aren't poor, they're 'economically challenged,' no one pays taxes, they pay 'revenue enhancements,' janitors don't exist, only 'building services attendants,' and don't even get me going on the him, her, they thing!"

"I'm going to leave at four tomorrow morning and pay a visit to the town of Motherly and a certain residence occupied by Mr. Pearson."

"Does that hour of the day really exist? It's hearsay!"

"I'm taking the soccer balls I bought in Motherly with me. I'll let you know what happens."

"Those blue soccer balls? I know you're a bit loony, especially when it comes to exercise, but when you bought those blue balls, I knew you had really gone bonkers, off the deep end so to speak, if not totally crazy!"

"I'll check out a car and leave from home tomorrow morning."

"No you won't! I'm going with you. You're likely to do something totally crazy and I'll be liable for you. How many of those balls did you get, by the way? A hundred?"

"Enough."

The next morning they arrived early in Motherly and drove to within a block of Bradford Pearson's house. Rochwal took a blue soccer ball and tossed it in the snow on Bradford's lawn, then returned to the car where they waited for Bradford to discover it.

The wait was long, but Daggett never abhorred sitting, and he kept up a stream of chatter about whales, politicians, women and what life was like for him as a boy. When Bradford appeared on his porch, it was evident he had seen the blue ball on his lawn from the window, for he went straight down the steps and onto the snow-covered lawn to retrieve it. After picking it up, he looked around to see if any children were playing, but there were none, so he took the ball over to his trash can at the side of his driveway and, angrily, threw the ball in before going back inside.

"What now, Rochwal? Do you expect him to go to the sheriff and confess?" Daggett let out a peel of laughter.

"Right now, we go back and return tomorrow morning. He won't do anything today."

"I wish we had something more than your intuition for a search warrant."

"It wouldn't do any good, he doesn't have anything incriminating at his house."

The next day, they repeated their routine, with the exception that Daggett had periods of silence and Rochwal placed a second blue soccer ball on the steps to Bradford's porch. Bradford must have checked the front yard immediately after he woke up, for it was much earlier when he came out on the porch, stood a few seconds looking at the ball with consternation, then took a step down and picked it up, holding it as if he were trying to determine if it was the same ball as the one on his lawn the day before. Clearly upset, he took it to the driveway trash can, and after checking the can and seeing that yesterday's blue ball was still there, he pushed today's into the trash, slammed on the lid, and stormed back into the house.

"Well, Rochwal?"

Rochwal looked at Daggett and shook his head slightly before starting the car to return to headquarters. "No, not today, he won't do anything," he said as they rounded a corner onto the main thoroughfare, "but he's bugged about what's going on."

The next morning, Rochwal placed a new blue soccer ball on Bradford's porch. Daggett was quiet for the most part, but their wait wasn't long, and he had barely warmed up his vocal cords on how conservative today's youth were, "Not like us, Rochwal, protesting and marching, determined to change the world—today's youth are too caught up in video games or, ugh, playing sports!" when Bradford appeared on the porch. He had yanked open his door quickly and without bothering to examine the ball, gave it a kick hard enough to bounce it down his walk into the street. He went back inside, but soon returned and marched down the steps of his porch, a determined look on his face. This time he didn't search for children, but for someone nearby who was perpetuating this joke on him—he looked angry enough to tear them apart. He picked up the ball and threw it like a baseball straight down onto the asphalt as hard as he could and watched as it bounced up, but its upward trajectory was not as high as he expected. He picked it up again and shook it, put it to his ear and shook it again, his face first looking doubtful, then concerned as he returned to the house with the ball. Fifteen minutes later he was on his porch again, the ball cut into pieces, and strode to the trash can, where he scanned the inside and saw both balls of the previous two days before he hurled the destroyed ball into the trash.

After Bradford went inside, Daggett asked: "Well, Rochwal, are you going to drive back and repeat this charade tomorrow?"

"No, we're going to wait here."

"Why do you think Bradford cut up the ball? He was angry, of course, but I also think he looked a little fearful."

"He cut open the ball to see what was inside for he sensed something was there, that's why he held it up to his ear and shook it. Following a hunch, I made a small slit in the ball last night and forced an old padlock key inside, then repaired it as best I could. I knew it would make him wonder if someone was on to him or had broken into where he's hiding the stolen goods. He's spooked now."

At ten that morning, Bradford came out of his house to his car, which was small, but had also been fitted with pedal extenders and a high seat cushion. Rochwal and Daggett followed him to an area south of Motherly, but still close enough that a few houses were scattered nearby. Bradford stopped where a group of leafless beech trees spread up a small hill, got out of his vehicle and walked up a snow-covered path which worked its way into the grove. Rochwal inspected the path and saw enough tracks to know it had been used several times. He returned to the car and called the sheriff, who responded quickly. All three made their way up the path, Daggett tempted to protest against the strenuous hike up the hill, but he held back not only because he didn't want to miss what they would discover, but also not to let talk give away their presence.

It was a quarter mile before they saw a storage shed with its door opened and tracks in the snow leading to it. Not far away was a very dilapidated farmhouse, its door missing and windows broken. The sheriff led the way to the shed and stepped into the doorway.

"Well, Bradford, I think the game is up. You can stop doing what you're doing and come with us."

Bradford looked up in surprise, then saw that Daggett and Rochwal were with the sheriff.

"Hello, Fatso!" he said angrily. "I suppose this was your idea!"

Daggett merely laughed.

Bradford had been sitting on a mail pouch in the shed with several other pouches nearby, and it was clear he was opening letters and packages to search their contents. Several ten- and twenty-dollar bills, and in one case, a fifty-dollar bill snatched from birthday cards were in a pile to his left, with new or replacement credit cards and their letters to his right. A boom box and a DVD player had been removed from their packaging, as well as a few other small items, all of them placed by the door.

After taking him to the station and locking him in a room, the sheriff said: "Let's go pick up Plum Meredith. That old farmhouse was her grandfather's and has been abandoned for years—the road in is impossible without a four-wheel drive. I want to know how much she helped him, just letting him use the shed or if she was at the accident helping him load up what he wanted to take."

Plum Meredith denied any involvement, but as they worked the two suspects separately, she began to break down, especially when they reminded her she would get a stiff sentence for obstruction of justice if she continued to deny her participation.

"And murder," the sheriff added to Daggett's interrogation.

"Murder?" Plum was incredulous.

"Yes, Picalo died in that accident you and Bradford created."

"That wasn't the plan!"

"It wasn't?" Rochwal asked. "You might only be charged with manslaughter, but it doesn't look good for you."

"Cooperate Plum, it will do you good when it comes to the DA charging you."

She looked away and a tear ran down her cheek.

After her confession and Bradford's continuing denial of guilt even though he was caught with the evidence and knew Plum would testify against him, Rochwal and Daggett headed back to headquarters. Daggett was in a good mood, gleeful, for he was certain that Mr. Bradford Pearson, Sir, was going to spend many years in prison. He looked at his partner, who was driving leisurely as if on vacation, and chuckled softly before he burst into laughter: "Well, Rochwal, it's the first time I've ever heard that having blue balls was a good thing!"

Side Pocket Bank Shot
William Kitcher

When I hit town early afternoon, I went to *The Crystal Duck*, next to the train station, took a stool at the end of the bar nearest to where the bartender was reading a really old hot rod magazine, and ordered a beer. He served me, looked around the bar to confirm no one else was there, and went back to his magazine. The bar was a little grimy, and the air was stale, like last night had never left.

The bartender was a little grimy as well. He was about twenty-two, with long unkempt blond hair, a faded Bugs Bunny t-shirt and jeans, and a smell of dried sweat.

Somewhere, ZZ Top was playing softly.

While contemplating the liquor bottles stacked behind the bar, I heard a familiar sound. A loud clack followed by a few softer clacks. I looked at the bartender but he didn't react. After two more clacks, I said, "Many people play here?"

The bartender looked at me, paused, then said, "Sometimes." He went back to his magazine.

I got off my stool, picked up my beer, and slowly wandered to the back of the bar. I pushed open a door that was slightly ajar, and stood in the doorframe.

There was a guy playing pool by himself. He apparently hadn't noticed me. He was an old forty, a big bear of a man who was flabby in places. He wore a crisp white shirt, khakis, scuffed black shoes, and smelled of too much cologne. A decent gray jacket hung off the beak of a stuffed swordfish, mounted on a wall that otherwise had only a few old liquor ads and a painting of dogs playing pool. Sunlight oozed through a smudged window opposite.

Side Pocket Bank Shot

The balls were scattered, and he made three shots easily, giving himself good shape each shot, before looking up at me briefly. He sank another shot, and then he missed what looked to be an easy one. That seemed suspicious to me.

He chalked up his cue and said, without looking at me, "You play?"

That sounded even more suspicious. Was this guy a hustler?

"I used to," I said. "When I was a kid."

He looked at me with an expression I couldn't figure out. Was he sizing me up? He concentrated on his shot and missed it. He circled the table to set himself up for another shot.

I waited and watched, and said nothing else. If he was first to speak next, he was definitely a hustler.

He made two shots, missed one, and with a handful of balls left on the table, said, "You want a game?"

What the hell, I thought. "Sure," I said.

He leaned his cue against the wall. "Take a few practice shots," he said. "Then we'll start a new game." He put four quarters on the side rail above the money slot.

I took a cue from the rack and stared down the shaft to see if it was straight.

"Put it on the table and roll it," he said. "You can tell better if it's warped that way."

I did as he said. The cue was good. I took a few shots. I wasn't very good.

"Ready to go?" he asked, picking up the triangle.

"Sure," I said.

"Put the money in. Make sure you hold it in until all the balls have dropped."

The balls rolled like thunder. He racked them up, handed me the cue ball, and picked up a cue ball from the other table.

"Lag for break," he said.

We did, and he won.

"Derek," he said, putting his big bear paw out.

"Bill," I said, shaking it.

He broke, and two stripes went in. He potted two more stripes, then missed.

"So I'm shooting solids?" I asked.

"Uh huh."

I sank the two-ball but left myself in terrible shape, and could barely even hit another solid.

He sank two more stripes, then missed an easy shot. He was definitely a hustler. It was only a matter of time before the topic of money would come up.

We finished the game. He won by a few balls.

"You from around here?" he asked.

Showing interest, I thought. Becoming my buddy. Classic hustle.

"No," I said. "Just in town for a couple of days, visiting friends. They're still at work so I thought I'd have a beer or two."

"What's your business?"

"I'm a spy. I sell arms."

He laughed.

"Nah," I said, "I'm a mechanic."

He looked at my hands, and I looked at them as well. Calluses. Cuts. Scars. Busted fingernails.

The bartender poked his head through the doorway. "You guys want anything?"

"Wanna play another game?" asked Derek.

I finished the rest of my beer and handed the glass to the bartender. "Sure," I said to both of them.

Derek hadn't been drinking. If he was a hustler, he'd order a whiskey or a shot of vodka or tequila. If he wasn't a hustler, he'd have a beer. Beer makes you go to the toilet too often, and hustlers don't have time to waste.

"Yeah," said Derek. "I'll have a Jameson's. Two ice cubes."

"Done," said the bartender as he left.

"What do you work on?" asked Derek.

Side Pocket Bank Shot

"Mostly motorcycles," I said. "I like Harleys."

"Great bikes. You got any quarters?"

"Yeah," I said. I put four in the slot and held it in. Derek racked the balls.

"Wanna make it interesting?" he asked.

Here it was, I thought. I wanted to see where this was going, so I said, "Sure. How much?"

"Ten bucks?"

Ten. Not too much to turn me off. Not enough to make me think he was hustling me. Not too little to not make it worth his while. But this would escalate, I was sure of that.

"Ten's good," I said. "Who breaks?"

"I do," he said. "I won the last game. House rules." He broke, sinking a stripe. He sank three more before missing.

The bartender came back, handed me my beer and Derek his Jameson's with two ice cubes which tinkled. I noticed that Derek put his drink down without even taking a sip. He didn't want to get close to drunk. He was in for the long haul.

I sank a couple, then missed. He sank three, then missed. I sank one, then missed. He ran the rest of the table.

"Again?" he said.

"Sure," I said. "I'm slowly getting the rust off." I laughed.

"Twenty this game?"

"Sure," I said. What the hell. This was fun. And it wasn't a lot of money for me. He probably had somewhere to go later that afternoon, so he wanted to make a few bucks as quickly as he could.

He won that game too. I was down thirty. So what? Thirty doesn't even cover an hour's work of a decent motorcycle mechanic.

We kept playing. I kept drinking beer. We raised the stakes. You've heard a version of this story many times.

I won the $50 game. I think he let me. He made a few suspiciously bad shots, the last of which set me up to clear my remaining balls.

Then I won the $100 game. I was playing better but he was still fumbling occasionally, setting me up for the long con.

And then it came. He won the $200 game, playing much better. His missed shots didn't look intentional to me, and there were very few of them.

He won the $300 game. He broke, methodically ran the table, and I watched, drinking my beer and chalking my cue tip pointlessly.

He put his cue back in the rack, came over to me, and put out his bear paw. I assumed he wanted me to put money in it, but I didn't want to do that.

"One more?" I slurred.

"Aren't you done?" he asked.

"One more," I said, taking his paw and shaking it. "Thousand dollars!" It was supposed to sound confident, but it sounded to me like false bravado.

"Do you even have that much money on you? You're already down three-eighty to me. You wanna be down another grand on top of that? Do you have the money?"

"Screw you, buddy!" I yelled, loud enough to attract the bartender's attention.

"What's going on, guys?" he said.

"This guy!" I said, waving vaguely at Derek. "This guy is accusing me of not having the cash to cover my debts. How do I know he can cover the debt if I win?"

"I can vouch for him," said the bartender.

"Yeah, of course you're gonna say that!"

"Look, man, don't you think you've had enough to drink?"

"Screw you too! I can hold my booze," I said as I staggered toward the bartender with a look on my face that meant I was ready to pound someone. "How do I know he's got the money? Just 'coz *you* vouch for him? Who the hell are you?!"

"OK, calm down," said the bartender, putting his hands on my chest. "I'll not only vouch for him, if he *doesn't* have the money, I'll take it out of the till and give it to you, I swear."

He'll take money out of the till? He keeps a grand in the till? That sounded as fishy as the swordfish with the blank eyes.

"Take your hands off me," I said, as quietly as I could. Quiet is scarier than loud.

He did. "OK, no problem, OK?"

"All right," I said, and stepped back.

"Now," said the bartender, "it's understandable that Derek would want assurances you can cover any losses you have."

"Fine," I said. I took my wallet out of my back pocket, opened it, took the cash out, and gave it to the bartender.

He thumbed through it. His dirty blond eyebrows went up in surprise. He handed the money back to me and looked at Derek. "He's good."

"OK," said Derek.

I said, "Get us a couple of whatever he's drinking. Put it on my tab."

The bartender looked at Derek, who nodded. The bartender left.

"Rack 'em up," I said.

"Are you sure?" he said.

"Screw you!" I yelled. "And you know what? Screw a grand! Make it two! Rack 'em up!"

"OK, two grand," he said. "You rack them up. Loser racks, winner breaks."

"Put your quarters in, screwboy," I said.

He let out an unintentional snort, and put the quarters in. I racked the balls.

He broke, and sank a stripe and a solid. He looked over the table, then sank a stripe. I was solid.

The bartender brought the drinks, put one on the table beside me, and one for Derek on the side rail. The bartender stood and watched.

Derek sank four more stripes before just missing on his remaining ball. He spun away from the table and swore at the wall. He turned back to the table calmly, knowing that he'd left me the cue ball behind the eight-ball without a clear shot at a solid.

"Two-ball," I said, and hit a two-bank shot on the two into a side pocket, leaving myself in good shape.

I ran the table after that, sinking the eight-ball with my eyes closed. I put my cue on the table and rolled it. "That'll be sixteen-twenty," I said.

Derek took his jacket off the swordfish's nose and removed a roll of bills from a side pocket. He took the rubber band off it, and counted it. He handed it to me, and said, "I'm four hundred short."

I took a few steps toward him.

"I'll cover it," said the bartender quickly, and went into the other room.

I went closer to Derek and pulled my fist back. He winced. I laughed, and put my fist to my side. "You prick," I said.

I took my whiskey off the table and had a small sip. It was good. I put the remains on the long rail. "You can have the rest," I said. I chuckled to myself at the double meaning.

Back in the bar, the bartender was standing there holding out his hand with $400 in it. He seemed nervous.

I gave him another hundred and said, "That non-alcohol beer tastes like crap."

I left the bar and made it to the train station in time to catch my train for the next town.

Never Bet Against Death
J. F. Benedetto

The Treaty Port of Tien-Tsin, China
Saturday, 19 May, 1901

No one goes to a sporting event expecting to witness a murder. Even in Occupied China in the wake of the failed Boxer Rebellion, they don't. It's just not cricket.

Hezekiah Sauer, USMC (ret.), paused at the top of the staircase and pushed back his Stetson. Peppery incense filled the air of the heavily-ornamented Oriental hall; to his left and right, impromptu booths lined the walls, each booth containing a native Chinese hawking drinks, foodstuffs, and tobacco to foreigners in top hats and capes. The former cowboy-turned-marine took in the place the way he would have a gambling den in Manila.

Behind him, the Englishman—Sir Michael Beauclerk de Barham, 11th Baronet of Allington and 'gentleman-adventurer-at-large'—put his hand in Sauer's back and shoved him out of the way. "If you please, old chap? Some of us have bets to place."

Sauer hitched up his trousers and followed the Baronet. "Don't look like any gambling hall I ever saw."

"Whatever did you expect?"

"Faro, to start with. Vingt-et-Un. A craps table. A roulette wheel. You know, games people bet on?"

"The game we are here to bet on does not occur *inside*," de Barham said with that smirk that always made Sauer feel like a stupid country bumpkin. "We must egress to the viewing wall."

Sauer smothered a growl and fell into step with the English Baronet, his spurs jingling as they strode past the booths of Chinese sellers. "So what is this 'Cu-ju' anyway?"

"*'Ts'u-chü'*" the Baronet corrected with the tone of someone speaking to a child.

Sauer took a slow breath. This was the **271st** 'correction' he'd received from the damned Englishman. It happened so often, he'd had started keeping count. "Which is…?"

"*Ts'u-chü* translates literally as 'kick-ball,'" the Englishman explained. "It is an ancient Chinese sport almost 2,000 years old. Ah! Here we are." He led Sauer out of the hall, through a wide pair of sliding wooden doors onto a narrow, roofed wall-walk running left to right, with a staircase down just in front of them. The wall-walk was a viewing space, one divided in the middle by the wide staircase that descended to the ground below. The murmuring group of viewers to the left of the stairs consisted of caped nobles, top-hatted men of position, uniformed military officers, and here and there a woman as well, as expensively-dressed as the rest.

To the right of the staircase, the louder-talking spectators all came from the opposite end of the social ladder: tradesmen, common laborers, some gamblers, and a few women who would spend tonight walking the streets, searching for customers. They were confined by social prejudice to 'their side' of the staircase, away from the wealthy and well-to-do. The one thing they all had in common was that not one of the spectators was Chinese. All were white; the only Chinese on the wall-walk were attendants or sellers.

And then Sauer's mouth fell open: two of the women in the upper-class group stood out, as the people near them had moved away, visibly snubbing them. The reason? The black-haired beauty facing his way had a lit cigar in her silk-gloved hand, and chatted amicably with a blonde woman who had her back to him, also holding a lit cigar.

Women? *Smoking tobacco?* **In public?**

Everybody knows a woman who smokes tobacco is immoral, promiscuous, and not to be trusted. And these two? Why, they were not only smoking in public, but were out in public *by themselves* at a sporting event, without a man escorting them. Back in the States shops, first class hotels and restaurants always refuse to serve a lone woman, because (and *Hell,* even schoolchildren know this!) no high-born woman appears in public without a man at her side; if she does, she must be a prostitute.

Damn. These two 'emancipated' women were flaunting every social more, doing it right out in the open, as if daring any man to try and tell them what they could and could not do. Sauer turned away before he caught their eye, nudged de Barham, and gestured at them with his head.

"What? Oh, them? Yes, very *sui juris,* doing things that are quite unacceptable in a civilized society. However, some women on the Continent do smoke, and apparently their menfolk don't seem to care much, especially in Spain." De Barham snorted. "A nasty business, that. Oh, I say!" he cried, pointing. "There he is." De Barham pulled Sauer toward a Chinese Mandarin standing with his back to the staircase as Westerners of both classes clustered around him. His clothing was shopworn and his face haggard; a former Imperial official who had backed the wrong side during the recent Boxer Rebellion? That would explain his presence here. He was the bookmaker, given the amounts of money being handed to him in return for one or more red chits with either green or white Chinese symbols painted on them.

Without a word, the Englishman joined the others crowding around the Chinaman.

Sauer threw up his hands, then moseyed over to an open spot at the edge of the wall to see what all the fuss was about.

20 feet below him lay an open rectangle of ground walled in on all four sides, an enclosed space for the game to be played within. Positioned in the center of the otherwise empty field stood two poles 30 feet high. Connecting the two poles together at the top was a wooden screen with a large circular hole in the middle, the whole of the affair adorned with carvings of Chinese dragons and lotus flowers. A pair of small flags, one bright green and the other dull white, fluttered from the

tops of the two poles in the midday breeze.

Whatever it was, this was what de Barham had dragged him here to watch.

The gentleman-adventurer returned holding several red chits with green symbols on them, beaming. "It would seem that everyone who is anyone in the gaming circle of the treaty port is here today. I just saw the Russian Consul pass by, and over there? That is the Japanese minister conversing with the Secretary of the German Legation, and I can name more than a dozen gentlemen of position. We should have a smashing time of it!"

It was only natural the Baronet ignored the entire half of the crowd Sauer had joined; they were 'below the salt'. Sauer pointed at the poles occupying the middle of the otherwise empty, walled-in field. "What is that?"

De Barham guffawed, as if the answer should be obvious. "*Ts'u-chü* is played here, of course!"

"Oh, of course," Sauer parroted. "So are you going to tell me what in Hell *tcu-ju* is?"

"'*Ts'u-chü*'" the Baronet corrected.

Correction #272. The former cowboy's eye twitched.

The Baronet did not notice. "You see, old chap, it is a game somewhat in the same vein as our own football—the kind they play at Eton, not Rugby. Important difference, that. There are six players on each team, which array themselves on either end of the pitch—"

Pitch?

"—facing the upright posts in the center. The aim of each team is to propel the ball through the *fengliu yan*, the wooden 'banner' with the circular opening you see there high up between the poles. One team starts in possession of the ball. They kick it up into the air, kicking to one another or to themselves—"

*Kicking **to** themselves?*

"—and thereafter must keep the ball from touching the ground; if it does at any time, they incur a penalty point. They must also not allow it to contact the wall surrounding the pitch; if it does, they incur a penalty point. If they are unfortunate enough to kick the ball over the wall surrounding the pitch, the game ends and the other side wins the match."

Sauer thrust out his chin. "Doesn't sound so hard to me."

De Barham raised a warning finger. "Ah, but the players are not allowed to touch the ball with their hands, arms or head! Doing so incurs a penalty point. They are permitted to use only their feet, legs and …, ahem, chests, to keep the ball in the air. The whole aim is to kick the airborne ball through the hole in the screen between the tops of the two poles, but only one player on each team is permitted to try, that individual being the team captain."

"And they stay on their own side of the field for the whole game?"

"'Pitch', old chap."

Correction #273. Sauer automatically rested a hand on the holstered .44 Smith & Wesson on his right hip, then deliberately lifted his calloused hand away. They'd fought the Boxers together. At Lang Fang, their stranded train was being overrun by unstoppable sword-wielding Boxers; it was de Barham who helped Sauer turn the tide by getting the British Marines to deploy a Maxim gun at the front of the train. Since then, his friendship with the English nobleman stood equal parts like and dislike, but they'd fought side-by-side and made a desperate stand against overwhelming odds together; *the blood of the covenant is thicker than the water of the womb,* and all that. No cowboy could turn his back on such a man.

But damnation, he'd become a real burr under Sauer's saddle.

"No," de Barham went on, oblivious to Sauer's simmering anger. "No physical contact between the two teams is allowed. I well imagine it would be an even more delightful event that way. Where was I? Ah, yes. A referee will station himself on that platform there on the far side of the pitch, between the two teams, and maintain a list of penalties incurred and points scored. When a team has the ball, they must keep it in the air and propel it to the team captain, but only where and when it is desired—a feat harder to accomplish than you may believe—and the captain kicks the ball at the open circle." His hand traced the flight of an imaginary kick. "If it goes through, that team scores one point. If it fails to go through, there is neither point nor penalty. In either case, succeed or fail, the ball is then passed to the other team. When the game ends, each side's penalties are deducted from the number of goals they scored, and the side with the higher number wins the match."

Sauer scratched the back of his head. Two teams of six men each faced off, with the aim of each team's captain kicking the ball through the opening in the screen between the tops of the two poles, trying to make a goal while avoiding penalties. There was something about a pitch or a throw of some kind that he didn't understand yet, but it all sounded simple enough.

He relaxed a touch. This might be fun to watch after all.

"I have saved the best for last, old chap!" de Barham declared, as an excited murmur ran through the crowd. 20 feet below, a withdrawn, inscrutable Chinaman … another down-on-his-luck Mandarin, based on his clothing … came out onto the field and proceeded to take his place on the raised platform facing them. He spoke to the crowd in Chinese, which Sauer didn't understand. Why couldn't Ch'ou Tzu be here to translate for him?

Not that she could show her face in public right now. God, why did he have to fall in love with a Chinese girl who was secretly a Red Lantern witch supporting the Boxer rebels?

No. With the anti-Boxer feelings still running high, it was best she stay away and out of sight.

Face downcast, he leaned on his elbows and watched without interest as doors at either end of the field below opened and the players came out. All Chinese, of course. One team wore green jackets and the other white ones, with both sides wearing matching red pants…

Sauer stopped, his eyes growing wide as his gaze darted from one player to the next.

No, he wasn't imagining it. All twelve of the players were female!

Women? And they're playing a sports match??
Women! And they're playing a sports match!!
Women smoking in public. Women playing sports. Palace officials reduced to making book at local sporting events. It was too much to take in. Apparently in Occupied China, the motto was *Anything Goes!*

De Barham took extreme pleasure in watching his stunned reaction. "Do you understand now why I insisted you accompany me, old chap?" The Baronet's grin was as broad as it was lecherous. "I should imagine that with the right monetary incentive, we should be able to engage one or more of the players in some private 'athletic exercises,' if you comprehend of what I speak."

Gambling and whoring? Sauer might have been back in Arizona Territory. He pulled the brim of his Stetson back down.

He watched as below them, the girls in green and the girls in white moved onto their respective sides of the field. The Mandarin-cum-Referee rang a gong, and atop the wall rich and poor alike fell silent. The silk-clad official swept his arms out to encompass the whole field, and spoke gravely about something, which various foreigners on the wall translated for those around them, in a half-dozen different languages. Next, he recited something, almost as if it were a poem…which it was, de Barham repeating it aloud in English.

> *"Their sweat-stained faces*
> *are like flowers under dew;*
> *their fair brows dusty from the toil*
> *remind one of willow leaves in the mist.*
> *Hidden are their slender fingers*
> *in the sleeves, while*
> *a pull at the red skirts*
> *shows their tiny feet.*
> *The ball is kicked time and again,*
> *the maids blushing but speechless.*
> *They are watched with envy*
> *by the gallant youths of Chang'an."*

Never Bet Against Death

"The noted Chinese poet Li Yu, describing the game he watched over 200 years ago. Why, *Ts'u-chü* has been played in China for 2,000 years!" His face beamed like a child about to get a handful of candy. "Just wait until you see it. A true native display of a sport stretching back into Antiquity itself. A millennia-old window into their culture."

"Riiiight. And their all being women didn't influence your decision one bit, did it."

De Barham smirked. "Never even entered my mind, old chap."

Down on the field below them, the Referee rang a gong.

Firecrackers erupted in the center between the two teams of girls, and a moment later also exploded amongst the Europeans atop the wall-walk, tossed there by the Chinese attendants. A male English voice cried out "Gunfire!" only to be answered by a female French voice "*Non, ce ne sont que des pétards.*" Detonated wholesale along the roofed wall-walk, the multiple explosions elicited cries of shock and surprise as the acrid, billowing smoke quickly engulfed all of the foreigners, turning the wall-walk into a smoky fog bank.

The overpowering odor of burning gunpowder pulled Sauer's mind back to another such cloud from the last day of his childhood. He was six years old, living at Fort Apache with his father the US Marshal, when the followers of the Apache medicine man Noch-ay-del-klinne attacked the outpost. That was his far-too-young introduction to hostile gunfire. An Apache bullet caught him in the left side of the neck, leaving the scar he now unconsciously rubbed.

But there was nothing to fear here, right?

Then a woman screamed in terror.

Sauer dashed the length of the lower-class section of the wall-walk, his hand on his holstered revolver's gunbutt as he ran through the pungent smoke. Shapes loomed up out of the white cloud: an hysterical woman being held by a man, her head buried in his chest. An empty space separated these two from the four individuals at the dead-end of the wall-walk: three men, one white, one black, one yellow, standing over a fourth man, a Westerner by his clothing, lying face-down on the stone floor in a spreading red pool of blood.

He drew his Smith & Wesson on the three. "Hold it right there!"

De Barham came up behind him but stopped short. "I say!" He ran over and knelt beside the dead man, lifting his head. After a moment the 'gentleman-adventurer' turned pale, lowered the dead man's head and pulled out a linen handkerchief to wipe clean the fingers that had touched a corpse.

As the smoke cleared, a few men of condition came up behind Sauer, but stayed back a couple of feet, giving him room while they watched. They were followed by a lot more people, whom the men in front held back, as they stood rubbernecking the scene of a murder.

"Well?" Sauer asked the shaken Baronet.

"He—" De Barham swallowed. "He is dead."

"I can tell that by looking at him, dammit! Who is he?"

It took de Barham a moment to find words. "He is … *was* the Russian Consul for Tientsin. He's been murdered."

Sauer kept the muzzle of his revolver aimed at the three standing men as he spoke over his shoulder to the crowd behind him. "Go fetch the police."

"*Je suis désolé monsieur. Qu'est-ce que vous avez dit?*"

Sauer blew out a hard breath, but an authoritative Russian accent spoke up behind him. "I shall depart and at once beckon the gendarmes."

* * *

In the wake of the Boxer Rebellion, the Treaty Port of Tientsin, China is now occupied by armed foreign troops of the Eight-Nation Alliance, who make the rules and keep the shaky peace. In Tientsin that's overseen by the Provisional Government, a military dictatorship made up of representatives from the British, French, German, Russian, Japanese, and American military—in fact, the newest member, Commander Casanova, the representative from Italy, just joined the council four days ago. For public safety they've created a dual police network: military police composed of foreign troops, backed by civil police composed of native Chinese under the command of European officers. The native police handle most day-to-day matters ... but when a foreigner gets murdered, it's the foreign police who handle the case.

This explained the tromping arrival of four Russian Army gendarmes wearing round black sheepskin caps and carrying pistols and sabers, each man wearing a black uniform trimmed in orange. The four were led by a heavily bearded Russian officer who had the disposition of a wounded grizzly bear. "*Otodvigat'sya!*" he shouted at the crowd. "*Ty! Proch's dorogi.*" He pushed through and stomped over to where Sauer waited, still holding his revolver on the three men, who now sat back against the end wall of the walkway. The Russian officer faced Sauer. "*Kto ty? Chto ty delayesh' s etim revol'verom?*"

Sauer kept his eyes on the prisoners. "One of these men murdered the Russian Consul."

The youngest of the four gendarmes spoke to the bearded officer, who gestured sharply, and the young gendarme stepped forward and came to attention facing Sauer. "My officer says, hand over this revolver."

"Why?"

The gendarme raised one eyebrow, then translated. His bearded superior almost shouted his reply, and the gendarme translated. "My officer says, you must give up this revolver. It is a police order."

Sauer stared over at the bearded officer, then handed the gun to the English-speaking gendarme. He handed it to his officer, who sniffed the gun's muzzle, then broke it open and shook out the bullets in the cylinder. They were all still loaded, and because it had been cleaned since the last time he used it, there was no smell of it recently being fired. The officer reloaded it. "*Kto ty?*"

"My officer asks, who are you?"

"I'm an American. Lieutenant Sauer, United States Marines, retired."

The translator's eyebrows climbed his forehead and he translated this with a bit more animation than before.

The Russian officer examined him with skeptical eyes. And why not? Sauer dressed far more like the Arizona cow-puncher he used to be, rather than the Marine officer he had so recently been.

The young gendarme spoke. "*Amerika*—? 'Cowboys, with Indians'?" He immediately got busy talking to his officer. As he spoke, the other Russians' eyes lit up and they spoke sotto voce amongst themselves. The officer spoke again, softly for once, and respectfully handed the loaded revolver back to him.

Sauer glanced sideways at de Barham with a sinking feeling. "My Stetson, a gun on my hip … he thinks I'm a gunfighter, doesn't he."

De Barham smirked. "Oh, yes!"

Sauer rubbed the side of his forehead. "Can we get on with this?" He spoke to the translator. "At the start of the game, firecrackers were set off up here on top of the wall, and some of the Europeans over there started shouting because they thought it was gunfire. Then that woman over there screamed; says she saw the Russian Consul get attacked, but that the smoke was too thick for her to see who did it. I was back there—" he pointed "—I heard her scream, I came running. The smoke was clearing and I found these four people here," he said, gesturing at the three sitting men and the corpse. "I drew iron on them, ordered them all to stay put, and sent someone to fetch the police. And now, here you are."

The young gendarme continued translating for Sauer. "My officer says he wishes you to stay here and … witness, this?" He paused, lowering his voice. "My officer, he desires your aid in this matter. Personally."

"Sure. Tell him I understand."

More guttural words in Russian. "My officer, he thanks you for your aid."

Sauer holstered his revolver and gestured the bearded officer into the scene of the crime.

Never Bet Against Death

The three suspects stood up, but the officer snarled at them and they all slumped back down. The Russian knelt on the stone floor next to the body, and Sauer joined him; three of the Russian gendarmes stood by, revolvers in hand, keeping an eye on the suspects, while the youngest gendarme crouched behind Sauer as his translator.

"Better keep the women back," Sauer told him. "They shouldn't see this."

"Yes, sir," the translator said, and passed the command to the men behind them.

A cursory search of the dead man's back showed no wound, nor any blood there, so they rolled the body over. His front was painted with blood, most of it on his left side, from the armpit to the waist. The Russian officer opened the shirt, then removed the shirt from the corpse's left arm, but there was no wound. He waved his hand over the body and asked Sauer something.

"My officer asks; can you see where the blood comes from?"

"I have an idea." Sauer lifted the dead man's left arm and pushed it backward, revealing a stab wound high in the armpit. The Russian stared, confusion painting his face; apparently people did not get stabbed there where he came from.

But then again, it wasn't all that common where Sauer came from, either.

The young gendarme translated. "My officer asks; this can be kill a man?"

"Yeah. I learned about it from a *bandito* in Mexico." Sauer gestured for de Barham to come over. The English nobleman did so, only to blink when Sauer spun him around so that his back was to Sauer and the officer. Sauer took out his belt knife and showed it to the officer, gesturing to stab with it. The officer nodded, and so Sauer sheathed it and repeated the gesture with his thumb out in place of the knife.

The Russian officer understood.

Standing behind de Barham, Sauer grabbed the Baronet's left arm and jerked it up and back, something de Barham did not expect. Before he could react, Sauer stabbed the "knife" up into his armpit and yanked the "blade" back towards himself. He let go of de Barham and explained. "The heart pumps blood from here," he said, pointing to his chest, then traced its path up to the armpit. "All the blood that goes into your whole arm passes through here. Cut a man open here, and he'll bleed to death damn fast." Without waiting to be asked, he drew his belt knife again and handed it to the officer.

The man smelled it, then licked the side of the blade, then used his handkerchief to wipe it clean before handing it back to Sauer.

"My officer, he says—"

"That there's no smell or taste of blood on the blade. Yeah." He'd seen Apache Scouts do the same thing.

The Russian knew his business. Despite the man's sour disposition, Sauer had a newfound respect for the bearded officer. He ordered one of his gendarmes to go to the three suspects, no doubt searching for the murder weapon, while the other two covered him with their drawn revolvers.

None of the three suspects appeared to be particularly stupid, so it was unlikely the killer still had the murder weapon on him. He spoke in a low voice to the Baronet. "I don't see any place to hide a knife on this stone wall. Maybe the killer threw the knife away in all the smoke and confusion. Head on down and take a look around the ground on both sides of the wall, see if you can find it. Oh, and one more thing."

A shakiness made itself known in the Baronet's voice. "What's that, old chap?"

"The Russian Consul … he's a fairly high Government official. Knows all the 'right sort of people'. Why was he over here among the peasants? He shouldn't be here at all. All of your kind stay on your own side, away from the 'cheap seats'. Even **you** did, leaving me to take up station on this side so you could go over there and be among your own class. Or did you assume I didn't notice?"

"I assumed you had," the Baronet said, "by the way you remembered your place."

Correction # … Hey, that wasn't a correction, *that was an insult!*

Before Sauer could answer that dirty remark the Baronet strode off on his quest to locate the murder weapon. Sauer cut short a rather rude reference to the Baronet's parentage and returned to the investigation.

As he expected, a search turned up no knife among the three suspects.

So who were they?

The yellow man, Nie Yukun, was a fallen Imperial Mandarin who worked now as the local bookmaker, but that alone probably wasn't a crime in China, given how the natives will bet on literally anything if you challenge them to. But the Russian Consul dealt with politics, and the bookmaker's former position as an Imperial official favoring the Boxers stood hard against him being the innocent party here.

The white man, Issac Tarris, a string bean of a fellow, wore dirty workman's coveralls and a 'newsboy' flat cap, with a battered red monkey wrench hooked to his pocket. Holding his hat in hand, he had the appearance of a country mechanic or a bicycle repairman, which meant absolutely nothing when it came to being a murderer.

The black man, Booker Franklin, was the best-dressed of the three, though it didn't take a genius to know why a man in such a nice suit was on this side of the viewing stand. Despite the fine clothing suggesting he was a man of means, he was also a negro, and it was a fact of life that too many people thought they were better than him because he wasn't a white man.

People like Sauer's own father, the US Marshal at Fort Apache.

The Russian officer made a disgusting sound in his throat and motioned for the only witness, the woman, to come forward; they moved to talk to her in a fashion that would keep her from seeing the pool of blood and the dead body. The bearded Russian spoke, and the translator said "My officer asks, who are you?"

The plain but still nice shirtwaist and skirt of the distraught woman suggested she might be a seamstress, more at home in Sauer's social circle than the Baronet's. She spoke English with a hard French accent.

"I am Marie-Anne Olympe Clicquot." She paused, taking in the stern faces of the men around her, and hung her head. "I heard that there is to be a 'fix' in this game, that the Greens shall be made to win and the Whites to lose. I had come here direct from bank with my savings—" She produced a carefully folded pile of money. "—250 Francs, to place all in a bet upon the Greens. When I arrived late, I seek for the, the Chinese 'man of the betting', *oui*? I came over in quickness to put my bet before the game, she start. But firecrackers, they explode, and everything, she becomes fog of smoke. I come into it, then see man— the dead man—and through smoke another man came behind him, took up his arm, and stab him. There was too much smoke for me to see who the man behind him was, and when dead man fall, other man already step back into smoke unseen."

Translating. "My officer asks, Do you recognize any of these three men?"

Someone passed a cape, which was draped over the body, and Mademoiselle Clicquot was brought close. She glanced down at the covered corpse, swayed slightly, and took a long breath as she turned her gaze to the three suspects. She swallowed, still shaken. "The smoke, she was too thick. I do not know which of these is the man."

Sauer had expected as much. The killer had waited until the smoke was thickest before killing the Consul. He would have gotten away, too, if the French woman hadn't come up suddenly and witnessed the crime, her screams alerting everyone else.

The young gendarme translated again. "My officer, he says that you must stay here. He says, perhaps you will see or remember something about the killer."

Mademoiselle Clicquot shivered, but agreed, stepping as far back as she could from the dead man.

De Barham reappeared. "I searched the area below the wall, both inside and outside the pitch. I found no knife."

"Of course," Sauer said, tilting his Stetson back again.

The Russian officer was now questioning Nie Yukun, the fallen

Mandarin.

"My officer asks, what were you doing when the murder occurred?"

Nie spoke. "I take bets, many people. I go first to rich foreigners, then come this side, take many bets, much money placed."

Sauer spoke up. "Was there a fix on the game?" When Nie just stared at him, he rephrased it. "Were the Greens going to win, no matter what?"

Nie did not answer for a long moment. "No. This would not be fair. All bets good bets. No one know which side win."

"Really? Maybe there *was* a fix, and the Consul found out about it." Sauer bent down and turned out the dead man's pockets. He had no less than five red chits, all bearing white Chinese writing on them.

"He bet White win," Nie said, his eyes cold, looking down his nose at Sauer. "He not only one. Many here bet White win. This mean nothing."

Sauer stared back. "Unless he just found out about the fix and confronted you about it and all the money he was about to lose."

"He not do so. Me not be killer. There be no 'fix'. Game good. Game real. Take bets, both sides, all folk, rich and not."

"Uh-huh."

The bearded officer spoke to Tarris. More translating. "My officer ask, who are you? He ask, why are you here?"

The man's twangy accent proclaimed he was an American. "I'm Issac Tarris, and I work for the Maritime Customs Office. I keep the steam launch runnin'."

"And what are you doing here?" Sauer asked.

"It's my day off, so I figured on comin' over and watching this-here game. I wasn't bettin' or anything, sir! I'm not a gamblin' man. An odd fellow, he don't take with gamblin'."

"You are 'odd' man?" the translator asked with searching eyes.

"The 'Odd Fellows'," Sauer explained. "It's a, a group of men who get together."

"Oh, it's more'n that, sir," Tarris said. "Our motto is 'Friendship, Love and Truth,'. That's why we're odd: causin' we think of others instead of ourselves. We promise to 'visit the sick, relieve the distressed, bury the dead and educate the orphan.' Means we'll always go and help our fellow man, no matter what."

The young gendarme raised an eyebrow. "You are priest?"

"What? Why I ain't no Catholic! I's a Methodist, sir!"

Sauer rubbed his chin as the gendarme worked to translate all that into terms his officer could understand. If Tarris was the murderer, he had a damn good disguise; most people would say a man as plain and simple as him could never be a cold-blooded killer. But Sauer had seen men like him before who were indeed murderers, polite manners and simple speech be damned. "So you came here just to watch the game, is that it?"

"Yes sir. I come here to watch this here game, that's all."

"Uh-huh." Sauer raised an eyebrow. "You work for the Customs people?"

"The Maritime Customs Office? Yes sir."

"You ever met the dead man before?"

"Well," he drawled, followed by a pause that said he was mulling over telling the truth or not. "Yes sir. I done met him just last night. He went out on the Customs launch, the one I'm a mechanic for? Went out to see one of them little Russian ships, the ones that are small enough to come upriver from the coast."

"The shallow-draft 300-tonners," Sauer noted as a former Navy man. "And?"

Another pause. "Well, that there man slipped in some oil on the deck and got hisself all dinged up. Tore his trousers open right in front of everybody. Wasn't pretty to see."

"And he was mad?"

"Powerful mad, sir."

"At you?"

Tarris' mouth became a crooked line as the young gendarme worked to keep up the translation into Russian. "Well sir, he was plumb out o' sorts, said he was all humily-ated and such."

Sauer gave a sympathetic nod. "And told you he'd get you fired."

"That there's the long and short of it, sir."

"So you came here to kill him, then!"

"Nossir! I did no such thing. I just came here to relax and watch this here Chinese ball game." His next comment was softer, and to no one in particular. "If'n I knowed it would be like this, I'da stayed home in bed."

More and more translating. The officer gestured to the black man, Booker Franklin. The young gendarme spoke up. "My officer ask, Who are you? What is black man doing here among good people?"

Franklin bristled. "I am Booker Abraham Franklin, and I run a store in the American part of the British Concession. As to what I am doing here 'among good people', I came here to talk with the Russian Consul about his outstanding debt in my shop. I confronted him and demanded he pay his account."

"And?" the gendarme asked.

"He told me to go to Hell."

Translation. "My officer asks, why is nigger allowed to—"

"Negro" Sauer corrected.

The young gendarme cocked his head but repeated himself. "Why is 'neegro' allowed to come among white men?"

"Because this isn't America?" Sauer suggested with hands spread.

Franklin sneered at him. "You believe I require a white man to take care of me? Is that it, Massa?"

Sauer narrowed his gaze. "It's been a bad day all around, mister, so don't push me."

"Oh, now it's 'mister'? What makes you think I want your help, *Massa*? You're just another dumb white cracker! Why do you care what happens to me?"

"Because I grew up at Fort Apache with the best damn horse soldiers in the US Army, the Buffalo Soldiers of the 10th Cavalry! And as the son of a US Marshal, I know what a lynch mob'll do to a black man, and that ain't justice. But hey, you don't want no help? Fine! Probably means *you're* the one who killed the Russian Consul. You've got as good a motive as any man here."

"That is patently ridiculous. If I took the man's life, I would not receive the money he owes me, would I?"

"He said he wasn't going to pay it. Told you to go to Hell. You weren't going to get paid, so maybe you took offense and decided to rob him of his life instead!"

"I would not kill a man over his outstanding bill. I would if it were *my* woman he raped, certainly, but never because—"

Sauer stopped him. "What do you mean, 'raped'?"

De Barham interjected himself into the conversation. "The, uh, rumor is that the Russian Consul was, shall we say, something of a lady's man? The kind who, well, was … quite forward in his affections? Someone who never took No for an answer."

Sauer pinched the bridge of his nose. "You mean he was a—"

"He was something of a rake," the English Baronet quickly stated, cutting him off. "Even in a case of murder, scandal is something to be avoided at all costs."

"He's dead! I doubt he cares now."

"His honor is at stake, old chap! Surely even a colonial such as yourself can see that."

Sauer lifted his face Heavenward. "Give me strength, oh Lord." He paused, then squinted hard at the shadowed ceiling over the wall-walk. He gestured one of the Russian gendarmes to come over. "Lock your hands together, give me a boost," he said, indicating with his hands what he wanted.

The gendarme holstered his revolver and did as indicated. Sauer put one foot into the gendarme's interlocked hands and jumped up toward the ceiling, then came back down to the wall-walk with a blood-stained knife in his hand.

There was a collective gasp from the onlookers as Sauer flipped the knife around, examined it, then gave it to the Russian officer. "That's got to be the murder weapon."

The bearded officer looked it over and pointed at the blade, whose tip was free of blood.

Sauer understood without asking. "The tip's clean, but only because the killer threw it up and stuck it in the ceiling to hide it; hitting the wood took the blood off of the tip. But the blood that was left on the blade is still there."

The gendarme started to translate, but his officer cut him short, obviously getting the gist of what Sauer had said. He stared hard at the three suspects, all of whom were nervous, but seemingly not nervous enough to show panic. He immediately set about showing them the blade and grilling them for answers, the young gendarme working overtime to keep up with his superior's string of harsh questions.

De Barham stepped in close to Sauer. "I wonder if the Russians will offer a reward for finding the fellow who murdered the Consul. My, that would be smashing!"

Sauer's voice became as sour as his name. "Seems to me a Baronet who owns a whole village and a castle and a manor house wouldn't need *more* money."

"I was thinking of you, old chap, not myself. The way you are managing the matter, that reward is money for old rope."

Sauer stared at de Barham. "'Money for old rope'…?"

De Barham stared at Sauer. "Money for old rope." He tapped his palm in thought. "How do you colonials put it?"

A Canadian voice in the crowd behind them offered up "Like money in the bank?"

"Oh," Sauer said. "A sure thing. 'You can take that to the bank, it's guaranteed.'" He paused, searched his memory, and then snapped his fingers. "Damn!" He spun around, quick-drawing his revolver and pointing it at Mademoiselle Clicquot. "Hold it right there! *Ne bougez pas!*" he added in the French his schoolmarm mother had taught him.

Mademoiselle Clicquot moved with a speed no innocent woman could possibly have.

Sauer dodged sideways from the knife she threw, but couldn't shoot her because of the group of spectators behind her.

She vaulted over the top of the viewing wall like an acrobat and dropped from view.

As the startled crowd erupted with shouts Sauer vaulted over the top of the wall after her.

He dropped onto the field 20 feet below, rolling when he hit the ground to cushion the impact. The cat-like Clicquot, however, was already on her feet and sprinting away. He got to one knee. "Stop or I'll shoot! *Arrêtez ou je tire!*"

She kept on running.

He hesitated; a real man won't shoot someone in the back, especially a woman.

That stricture did not hold true for the Russian officer, who fired and dropped her on the first shot. The bearded policeman dropped to the ground alongside him, revolver in hand. The two exchanged a look and went over to the woman lying sprawled face-down on the far side of the field.

She lay motionless. The Russian drew his saber, jabbed her with it, and got no response. Sauer knelt and rolled her over. The fixed, sightless eyes told him all he needed to know, and he stood up and holstered his revolver.

"*Otkuda vy uznali, chto ona ubiytsa?*" the bearded Russian officer asked him, holstering his own gun.

Only some of the crowd atop the wall-walk had come down after them, all of them using the central staircase rather than trusting their skills in leaping down two stories to the ground. Thankfully, the person leading that group was the young gendarme who spoke English.

"What did he say?" Sauer asked him, suddenly tired.

"My officer ask, how did you know she was the murderer?"

"Indeed!" de Barham said, running over to join them. "How **did** you know?"

"I remembered something that she said early on, when we first questioned her. She told us that she had withdrawn all of her money from the bank to make a big bet on a fixed game."

De Barham looked puzzled. "Yes, I remember, old chap. So what of it?"

"This is Saturday, 'old chap.' None of the banks are open today, remember?"

De Barham's eyes went wide. "Good Heavens, you are correct!"

The young gendarme translated it, and the bearded officer's face lifted with his raised eyebrows. Words were exchanged, and the officer saluted Sauer. "My officer says, you are a brave man, gun-fighter. You have served Justice. He salutes you."

Sauer formally came to attention and returned the salute.

"My officer says, you have our thanks. We shall manage this from here on."

"Fine by me." With a silent *It's your problem now* gesture, Sauer walked back to the staircase, with de Barham trailing alongside.

They were halfway up the stairs before de Barham spoke. "I confess I am a touch perplexed."

"At?"

"Her saying she had been to the bank just before the game began. A poor excuse, that. Why did she use a bank as her *alibi*?"

"In case we searched her."

"I'm sorry?"

Sauer paused at the top of the stairs. "She was carrying a pile of money and needed an excuse for it being on her person if we found it on her. How else would a seamstress be able to explain having so much cash in her pocket? It didn't come from a bank! It was what she was paid to kill the Consul."

"Paid to kill?" De Barham's eyebrows came down, his eyes flicking from one thought to another. "But that would mean—"

"She was dressed like a seamstress," Sauer pointed out. "Do you think an ordinary seamstress could be that good with a knife? Know how to kill a man in that way? Know how to get rid of the killing blade by heaving it up into the ceiling from inside the smoke cloud? And the way she moved. Like a circus acrobat! Nope. She wasn't the offended party; she was someone hired to kill the Consul."

"By God's teeth! She was an *assassin*?!"

"That's my guess."

"A woman assassin. Amazing! But who hired her?"

"No idea, but the payoff was in French money, which suggests she or the one who hired her is French. Anyway, the Russians said they'll handle it from here and told me to skedaddle. It's their problem now."

"Hold up a moment, old chap! We need to inform the Russians of what she was! Of how she was in the pay of someone else, who—"

Sauer's tone stopped the Englishman. "He was a rapist who thought he was untouchable. But he wasn't, and he got what was coming to him. If the Russians want to take it further, let them. As far as I'm concerned, Justice got served."

As Sauer led de Barham from the viewing wall and back into the building, the black-haired French woman smoking the thin cigar watched Sauer leave, took one last puff and tossed the cigar, giving a smiling exhale as the dead rapist was wrapped up for the undertaker.

You May Already Be a Winner
A Vermont Radio Mystery
Nikki Knight

Do you know why radio stations don't give lottery numbers or school closings over the phone?

Most don't want to give away desirable information without an ad they can sell.

It's a good enough reason in a world where local radio stations scrape by on hope and minimal margins.

But it's not why I don't do it at my little station, WSV in Simpson, Vermont.

Not since the arson, anyway. And everything after.

Let me start the next set—some anniversary Barry White and a Celine Dion breakup wail—and I'll explain how I ended up going from full-service DJ to amateur sleuth. Again.

It really shouldn't have surprised me; in small-town radio you do everything. I've spent most of the last year getting used to that again—the hard way.

Over a few weeks last July, my comfortable job as your happy and friendly midday DJ at a top New York City music station evaporated and my marriage exploded. Neither disaster was my fault: my husband survived cancer and decided life was too short for monogamy…and my employer decided the *Bully Ballers Show* was a better bet than *Jaye Jordan's Light Rock at Work*.

Try making all that into lemonade.

Actually, I wasn't doing too bad. I used my severance to buy the radio station where I'd had my first on-air job and moved into the apartment over the studio with my tween daughter. By April, Ryan was settled and thriving, the station was edging toward break-even, and I'd re-connected with an old crush.

That's where it stood when I found myself in the middle of somebody else's bad movie.

It started the night of that big MegaCash drawing. The balls had just been drawn for the 723-million-dollar pot, and I'd copied the numbers over for our website. (The Chen's Minimart Lottery Update, if you're keeping score.)

The phone lit up at 11:09. Everyone knows the All-State Lottery balls drop just after eleven, and they expect to see those numbers posted pretty quickly on big jackpot nights. And I oblige.

So I was a little surprised when my cheery "WSV, what's your request?" was greeted with a snarled demand:

"Where are the numbers?"

As it happened, I was just clicking "post" at that second. But I don't like being snapped at.

"Thank you for asking," I said in my coolest and most professional tone. "They'll be up very soon."

"Good."

Click.

Sure, the odds of winning are lower than getting struck by lightning. But there are always a few folks who think they're the one.

Whatever.

One snotty listener wasn't going to ruin my night. I racked up "The Way You Look Tonight" for a golden anniversary couple and some Beyoncé for the new parents on their first date night, and went on with the show, enjoying one of the best parts of my day.

Sure, my life was nothing like it had been, but I also had a lot more freedom to play what pleased my listeners…and myself.

I didn't think about the lottery again for a while, because the next morning I was doing two more of my many jobs: mom, and reporter.

Just before eight, I was driving back from dropping my daughter and my business partner's son at Madeline Kunin Elementary when I saw smoke.

Not a little smoke, either.

If it was visible from the school at the top of the hill, it was pretty bad.

Thirty seconds later, as I pulled back into my spot at the station, I could see it was coming from the MobileHut phone store catty-cornered from our building, pouring out the open door of the storefront. As I hopped out of my old Wrangler, I saw several firefighters rushing in, carrying hoses.

Time to dust off my news skills. Better find the audio recorder and get out to the fire. If I could remember where the recorder was.

Just inside the lobby, Rob Archer, my morning DJ, business partner, and neighbor, was waiting. He handed me the news kit with a wry smile. "Time to see if you remember how to do a live shot."

"Oh, yay."

As I stepped back outside, patting my jacket pocket to be sure I had my phone, I saw another fire truck pull up—a yellow one from the next town over, pulling up behind one of the red Simpson rigs.

All three of ours were already there, and so was Fire Chief Frank Saint Bernard. I only knew because I saw his red SUV—he was on the line somewhere.

It looked like the Chief and his men were winning, because while there was smoke pouring out of the first floor, the upper floors seemed quiet.

The building, like most of our tiny downtown, was a store on the first floor and apartments above. Back in the day, there were plenty of local families who ran small businesses and lived over the store. Never mind back in the day. These days, my daughter and I do, and so does Rob, his husband, and son, over the restaurant that is Rob's *other* full-time job.

The phone store on fire was one of the few things in town really doing well. If the day I changed my plan last August was any indication, they had three or four people working there, and it was pretty busy.

I remembered they opened early, and I ran across the street, taking a new, worried look at the scene.

A small knot of people was just outside the line, most holding minimart cups of some hot drink and looking shellshocked. I recognized the scruffy blonde woman who'd walked me through my paperwork. She looked even more tired now.

I didn't remember all the details, but her name was Tina and her son had some kind of special-needs issue. We'd talked about Kunin Elementary, and Tina had assured me the staff was terrific, citing her own experience as a single mother with a child who didn't fit the usual mold.

The other workers looked vaguely familiar—a couple of guys in their 30s I'd probably seen at the minimart and a very pale older lady who was the grandmother of one of Ryan's classmates, but I didn't know them well, either.

Fire Chief Frank (the "good friend" of Rob's aunt, and therefore family) came out of the building as I approached, and spent a few moments talking to the workers, shrugging and shaking his head.

"The desk?" I heard one of the guys say.

"I'm sorry," the chief said.

Both guys swore, and Tina seemed to collapse inward. The older lady looked like she wanted to cry.

What was up with that?

"Oh, hell."

I turned to see Penny Chen, owner of the minimart, running up with another go-tray of coffee, probably for the fire crew.

"What's wrong?" I asked.

"They had the winner," Penny shook her head. A plump little woman with salt-and-pepper hair, she had a light Southern accent from learning English in Texas decades ago. "They called ten minutes ago. I was just thrilled. You know about Tina, Mark's wife is sick, and Mrs. Linsey's been answering the phone because she can't afford to retire. Seven hundred twenty-three million dollars. Burned to a crisp."

"What rotten luck."

We shook our heads together.

"Just cruel," Penny said, her accent stretching out the description into a long, mournful sigh. "So close to everything getting better, and then…"

"Come on, we have to go in there!" one of the guys shouted.

"It's too late, Mark," said the other. "They won't let us."

The two voices were so similar it was like one person talking to himself. Weird.

Of course, it might not have been so weird to anyone else. Being a jock, I hear voices differently than most folks, and they might well not sound so alike to someone who doesn't pick up tone, pace, and emphasis the way I do.

"But it's—"

"Just let it go for now. We can look later."

The voices weren't just similar.

One of them had been the guy who called and demanded to know what the numbers were.

Made sense, I supposed, if he'd been watching the lottery balls drop on TV and wanted to see it print to be sure.

Chief Frank saw me standing a bit further away and walked over, his round face smudged—and troubled. "Don't have anything official yet."

"No rush." I met his gaze. "Off the record?"

"Lithium-ion battery charging at the desk where the ticket was locked in a drawer. Burned to a crisp. Because of course it did." He scowled.

I heard something in his voice. I waited.

"Don't know, Jaye. Just a bad feeling."

I nodded. My Uncle Edgar had spent thirty years with the Mineral County, Pennsylvania, Sherrif's Department, so I knew about that feeling: "Hinky."

Police Chief George Orr, a fellow transplanted New Yorker, and husband of a friend of mine, walked up just then to hear me use the magic word. His usually amiable brown eyes sharpened and his friendly caramel face tightened into a scowl. "Not planning to play amateur detective again, Jaye?"

"Just keeping my ears open. I heard a few things. Maybe you two want to come over for a cup of good coffee after you finish the mop-up?"

The chiefs exchanged glances. Smiled.

You May Already Be a Winner

The coffee, from a high-end subscription service I bought after narrating an incredibly boring—and lucrative—corporate training video, is always a draw.

Today, though, the info was probably better.

* * *

An hour or so later, our chiefs were happily ensconced in my office with the promised coffee and a couple of Rob's infamous pecan sticky buns. No, not bribery, merely a little thank-you from a grateful local business owner.

"It's all just too simple," the fire chief said. "Those batteries catch fire every day…but today's the day it goes, when a 723-million-dollar ticket is in the desk by it?"

"You thinking arson to cover a theft?" A bit of the Bronx crept into Police Chief George's tone, a sign he was thinking hard and not trying to be low-key Vermont friendly. He usually calibrated very carefully, since he stood out more than a little, being six-foot-three, Black, and formidable, even without the leather trench and fedora.

"Be a really rotten thing to do," Chief Frank said. He still lives in the house his parents—an earlier Fire Chief and a Sunday School teacher—brought him home to from Simpson Memorial Hospital. Even after most of a half-century on the fire line, I knew he had a hard time seeing anything bad in his neighbors. "And why? Plenty of money to go around."

"To us, sure," Chief George said, nibbling contemplatively on a square of sticky roll. "But that kind of money makes people crazy."

"Maybe in New York, Chief, but…" Chief Frank shook his head. "They all know how much the others need the money. Surely nobody would…"

"All due respect, Chief, but 723-millon-dollars changes everything."

It was unintentionally funny, the odd couple effect of the small, older—and very pale—fire chief, sparring gracefully with his opposite number. Despite a surprisingly close and supportive friendship, they always address each other by title, as a standup guy respect thing.

"Maybe so, Chief," said the older man. "Maybe so. What do you think, Jaye?"

"I told you about the call and the voices. I think we all agree something is wrong here."

"But that's all," the fire chief said.

"Could be any one of the four," Chief George said.

Technically true. Tina, I knew, needed the money, and I didn't doubt she'd do whatever she had to do to take care of her child. I would. But I wouldn't get greedy, and I didn't think she would either. Penny had said Mrs. Linsey couldn't afford to retire, which made sense, considering her age and the depressing nature of the job as a greeter. I didn't know the brothers at all, but I had heard them.

"I think it's one of the guys," I said. "The voices."

"Which one?" asked the police chief.

"I don't know them. They sound so alike—are they related?"

"Cousins," said Chief Frank. He'd stopped eating, a definite sign of concern. "Mark and Ezra Gray. Ezra's the store manager, Mark's sort of the family ne'er do well so Ezra gave him a job."

"Mrs. Chen said Mark's wife was sick?" I remembered only other thing I knew about them.

"Some kind of chronic illness, I think." Chief Frank shrugged. "I know the grandparents. I don't know any of the younger ones well."

"Be an awfully nice score for someone whose life wasn't going too well." Chief George took a sip of his coffee.

"I hate this." Chief Frank drummed his fingers on his mug. "We're talking about our neighbors like potential suspects."

"Unless that battery caught fire at exactly the right moment, they are." Chief George gave his friend a sympathetic smile. "I know it's hard for you."

We all sipped our coffee.

"Well," I said. "I might be able to help a little. I've got a friend in Montpelier who could make a call to the lottery folks and give them a heads-up, maybe get them to help us flush out our suspect."

"Really?" Chief George's brow flicked.

"Think so?" Chief Frank smiled a bit.

"Absolutely." I topped off our mugs. "Let's figure out a plan."

After they left, I made a call to a private line. My friend in Montpelier was more than happy to help. I would probably end up owing him a favor, but that's how the game is played.

And we were ready to go.

* * *

It was actually pretty easy. The next morning, I made sure to work the announcement the Chiefs had cooked up into the news updates:

> "And in other news, authorities say the damage to the cable office may not have been as bad as initially believed. Fire officials plan to go in for a search later today. State lottery officials have confirmed the winning ticket was sold at Chen's Minimart…and tell WSV Radio they're waiting to see if it can be produced."

Factually true—the authorities were the chiefs. My connection had convinced the lottery to put out a statement confirming the sale of the ticket and explaining that they could not pay out without a physical ticket. So, the report wasn't the biggest violation of journalistic ethics ever. Anyhow, I haven't been a real practicing journalist in a couple decades, and my own ethics lean strongly toward making sure creeps don't steal money from good people.

While Rob spun the usual morning mix of what I like to call "mom bangers"—bright, up-tempo songs suitable for the morning carpool—I recorded the news updates, got my daughter fed, dressed, and ready, and kept looking out the window at the cable office every chance I got.

Nothing.

Headed up the hill to school for drop-off, then swung back to the mobile phone office. In the lot outside, Chief Frank and a couple of burly firefighters were waiting with three people.

Three. Not four.

I was right.

Partly, anyhow.

As I parked, I saw Chief Frank patting Tina's arm and reassuring her.

That was a relief, anyhow. I really didn't want her to be involved.

But both guys were there. I guessed the shorter, pudgier one in a MobileHut branded yellow fleece over an oxford was Ezra, the manager, and the younger, scruffier man wearing a rumpled gray official polo with a stain was Mark, the ne'er do well.

I greeted Chief Frank with a smile and a friendly handshake.

"I'm not sure if you've met," he said, motioning to the men with a social smile. "Jaye Jordan, from WSV, Ezra and Mark Gray."

"Nice to meet you." I held out a hand.

"I feel like I already know you," said Mark. "I listen."

"So do I," Ezra said.

"Thanks." I realized I would not have noticed the similar voices if I'd seen them face to face first. And I still had no idea who'd called.

Interesting, though, that they didn't mention hearing the numbers or this morning's story.

With a quick glance to Chief Frank, I turned to Tina. "How are you holding up?"

"Been better." She tried for a smile, but couldn't force her mouth to do it, never mind her eyes.

"Got that." As I reached to pat her arm, the Simpson police chief's cruiser turned into the lot.

Everybody watched as Chief George pulled up to our little group and rolled down the window.

"Thought you folks might like to see who I happened to pull over at the exit for the interstate just now." said the police chief, leaning out the window. "Heading to Montpelier."

On the way to Lottery Headquarters.

In the back sat our fourth suspect, Mrs. Linsey, staring straight ahead.

"What?" Ezra Gray gasped.

"Montpelier?" Tina breathed. She got it.

"Rotten old bag!" Mark snapped.

The two chiefs exchanged glances.

Showtime.

"Shut up, you little snot!" Mrs. Linsey snarled at Mark.

As she spoke, the police chief helpfully lowered Mrs. Linsey's window to make it easier to hear her. Probably also to avoid cleaning off the spit later.

I noticed the town's other police cruiser pulling up, too. Good thing.

Ezra wheeled on his cousin. "What did you do?"

"Oh, stop that, Ezra." hissed the old lady. "You think I didn't see you move the charger to Mark's desk yesterday morning?"

The ne'er-do-well turned to Ezra. "You said it had to be my desk so nobody would think it was-"

"Stop it, Mark," Ezra's soft, amiable face hardened into cold fury. "Why would anybody believe you?"

Tina watched them, speechless, her eyes widening.

"You two don't deserve it anyway!" Mrs. Linsey hissed, shaking a fist out the window. "Arrogant jerks, always ordering me around like I'm your maid or something."

"Back off, old woman!" Ezra shot back.

"Don't you talk to her that way!" Mark practically exploded. "You're not sticking me with this one, Ezra."

Ezra didn't break. "With what? Not my fault you and that crazy old hag tried to cheat me and poor Tina here out of our shares."

He tried to put an arm around Tina, and she flinched away.

"Chief!" Mark stepped over to Chief Frank. "Listen to me. It was Ezra's idea. He said—"

Ezra drew himself up, trying to look like a pillar of the community, and made eye contact with the police chief. "I'm sorry, sir, but I'm going to have to come forward and report my cousin."

Mark went for Ezra, and Chief Frank held him back with strength that clearly came as a surprise.

"Go ahead, Mark." Ezra taunted.

"Enough." Chief George stepped out of the cruiser, narrowly missing Ezra with his door. As Ezra tried to pull away, the police chief grabbed him. "You're both under arrest. We'll let the DA sort out who's getting charged with what."

"Arson, for starters." Chief Frank pinned Mark's arms and held out a hand to his counterpart. "Got any zip-tie cuffs, Chief?"

"Sure thing." The police chief pulled one from his jacket pocket with his free hand, then looked down at Ezra. "You want some too?"

"No, sir." Ezra suddenly sounded small and defeated.

Mrs. Linsey saw her chance and tried to open the cruiser door.

"Stop!" ordered Chief George.

"I didn't set any fires!"

"No, you just took advantage of it," snapped the cop.

"I bought the tickets every week. It was mine!"

Mark and Ezra started another round of grumbling.

"IT WAS OURS!"

Tina's wail cut through everything.

All eyes turned to her.

"We won together. It was supposed to make everything better. And now…"

For a moment, the only sound was Tina's ragged breathing.

"It still will, at least for you."

As he spoke, Chief George handed Ezra off to the backup officer.

Then, he turned to Tina and reached in his jacket pocket.

"She had this in her purse." He held up a small plastic evidence bag.

The bag held a small square of paper worth more than the entire town. More than enough to share if nobody had gotten greedy.

Tina stared at the ticket, and a single tear oozed out the corner of her eye.

"We really won."

She might even feel like a winner someday.

* * *

It was no surprise when my cellphone buzzed a few hours later during the nighttime all-request show. My friend in Montpelier wanted to know how it ended.

"I hear there's been an arrest."

Governor Will Ten Broeck, my old crush and new man, sounded as happy as if he'd cracked the case himself.

Yep. The twist.

During my first hitch in Vermont, Will had been the hot politician on his way up, happily married, with a couple of kids. I'd had a huge late-adolescent crush, which was fine, because I *was* a huge late adolescent. Of course, I would never have done anything about it, even if he'd indicated interest, which he never would, with an ethical code every bit as strong as mine.

But he'd been aware of me.

So when I ended up back here, not all that long after he did, after his own trip through the career and marital blender, the chemistry was still there. And this time, we could do something about it.

We'd only been dating for a month or so, but it was clearly exclusive and serious. Neither of us was ready for declarations and official designations, but there was no doubt where it was going.

No doubt also about some very careful rules of engagement. He doesn't take advantage of the fact that he knows a radio station owner who would give him the benefit of the doubt, and maybe some airtime to go with it. I don't take advantage of the fact that the governor takes my calls.

But I might tell him about a situation where he can help good people by using his influence. The lottery commissioner had been very glad to earn a favor with that press release.

"Actually, a few arrests," I said. "I owe you one."

I had to offer the marker as a matter of honor, even though we're together.

"Nah," he said with a little chuckle, "this one is on me. I just like seeing the right thing happen."

"So do I."

"One of the many things I love about you, Jacqueline."

"Right back at you."

It was enough of a declaration for the moment. And if I felt like maybe I had a winning ticket of a different kind, well, that was my business.

Major League Collectibles
Mark James McDonough

I got the call as I was lying drunk on the couch waving both middle fingers at my cat. I didn't recognize the voice on the other line, but they were asking for the Albino Detective. Nicknames have a way of sticking, and I couldn't shake this one even though it was a misnomer on both accounts. I've got alopecia, not albinism, and people pay me to commit crimes, not investigate them. Even so, I'm tired of arguing. You can call me the Albino Detective or you can call me what I am; *the* yegg. Ask any well connected creep on the Eastern seaboard and they'll vouch for me. I'm the best. I steal the unstealable.

I've got eight million stories (seems a little high) but this unsavory yarn starts back in 1999. No one remembers anymore, but people used to love baseball and for a brief moment during the spring of that year, people loved a fella named Tommy White. White was tall and dull and gassed to the gills and had a meaty bum and was as American as assault rifles. He hit 47 homers in 137 games for the Tampa Tarpons, a single-A Florida State League club. Astronomical figures for a relative nobody. Everyone figured it was just the rich getting richer when the young stud was set to join a stacked New York Yankees roster the next year. That never happened though, because Tommy White up and vanished.

What concern of mine is he in the year 2024 when the world has gone to hell in a Whole Foods tote? Well, the thing is, Topps came out with a set of rookie cards for that 2000 season and, aside from the general mystery and intrigue around his disappearance, the card they released was spooky for another reason. The photo they used, one of White rounding the bases with his hand raised in celebration, was set in front of a centerfield billboard advertising the movie *Final*

Destination. I'm not one for that horror crap (I like the movies where it's a guy in a big stupid suit and a lady in a fur coat trying to kill each other) but the general premise of the film is that death is out to get you. I guess that's kind of ominous. They released 250 of these cards into circulation before he went vamoose . They can range in price from 25 to 50 bucks depending on their condition, but the plot is about to thicken like your great aunt's thighs. Topps releases a checklist every year and the 2000 edition shows that there were also five signed cards put out into the wild. No one knew where any of them were. Except maybe one.

Every few years on social media, whether it be Yik Yak, Friendster, Yahoo!360, or iTunes Ping, someone brings up the story of the missing cards and there's interest for a week or two before everyone gives up again. Buried in one of these comment sections on Twitter however, was a now deleted tweet showing what looked to be the genuine article. Baseball collectors are nutso (only finishing behind Abe Lincoln fanatics on the insanity scale) and so after I found out about the missing cards, I wasn't surprised one of them contacted me to track one down. The only lead I had to go on was the username of the person who posted the photo of a seemingly real card. That turned out to be enough. Whoever it was had an Etsy store under the same name. Listen, this wasn't my favorite case by any means. Etsy? Horror movies? And, worst of all, baseball? Yuck. I would have stayed far away from it if the money wasn't so damn good. If we're talking turkey, consider me Ben Franklin.

I never kept an ear to the ground for fear of someone stomping on it. These wackos sought me out and not the other way around. The guy that hired me went by the name Kris Kristofferson (different Kris Kristofferson). He didn't have much choice but to do what I said. Kris agreed to order something off of the Etsy site so that we could get a return address. I figured he had so much baseball paraphernalia that it wouldn't look out of the ordinary for him to have something delivered from the store. Kris bought a San Diego Padres shirt and I was astonished to find out there was a team with that name. Never underestimate the athletic prowess of priests.

Speaking of baseball, let me reiterate that I hate baseball. When you're a kid and look differently than everyone else in your neighborhood, you better be good at sports. I wasn't. I played little league one year and that was enough. As I was up at the plate my own teammates were calling me things like "Smeagol" and "Baseball". To make matters worse, the parents of the players on both teams would stand up and cheer me on like I was dying or something, like physical ability was measured in strands of hair. My being bad at baseball had nothing to do with my alopecia. Damn. You can see this case dredged up poisonous old memories and I wanted it closed quicker than your great aunt's thighs. Kris gave me the address on the label and it shared the same address with a shop called Major League Collectibles in Tampa, Florida. I filled the automatic cat feeder, bought a gallon of the heaviest duty sunscreen I could find and then headed down to the Sunshine State.

For those unfamiliar, Tampa is a little 2,898 hotel town on the Gulf Coast. People say it's the sanest city in Florida, but that's like being the cleanest guy in a hot dog eating contest: you're still slobbering all over the place. Tampa's one of the best places in the world to get drunk in the sun. Go and watch the overly tanned alcos crawl around you like drugstore beetles as an Uncle Sam on stilts sways and makes vague threats at the crowd. Not exactly my scene. I had to make a few alterations in order to blend in.

Let's get something out of the way right now, yes, okay, fine, sometimes I have to wear a disguise. How do you picture your favorite criminals? Probably not drawing fake eyebrows on with makeup. Nevertheless that's what I have to do and after extensive research (watching teenagers on YouTube) I've become an expert. Beauty isn't necessarily in the eye of the eyebrow haver, but they do help me to blend in when I'm working a case. I also have a wig that I'm less thrilled about. I ordered it because the wig in the picture made the model look like Jason Mamoa but whenever I put it on I look more like Phil Spector. I have to put a hat on top of it to make it look more natural. This was the getup I was wearing when my 1994 Ford Aspire pulled up in front of the card store.

Before I entered, I did a quick Google of "best baseball players of all time" in the event that someone struck up a conversation with me. I had heard of Babe Ruth but he seemed too dated so I decided to memorize the first paragraph of Willie Mays' Wikipedia. Trying to seem casual, I walked inside and started looking at balls, bats, hats, gloves, jerseys, and thousands and thousands of trading cards.

"How can I help you?" said the man behind the counter.

"Willie Howard Mays Jr. (born May 6, 1931), nicknamed "the Say Hey Kid"[a] and "Buck",[7] is a former center fielder in Major League Baseball (MLB). Regarded as one of the greatest players ever, Mays ranks second behind only Babe Ruth on most all-time lists, including those of The Sporting News and ESPN.[8] Mays played in the National League (NL) between 1951 and 1973 for the New York/San Francisco Giants and New York Mets. Mays is the oldest living member of the National Baseball Hall of Fame," I said.

"Wow, big fan huh? Me too," said the man. "Bob Dentist. Forget the name, I've got no interest in your teeth. Nice to meet you." Strange man with a strange name, short in stature, wiry and leaning forward like a potted plant trying to find the sun. His spectacles were as thick as the glass on submarine windows.

"Ross Geller," I said, giving him the first name that came to my head. "Who's your favorite fella? Player I mean."

"Ken Griffey Jr. of course. Kind of like the modern Willie Mays," said Bob Dentist.

"The Say Hi Kid I call him!"

"Ha! That's pretty good. Anything in particular you're looking for?"

A signed Tommy White rookie card with the Final Destination billboard in the background. "Ummm, well my collection is so large already. What I'm really interested in is the rare stuff. Not even necessarily for the big names, I like kind of odd, potentially spooky baseball cards?"

"Spooky baseball cards? Never heard of them," said Bob Dentist.

"Well, to each their own. I'll just take a look around."

I pretended to peruse the memorabilia and couldn't believe some of the names ('Oil Can' Boyd? Coco Crisp? Dick Pole? And that was just on the Red Sox!) but I tried to stay focused. Futile! No matter how hard I looked, I couldn't locate the Tommy White card and if I came right out and asked for it, it might tip the little nutso off. I did the only logical thing, which was waiting until the shop received a phone call and then hiding underneath one of the display tables. I squeezed in between two boxes and was granted cover by a tablecloth that hung almost to the ground. After a while I got bored and put my headphones in so I could watch videos on my phone. When I woke up the shop was dark. I crawled out, sore and cramped but in the clear.

Hanging beads, like the kind perverts have, blocked off the backroom so I just pushed them out of the way and found a safe. There was an electronic keypad to enter the code and I thought for less than a half a second and then looked up Ken Griffey Jr's birthday. I gleefully typed in 112169 laughing preemptively at how stupid this nerd was. And I was right to! Open sesame, jackass. It seemed like Lady Luck was by my side and that we were about to French kiss… but not so fast. The safe held a few cards I wasn't interested in, a framed and visibly photoshopped picture of Bob Dentist and Griffey at SeaWorld together, and a completed Topps checklist from the year 2000. Chances are that Dentist moved the card to his house after being foolish enough to post a picture of it online.

The next day, I followed him home from work. The morning after that, I waited until he left and then made my move towards his house. I always brought a brown shirt and shorts for occasions such as this. The neighbors would just think I was a UPS worker dropping off a package, and even if I got caught, there were no laws against impersonating a delivery driver. Or were there? I mean probably not, right? The bad news was that Ol' Bob had a Ring camera under his doorbell. The good news was that I caught sight of it before walking up onto his porch. I'd have to try the backway around. One thing that really ticks me off is that my clients always assume that I can sneak into places easier because my lack of hair makes me sleek and slippery. This just isn't true! But in this specific instance, I really slid quite easily into a basement window.

The cellar was filled with a bunch of embarrassing weird stuff just like the shop was (a cutout of Mark McGwire eating a cheeseburger?) but my gut told me I wouldn't find the Tommy White card out in the open like that. Then I saw it. Not the card, exactly, but the place where it might be. In the back corner of the room there was a padlocked door. I took one of the bats that was laying around and took a big swing. Okay, it took me two swings because I missed on the first one then spun around like a Skip-It and then crashed into the Mark McGwire cutout. But on the second swing I smashed the thingy and was able to open the door.

There were no lights in the room and the sunshine that had lit up the basement proper didn't reach that far. The flashlight on my phone revealed the card sitting on a shelf on the back wall. It was in a protective case and in phenomenal condition. When I turned to leave with it however, my foot caught on something on the floor and I fell hard onto the dirt ground. I used my flashlight to see what I had got snagged on and found the end of metal restraints attached to a hook in the ground. My hand shook violently as I moved the light up the length of the chain and finally to the skeleton leaning against the wall. I had never been so close to the end, never looked it in the eyes and lost that horrid staring contest. The reaper was unkind enough to provide me a preview for what lay ahead for me, what lay ahead for all of you. There is no escaping death, that dreadful thing, but I used to be able to bury the thought of it in the back of my mind like clipped toenails behind a couch. Now it's ever with me, using Tommy White's remains as a conduit for its laughter.

I ran as fast as a cat from a plastic bag and then jumped back out the window. The second after I reached my Ford Aspire, I turned the ignition key and stomped on the gas pedal as hard as I could. Despite everything I was really in the mood for McDonalds. I pulled into one of their 13,509 U.S. locations and mashed burgers into my mouth in the parking lot. Mmmm. Mmmm. Mmm… Mmmm! Oh. I knew I had to do something about Tommy White's bones but I didn't want to blow up my whole operation. Thankfully there was this neglectful mother not paying attention to her kids or anything else and I was able to effortlessly steal her Android. I called the fuzz from her phone then snuck it back onto her table. One of her idiot kids noticed me but they were too immobilized by their own cowardice to do anything about it. I may have looked a little scary, what with the makeup for one of my eyebrows missing and the dirt and cheeseburgers all over my face.

I was about an hour into my drive home when the news came on the radio. The police had reason to believe that the remains of Tommy White had been found in card collector Bob Dentist's basement. Dentist was on the lam. The police didn't know which way he was headed but they considered him armed and extremely dangerous. When I got back home, I dropped off the card with my client, Kris Kristofferson. Of course he still wanted it. I told you these guys have got something wrong with them. At first I thought the payday had been worth it, even with the corpse, but now I'm not so sure. I see White, sometimes in dreams, sometimes in nightmares. But the real kick of the thing was, that wasn't the last time I'd rub up against Bob Dentist. A tale for another time I suppose. The moral of this story is—don't collect stuff.

The Baby Lawyer
Paul R. Paradise

Jeff Little, a founding partner at Polk & Little, called. "It's that damn street peddler," Jeff said, exasperated. "He's back."

"What? Back again?" Jeff and I had served a cease and desist letter on the street peddler two days ago.

"Yes, the Commissioner is furious. I'm calling the police. I need you here this afternoon if you're free."

I left the office and took a cab.

For over a month Sam Drake, Commissioner of the National Basketball Association (NBA), had to pass a stubborn street peddler hawking knockoff NBA sports jerseys featuring a well-known design of basketball legend Jerry West dribbling a basketball. The street peddler also hawked jerseys of the New York Nets, Cleveland Cavaliers, and other NBA teams with their basketball-themed sports logos.

The Commissioner was involved with NBA Properties which handled the merchandising and licensing of the NBA's intellectual property, and he was not amused by the peddler who beckoned passersby with knockoff jerseys in front of the NBA's corporate office, located in the Olympic Towers on Fifth Avenue. However, the Commissioner's efforts to remove him were unsuccessful, which is why he had turned to Jeff's law firm.

I took the elevator. The receptionist told me Jeff was waiting in his office.

A young man sat next to Jeff. I knew the signature look of expensive Brioni cashmere suits, which were worn only by partners. Jeff was wearing a Brioni blue pinstripe. However, the young man seemed to be batting out of his league in his ten grand Brioni brown tweed suit. He had pink cheeks and tousled brown hair that gave him the distinctly preppy look of a college freshman.

"Have a seat," Jeff said. "I want you to meet my son, Kevin. You're going to be working with him."

"Pleased to meet you." Kevin reached over and shook hands.

"Kevin's a bright kid," Jeff said. "Chip off the block. Just graduated from Yale Law."

"Congratulations," I said, apprehensive at Kevin's being assigned. I sized him as a 'baby lawyer' destined to make partner but inexperienced and too young to work with me.

Jeff didn't waste time. I knew he was peeved. His fists clenched as he updated me on the street peddler.

I felt sorry for Jeff's having to deal with this low life. He was a high-powered attorney who pulled in seven big ones handling trademarks for fashion brands and the major leagues. In addition to trademark prosecution, the firm handled trademark infringement and executed trademark counterfeiting seizures. Petty criminals hawking knockoffs were the bottom rung and usually handled by new associates who worked with me.

"Commissioner Drake's in a fury about this street vendor." Jeff's voice reeked with frustration. "Wants to know why we can't get rid of this guy."

"Where's the street peddler?" I asked.

"Right now, he's selling counterfeits nearby. I called the police and demanded they send officers. I want you and Kevin to serve another cease and desist letter on this jerk. See if you can hold him till the cops arrive."

Jeff handed me a manila envelope with the c&d letter.

"Don't worry, Dad," Kevin said. "We'll get this guy."

Jeff smiled. "Thanks Kevin. I know I can count on you."

With no time to lose, Kevin and I left the building and hailed a cab. On the ride uptown, I questioned Kevin and learned he had started at the firm a week ago and knew little about the street peddler.

I thought it best to give him background on our adversary:

I told Kevin the quality of most knockoffs I had been seizing for designer brands like Gucci, Ralph Lauren, Luis Vuitton and sports apparel for the major leagues had been getting better and better over the years. Consequently, the Commissioner was concerned about the quality of the counterfeits being sold by the peddler and assigned the head of quality control to buy a few sports jerseys.

"You dad told me an in-depth examination left everyone baffled because even the usual factory flaws were missing. The counterfeits could not be called counterfeit in court without proof. Were they genuine? Parallel imports from overseas? Overstock? However, quality control discovered the dye ran out when the jerseys were washed."

Kevin chuckled. He'd heard snippets about the street peddler who was causing so much trouble.

Jeff learned that the Commissioner had called the police who either didn't respond or came the next day. Incensed, the Commissioner tried to roust the street peddler himself, but the peddler laughed and told him to get lost.

"That's when the Commissioner called your father," I said. I told Kevin his father's cease and desist letter was a clever strategy.

"When Jeff called two days ago, I hurried to the law office," I said. "We headed to Olympic Towers where we spotted him selling knockoffs from two plastic bags. Damn, the vendor looked like Matthew Barnes of the New York Knicks. He stood over six feet tall and muscular. No wonder he was successful selling jerseys with basketball logos. I didn't want to fight him if trouble started. I served the c&d letter which Jeff had addressed to an unknown John Doe Street Peddler.

"The peddler actually looked scared and read the c&d while we waited for him to comply. The c&d threatened all sorts of legal mayhem if he didn't surrender his counterfeit goods and cooperate in identifying his source. The c&d was a bluff. Without a police backup, Jeff and myself were powerless to enforce it.

"When he had finished reading the letter he threw it to the ground.

Fuck you! he snarled. He refused to identify himself and cooperate. However, the c&d letter was effective. He packed up and left."

Kevin nodded. His father had told him about the c&d letter.

"Why did this jerk return?" Kevin asked.

"Money," I said. "Midtown is lucrative for street peddlers. They sell next to stores like Macy's and Saks Fifth Avenue where there's a large pedestrian traffic."

"What about the police?" Kevin asked. "Do you think they'll show?"

"I doubt it," I said. "They usually don't want to be bothered with street vendors and take hours to respond."

The baby lawyer assessed the situation. I could practically feel the wheels turning. "What happens if the street peddler walks away?"

"Just let him go. Okay? Follow my lead."

The baby lawyer pondered the situation which made me nervous. This was the kid's first time in the field and he was green as grass.

"Listen Brian. I'll follow your lead. But Dad said I'm in charge of this operation."

My worst fear. The baby lawyer was pulling rank. Technically, he was in charge.

"Okay Kevin. But listen to me. I've been doing this for over twenty years."

We arrived at Olympic Tower, where the street peddler was holding up knockoff sports jerseys with his right hand. He was hard to miss because of his height. He had a bushy mustache and wavy black hair, and he was wearing blue denim jeans and a green pilot's shirt.

Two sturdy plastic bags rested at his feet. The NBA team basketball logos being counterfeited were the New York Knicks and the Los Angeles Lakers. He beckoned passersby with a sales pitch. However, his eyes narrowed as we approached.

"Oh shit, not *you* again—" He spat the words.

"Yeah, and I've got a present." I tried to hand him the manila envelope.

"Hey, get away from me! I don't want it."

I tossed the manila envelope at his feet. "Too late, you've been served. This is a cease and desist letter ordering you to cooperate with us. I suggest you read it. The police are on the way to arrest you."

"My name is Kevin Little," Kevin said. "I'm an attorney with the firm of Polk & Little."

"Listen fancy pants I don't care who you are." The street peddler stuffed the knockoff apparel into the plastic bags and sealed them.

"Blow it out, get lost." Without another word, he shouldered the plastic bags and walked away.

I turned to Kevin and said, "Well, that's that—"

Kevin scowled, "What do you mean? He's getting away!"

"Let him go. Our job is done."

"No! We're supposed to hold him until the police arrive."

I immediately sensed trouble. The inexperienced baby lawyer was becoming too eager. Having an attitude worked in court, but not in the field. He didn't know how dangerous street peddlers could be. When I worked peddler sweeps, I always had a police backup. Despite their living on the street, peddlers didn't take kindly to having their livelihood being seized. Over the years, I'd been kicked, punched, and had bricks and firecrackers thrown at me.

Kevin insisted we follow the street peddler. I tried to dissuade him, but Kevin refused to listen and demanded that I follow. Reluctantly, I fell in line, more to protect the baby lawyer who I was certain was heading for trouble.

Burdened by the plastic bags, the street peddler was unable to lose us. Finally, he stopped, turned and hissed: "Stay the fuck away from me!"

"No way, man," Kevin said. "We want to see where you're getting this stuff."

"Listen, Kevin, let him go," I pleaded.

"No, my Dad wants us to get this guy," Kevin said.

The peddler walked down the cement stairs leading to the underground subway. Kevin followed him. I followed a step behind, not wanting the baby lawyer to continue following the peddler but not knowing what else to do.

Before I could stop him, Kevin ran ahead and tried to stop the street peddler before he passed through the subway turnstile by grabbing one of the plastic bags.

The street peddler became a cornered animal. His eyes narrowed with pure venom. He tugged and tried to pull the plastic bag free, but when Kevin refused to let go, he roared like a vicious lion, "Let go, you bastard!"

"No! You let go!" Kevin roared back.

I raced to the rescue, but I was too late.

The street peddler let go of both plastic bags. It seemed as if Kevin had won the tug of war because he was still holding onto the plastic bag. I was horrified to see the street peddler reach into his pocket for a Filipino butterfly knife. He flipped it open with impressive expertise and held it hip high the blade pointing outwards ready to thrust.

Taken by surprise, Kevin appeared to be too terrified to move. He was still holding onto the plastic bag.

My heart raced. I'd had these knives pulled on me by street peddlers hawking knockoffs in Chinatown. If not for a police backup I'd have been killed. I was certain Kevin was about to be stabbed. I rushed forward anxious to grab the baby lawyer and pull him to safety.

Suddenly, out of nowhere, a woman screamed. Everyone turned and surrounded us to see what was going to happen. All eyes were on the street peddler who towered above everyone. The peddler hesitated for just a second with the knife held hip high. And then he lunged, with the grace of a fencer, his hand made a circular slash with the speed and skill of Zorro.

"*Ieeeee.*" The baby lawyer yelped as he let go of the plastic bag and jumped back as if struck by a bolt of electricity.

I knew Kevin had been stabbed. I pulled him away to prevent further harm. I heard gasps and moans from the bystanders who were mortified by what they'd seen. None of them, however, dared to intervene, as the street peddler with a quick flip of the wrist closed the knife and pocketed it and then he jumped the turnstile and disappeared, all with a bravado worthy of a swashbuckler.

Fortunately, the baby lawyer was unharmed. He checked to see where he had been struck. The butterfly knife had not pierced his skin but sliced through the sleeve of his Brioni suit. I was thankful. If Kevin had been injured, I would have been responsible.

"That was damn foolish," I said, letting my voice raise.

"I can take care of myself," Kevin said. "I know Aikido."

"Jesus Christ, shut up!" I yelled. I was furious at the kid. He could have been killed. "Come on. You grab a bag, and I'll grab one. Let's get out of here."

Kevin's face turned crimson. Probably no one had yelled at him in years. He grabbed a bag, and we left, pushing our way past befuddled, wide-eyed people.

We took an Uber back to the office. Seated next to me, he fingered his torn sleeve. 'His Brioni suit jacket was ruined. I believe the gravity of what he'd experienced hit him. He let out a slow breath and then apologized.

"You're right," he said. "I should have listened to you. I hope we're still friends."

Kevin extended a hand, and we shook hands. "No hard feelings. We're still friends. But I don't know how I'm going to explain what happened to your father."

"Don't worry, let me handle him."

We took the bags into the elevator and marched past the receptionist.

I let Kevin lead the way into his father's office. Jeff was thrilled when he saw the two bags of counterfeits.

"Wow, you got the guy!" He opened a bag and examined the jerseys with their basketball sports logos. "What happened? Where's the street peddler?"

"We followed him," Kevin said. He paused and then somewhat

embarrassed said, "When I saw him head for the subway, I did something stupid. I grabbed a bag. The peddler pulled out a knife—"

"A—a knife?" Jeff was flabbergasted when Kevin showed him the torn sleeve. He told his father not to get angry or to blame me. "Brian, told me not to follow the street peddler, but I wouldn't listen."

"I'm glad you're all right," Jeff said, relieved. He slowly let out a breath. "Anyway, we got the job done. I suppose that's all that matters. I want you to go home. I'll call the Commissioner and let him know we took care of the street peddler."

"Look Dad, I'm fine," Kevin said, trying to reassure his father.

"You did great, Kevin," Jeff said. "I can't have you walking around the office in a torn suit. Put on a new one and come back. I want you to write up a memo and address it to Samuel Drake, NBA Commissioner, and let me see it."

Jeff shook my hand, thanked me for my service and told me to send in my bill.

I left thankful the day was finished. Despite everything, I believe the baby lawyer accomplished the first goal a lawyer must do to make partner: keep the clients happy.

The Perfect Game
Robert Petyo

Donnie spent a minute drying his hands on the towel hooked to his belt before picking up the bowling ball. He knew everyone clustered around the center lanes in the bowling alley was watching him. That made his nerves jangle even more than usual. He had never bowled a perfect game before, never even been close. Now, standing at the head of lane number ten at Chucky's Bowling Alley, holding the ball up under his chin, he was about to go for his ninth strike in a row.

"You can do it, Donnie," Rachel shouted.

Not what he wanted to hear. His shoulders sagged and he let the ball drop a few inches. He spun toward Rachel who was seated at one end of the arc of chairs behind the lanes. He managed to snap off his anger and keep quiet. Rachel always said he was too quick to lose his temper.

Her pained look scared him.

"Quiet, Rachel," somebody said. "Let him concentrate."

Concentrate, he thought, as he turned back toward the lane. That's it. Don't think about a perfect game. Just roll the ball.

There were twenty lanes in the facility and most were empty on an early Wednesday afternoon. Donnie and his friends worked the late shift at the Post Office so this was a good time for their weekly bowling league. They had six teams and tied up six of the lanes at the facility, each match held on one set of two lanes.

Donnie was bowling in the middle set of lanes. The rest of his league bowlers were waiting and watching. He was the center of attention, just what he needed to make this even more difficult.

"Come on, Donnie. You can do it."

"Quiet."

The Perfect Game

"Shut up. He can handle a little noise." As Rachel said that, the clatter of pins from the other end of the building, where the only other bowlers in Chucky's Bowling Alley were, seemed too soft, like pebbles dropping on a table.

Donnie looked down toward lane number twenty. He felt a hush pressing down on him. He usually relished the clatter of pins, and the noise of the balls banging on the hardwood. For him it was a way to silently release his anger.

But now he was just too nervous.

"Do it, Donnie."

Most of the Postal league competitors sat in the semi-circle of plastic chairs, set back from the bowling ball rack and behind the scorer's table, a five foot wide table with two computer screens and two chairs.

Donnie had only started bowling two years ago finally giving in to the urging of his father who had bowled in amateur leagues for almost thirty years. He even offered to let him use his lucky ball. Not wanting to risk the repercussions if he damaged or lost the ball, he declined.

His father checked his scores weekly and always told him he would have done better with his ball.

Great! Donnie thought. Put more pressure on himself.

Because now, he was finally using his father's bowling ball.

"You can do it," Rachel said.

He glanced up to the high ceiling. His father was watching. He knew it.

Now or never, he thought as he swung his arm back, took four strides forward and released the ball. Then he stepped back and held his fists under his chin, squinting, but not quite closing his eyes.

The cheers when the pins went down deafened him and he titled his head back and let out a weak chirp. One more strike was all he needed for the perfect game. He felt Rachel's arms hugging him from behind. He glanced upward and pointed to the ceiling. "Thanks, Dad," he said softly. His father had died of a heart attack six months ago. And he had always wanted to bowl a perfect game. Thirty years of bowling, but never a perfect game.

He turned and kissed Rachel quickly on the cheek.

"Come on now," someone snapped. "The game's not over yet."

Donnie turned and saw Garfield standing near the small scorer's table. A dark haired woman punched some buttons on the small screen. "You guys are still losing," Garfield said as he patted the woman's shoulder. "And there's still one more frame to go." He waved his arm like he was shooing flies. "Clear out. It's my shot now."

Donnie tried to avoid shouting at him as he and Rachel moved to one end of the semi-circle of chairs. She always tried to control his temper. Garfield was a pain. And he was also the only member of their league who had bowled a perfect game. In fact, he had three, and never tired of pointing that out to everyone.

Garfield strode to the rack between the two lanes they were using and found his ball, a dark blue one with a goofy logo of a bowling duck visible near the finger holes. He kissed the logo for good luck.

Someone chuckled from the semi-circle of seats just behind the ball rack.

Garfield spun, his ball held up before his chin. "Who was that?" he shouted.

"Just take your roll," Donnie said.

"No." He spun and set his ball back on the rack, then faced the arc of chairs, his fists planted on his hips. "Who was that laughing at me. Come on, you coward. Who was it?"

There were six people seated in the semi-circle. Two were Garfield's teammates in matching blue shirts with wine glasses on the front. Two were Donnie's teammates, their white shirts splashed with a garish logo from Milano's Italian Restaurant, the business Donnie's father had owned. These were the same shirts his father and his team had worn.

This one's for you, Dad, Donnie thought. One more strike to go.

He and Rachel sat at the edge of the semi-circle. Each team had a scorekeeper seated at the small table in front of the arc and both stared at Garfield like he was a college lecturer.

"Who was it?" Garfield demanded again.

"Just bowl," Donnie said. "One more frame to go."

"Shut up." He spun to him and raised a fist. "Somebody's trying to make fun of me, and I'm not going to stand for it."

"Oh, come on, Garf." That came from Chet, a thin man with long arms and an oversized baseball cap. He was one of Garfield's teammates. "Roll the ball. Or, are you gonna have to kiss it again."

"That's it." Garfield started toward him but Kristy, the dark haired scorekeeper, stood and blocked his way. "Calm down, sweetie. Just bowl, will ya."

Garfield shoved her back against the table. The chair slid away and she grabbed the edge of the table to keep her feet.

"Hey." Donnie jumped up. Rachel grabbed his arm, trying to hold him back. He knew she didn't like it when he lost his temper, but he had to act.

Chet stood and moved to the table to help Kristy back into her chair. "Let's all settle down," he said.

"Get lost." Garfield shoved him away, knocking him on his butt.

"Hey." Chet grabbed one of the chairs for support as he struggled to his feet.

Garfield stepped toward him, fists raised in a boxer's pose.

Donnie shrugged Rachel off and ran in front of Garfield to keep him from hitting Chet.

Other players jumped up and started shouting. Someone threw a punch.

"Stop it!" Rachel shouted as somebody flopped back over one of the chairs.

And, down at the other end of the building, pins clattered normally as those bowlers were unaware of the brewing riot.

Donnie grabbed Garfield's arm and had to duck to avoid a wide swinging fist. He shoved his shoulder into his chest, forcing him back until they bumped up against the chairs to the right of the lane.

Garfield flung him to the side and he landed on his arm before rolling face first onto the floor.

"Hey, look."

Donnie rolled onto his side and sat on the floor. Garfield had moved near him but now stared out toward the lanes. Chet had swung around to the ball rack and removed Garfield's blue ball. He held it aloft like a precious gem. Then, he lowered it and kissed the logo.

"You bastard," Garfield shouted. He shoved Donnie side as he circled the table to get at Chet.

Laughing, Chet held the ball over his head as he ran down the bowling lane.

"Hey!"

All of the Postal league bowlers stopped their shouting and struggling, some frozen with their arms in the air, one holding his fist before him like a glass of rum, and they laughed as they watched Chet run down the lane toward the pins, still holding the ball aloft, and struggling to keep his balance on the slick hardwood. Even the people down the other end of the building finally stopped their game.

"Stop."

Chet lost his balance and pitched forward, stretching the ball toward the pins as he plopped onto his stomach. He slid a few feet forward and the ball crashed into the head pin knocking it and two other pins over. The ball rolled to the side and dropped into the gutter. As Chet struggled to his feet, he screamed and stepped forward, swinging his arm like a gate and knocking all the pins down.

There were cheers from both teams.

Lights were now flashing throughout the arena and a pulsating alarm sounded.

Donnie turned and saw two big guys with ill-fitting black uniforms coming from the back office that was behind the tiny snack bar, currently empty. "What's going on out here?" one shouted.

No one responded.

Chet, on his hands and knees, crawled back from lane number ten.

"Buddy, you're not allowed out there," one of the guards snapped.

The other man had moved into the semi-circle and rested a hand on Garfield's shoulder. "That's it, boys. You guys are out of here."

"But—"

"Don't give me no lip. Get out of here now." He scanned the competitors like he was taking inventory. "And I don't want to see any of you here for at least a month. I'll have to check with Mr. Eastwood to see

The Perfect Game

if you're ever let in here again. Now move it. Pack it up."

"Mr. Eastwood's a friend of mine," Garfield said.

"Good for you. I'm sure he'll be glad to hear about your antics. Now, get out."

The grumbling grew as the bowlers collected their balls and put them in their bags. Garfield's blue ball came up through the ball return and he checked it carefully, looking for scratches. Then he kissed the logo. Chet limped to the rack and looked for his ball.

Donnie found his father's ball and carefully secreted it in the carry bag, then took Rachel's hand and walked toward the main entrance. He wasn't a bowling freak like his father had been. He was only in the league to socialize and have some fun. And spend some time with Rachel. Surprisingly, he found today's semi riot a bit relaxing, a harmless way to vent his inner anger. Maybe it even made joining this league worth his time.

But he almost had a perfect game, something his father had never done. He would have been so proud.

Almost a perfect game.

Almost.

He slid his arm around Rachel's waist as they exited the building. "Too bad you didn't get a chance to finish," Rachel said. "I would have loved to see the look on Garfield's face if you got one more strike and bowled a perfect game."

Donnie stopped.

"What's wrong?"

He released her and turned back to the bowling alley. Through the glass doors he saw Garfield and Chet, both lugging their bags, as they laughed and slapped each other on the arms. Two good old boys enjoying themselves.

Because Garfield was still the only league member with a perfect game.

"What's wrong?" Rachel asked again.

"Nothing," he said. He kissed her on the cheek and slid his arm around her waist again. "Absolutely nothing. Those guys played a perfect game."

Dust in the Field
S. B. Watson

I was kneeling over the transom of a nineteen-foot Savage runabout, hot august sun beating mercilessly on my back, trying unsuccessfully to hammer a seized steering cable from the outboard motor's tilt tube. Between the blazing sun, and the heat rising from the marina's cracked asphalt lot, I felt like a grilled cheese sandwich. But in a dry-docked boat, and with a hammer.

I put the hammer down and sat up. The bay glittered in the distance, shimmering in the baked air. I shielded my eyes from the sun and took a moment, looking out across the arid lot towards the water.

A hot wind blew through the marina, picking up some dust as it swept along through the old dry-dock sheds, and swept out across the inlet. For a moment, I went back thirty years, to another hot, dusty, summer. Back when we were kids in Madras, Oregon. Back before Snuffles Morgan went to Iraq, and never returned. Before Terry Broadschalf made a fortune in banking and then lost it in the '08 financial crash. Before Hub McGruddy got married and moved away. When Stork Faulkner was still a string-bean kid in Iron Maiden t-shirts and oversized tennis shoes and Ed Ramirez threw the hardest fastball East of the Cascades.

Under the sticky heat of the sun, roasting on the white-painted transom of the runabout, for just a moment I was back in the shaded outskirts of Jackson Field, where it all started. Watching Snuffles, squinting through his owl-shaped glasses, try to throw sliders to little Ed Ramirez...

* * *

The ball flew like calf-skin lighting into Ramirez' mitt like they'd been magnetized. *Thwack!* Ramirez shook his head, frowning at Snuffles, and pulled the ball from the mitt. He turned it in his fingers, feeling for the seams.

"Look, Snuffles," Ramirez called across the grass to the scrawny kid standing in the shade of the next tree over, "you just gotta *huck*." Ramirez made like he was throwing, to demonstrate, leading with his elbow, his hand whipping behind it. "You want Coach to put you in the pitcher rotation, you're gonna have to get that speed up, man."

Ramirez took a breath and stood still, tall and rigid, hands brought together in the pitcher's prayer, sighting the distance to Snuffles. Then he brought one leg up and started the long, slow step, suddenly coiling into motion. The ball leapt from his hand, cutting a whistling curve through the air to Snuffles' mitt. We could see the dust leave the old mitt from where we sat around the tree behind Ramirez.

Stork Faulkner shook his head. "Gosh," he muttered.

"You gotta get it like *that*, Snuff," Ramirez said.

Snuffles dropped the mitt and shook his hand out.

Ramirez turned to us and grinned. "He's accurate enough," he said. "It's just that speed. He's gotta get some power behind those throws."

Snuffles wanted to be pitcher. He'd wanted it for two seasons. But our team, the Wool Hawks, had Ramirez. And stocky little Terry Broadschalf. Hub even threw, sometimes. Snuffles was tall, and lanky, and wore great big horn-rimmed glasses. He just didn't *look* like a pitcher…

"Alright, come on, man," Ramirez said, lifting his mitt towards Snuffles.

Snuffles stood, side-facing Ramirez, hiding the ball in his mitt. They stood still for a moment, and then Snuffles raised his mitt to shield his eyes from the hot summer glare and peered out past Ramirez, and us.

"Isn't that coach's car?" Snuffles called out.

We all turned and looked around the tree.

The car was way down there, at the low, bushy far corner of the field. A blue SUV, cruising slowly through the shade of the overflow parking lot.

"How the heck can you see that from over there?" Hub quipped.

Snuffles walked over to us, still shielding his eyes with his mitt.

We watched the SUV turn in under a tree, and stop beside a little red sports car; the door opened. We couldn't make out exactly who got out; the door blocked our view. A woman in the sports car jumped out from the drivers' seat and walked around to the SUV. The two forms seemed to merge behind the SUV's door.

"Blegh," Ramirez said, screwing his face up. "They're kissing."

"Isn't that Mitch Lavery's wife's car?" Stork asked.

"No way," said Terry. "Is it?"

Ramirez shielded his face now too. "It *could* be," he said.

Mitch Lavery was the coach for The Madras Wildfires, the best team in our region. And our direct rivals. We hadn't won a single game the entire season; The Wildfires hadn't lost one. They hit runs, they pitched outs, they stole bases better than anyone else. We were scheduled to play them in four days, on Saturday.

The woman opened the driver's-side passenger door and got in the SUV.

"Why'd she get in back there?" Terry asked, leaning his stubby bulk against the tree.

"So nobody sees her," Stork muttered. "She's sneaking."

"If she's sneaking," Snuffles said, "why'd they meet here? Pretty public, no?"

"Nobody really uses Jackson Field," said Stork. "Everyone goes to Juniper Hills or Sahalee. And if they *do* use Jackson, they go over there," he turned and pointed towards a small baseball diamond, dug into the dirt. Beyond that, an unshaded play-structure wilted in the sun. "The only people who hang out at that parking lot are druggies," Stork said.

Snuffles shrugged. "I dunno," he said. "Still seems kinda dumb to me."

"Well, whatever they're doing," said Ramirez, turning back into the field, "they're not helping your pitching any, Snuff. Come on and throw."

We all went back to watch Snuffles pitch. Whisps of dust curled around Snuffles' tennis shoes as he trudged back to his position. We all sat, again, in the shade of the tree behind Ramirez. It only took moments to forget about the SUV, and the sports car, and the woman who looked like Mitch Lavery's wife.

It all came back fast, though, the next day when we heard the news.

* * *

We watched from the treehouse as Terry labored up the long, high-desert road on his bicycle, ploughed through the line of decorative grasses bordering Stork's front yard, and stood on the pedals as he spun through the field towards the tree.

It was another hot, dry Madras afternoon. The sun was high in the naked sky, beating down relentlessly on Stork's neighborhood. The scent of heated foliage and baked dirt littering the summer breeze. Far to the east, the white-capped peak of Mount Hood blazed on the rolling horizon.

Terry chucked his bike into the bushes and clamored up the old ladder to Stork's treehouse. A dry wind rustled the leaves as he rolled onto the plank porch and scrabbled through the crooked door into our group.

"Did you hear about Coach?" Terry hissed, even before he'd caught his breath.

We were all there. Ramirez, Snuff, Hub, Stork, and me. And now Terry, whose eyes were as wide as Snuffles' glasses as he stared back and forth at each of us.

"What about him?" Ramirez asked, spinning a baseball on the uneven wood flooring.

"He's dead!" Terry coughed up, between gasps for breath.

Everyone stopped what they were doing and stared at Terry.

"No way," Ramirez said.

Terry caught his breath, and the next words all came out in a stream. "I went shopping with ma this morning and was walking around the produce and saw Mark Gloss, you know, Sheriff Gloss's kid, and he told me they found him late last night out by Metolius, on Bear Drive, by the side of the road with his bike. They think it was a hit and run."

"What do you mean… Dead?" asked Hub.

Terry lowered his voice. "Like, roadkill-dead," he said.

"No kidding?" Stork murmured.

"No kidding," Terry said.

"Do they know who did it?" Hub asked.

"When did it happen?" asked Ramirez.

"*Why* did Mark Gloss tell you?" Snuffles muttered, under the rest of the voices.

Terry was shaking his head, waving his hands. "Look, I don't know any of that. Mark just said they found him last night."

"How?" asked Snuffles.

"Mark said his dad got a call from the office and lit out from home around nine-thirty."

Stork sighed, and looked out the door at the sunbaked hills. "At nine…" he said. "I was in my room, playing Zelda."

Snuffles leaned back and put his finger along the bridge of his nose. It was a thinking posture for him. The same one he used to ace math tests and win at Stratego.

Stork cleared his throat and shifted where he sat. "Was it…murder?" he asked.

We'd all thought it.

"Gosh," Terry said. "I dunno. Mark just said it was a hit and run. I think they think it was an accident."

"You guys know who lives out by Metolius?" Snuffles said, suddenly.

"Yeah," said Hub. "Mitch Lavery."

Snuffles pulled his wrist up to his face and peered at the scuffed Casio watch. "If we ride now, we can make it to Lavery's before sundown. No. Let's wait an hour, then we'll get there just after dark."

Terry's eyes got even wider, somehow, and he said "You think we should go over there?"

"Come on, Snuff," said Stork. "What if we go over there and he didn't do it? We'd look like idiots."

"Screw that," said Ramirez. "What it we go over there, and he *did*?"

Snuffles shoved the glasses up on the bridge of his nose and glared through the great big lenses. "We're gonna play The Wildfires this Saturday. We're gonna run our asses off. And we're gonna lose. We know it. So, what if Mitch didn't do it? Nothing. We lose. Whatever. But what if he *did*? You want to lose to the son-of-a-bitch that killed our coach? Or, you want to lose, and *not know* if you lost to the son-of-a-bitch that killed our coach? I don't. I wanna know."

Everyone was silent. Ramirez picked the ball up from the floor and turned it in his fingers.

"We go over there tonight," Snuffles said, "and we find out for ourselves if Mitch killed Coach. Cops think it's a hit and run. If he did run over Coach, there's gotta be something on his car. Blood or something. Easy. We just can't get caught."

* * *

It wasn't completely dark when we reached the Lavery property. The sky glowed dark-purple above us, a few brighter stars glinting through the haze, as we stashed our bikes in a field of sagebrush a few hundred feet from the two-story farm house where Mitch and Nancy lived.

"Keep the lights off," Snuffles whispered, "and stay low."

He lowered himself to the height of the desert scrub and crept quickly towards the house. At first, none of us moved. Were we really doing this? Then Ramirez said a very, *very* bad word, and slunk after him. We all followed, after that.

The lights were on in the Lavery house; it was early enough the blinds weren't drawn, and we could see into the warm kitchen as we swept around the border of the yard. Nobody sat at the supper table, but it looked like plates were set for a late meal. We moved quietly up to the house, following Snuffles. How he saw that well in the dark, I'll never know.

The garage was separate from the house, with a portico reaching out towards the road. Snuffles waited at the corner of the house, listening to the sounds of the hot night. Someone moved across the window above us, their shadow crossing the swath of light the room cast upon the yellowed grass at our feet. We pressed against the siding beneath the window, hearing the plastic shingles creak against our bodies.

The shadow moved on, back into the house. Snuffles darted forward to the garage. We followed like baby ducks chasing their mother, rushing into the darkness beneath the portico and slipping around the building. We piled up in a crush around the garage's side-door.

Terry let out a fat sigh. "Gosh, that felt close."

"We're fine," Snuffles said, testing the knob. The door swung open easily. The garage was pitch black. The deep-purple sky had already darkened to a great curving abyss, broken only by a line of orange on the western horizon. "They're not expecting us, anyway. We're fine."

Snuffles snapped on his little flashlight and walked into the garage.

The red sportscar was right inside the door. It glistened like a wet cherry beneath the sudden bristle of lights as we all turned on our flashlights and swung them around.

"So, I guess it *was* Mrs. Lavery we saw," Hub said, walking around the little red car.

Snuffles shone his light on the front bumper. Then he walked over to the wheels, sweeping it along the chrome trim pieces running the length of the car. "It's been washed," he groaned.

"So what?" Ramirez said, walking past it and putting his light on Mitch's car, a big brown-and-cream wagon. "If Mitch ran over Coach, it was probably in his car, right?"

We all converged on the wagon, lights probing the windows, flitting underneath, flashing up and down its lines and edges.

This time Ramirez groaned. "It's been washed too," he said.

"Well," Stork muttered. "Shit."

"You got a ball on you, Ed?" Snuffles asked, turning to Ramirez.

Ramirez shrugged. "Sure." He pulled a worn baseball from his jacket pocket.

Snuffles took it. "I need something to write with," he said, making a clicking motion with his thumb and looking around the garage. "And something to write on…"

Stork pulled a page from the comic book he had rolled up in his back pocket---the latest Swamp Thing. Terry had a pen on him. Snuffles took them and scribbled a message, overwriting it multiple times to hide his handwriting. "I SAW YOU," was all it said. Then he crumpled it around the ball and tied it with one of the extra shoelaces Hub was infamous for always carrying.

We turned off our lights and crept back outside into the heavy darkness.

"What you gonna do?" Stork asked Snuff.

"Just everybody get back to the bikes. When you're all there, get set to light out of here in a hurry. Flick your light once, towards the house. I'll flick back. Then wait for me."

So that's what we did, each creeping their own silent path through the sagebrush in the dark. I lost sight of everyone within seconds, but kept the soft glow of the Lavery's house behind me, and eventually stumbled out onto the road.

For a moment, I thought they'd left without me, it was so dark, but then Ramirez grabbed me by the collar and pulled me over to where Terry was lining up the bikes. Hub slipped from the brush a few seconds later, then Stork.

When we were ready, Stork flicked his light out into the darkness.

We all held our breaths, then saw a little pinpoint of light flicker back, next to the house.

A moment later we heard the distant sound of breaking glass.

A light erupted from the Lavery's back door, painting their backyard blue-white.

Then Snuff burst from the sagebrush and leapt onto his bike. We rode like bats out of Egypt, never slowing until our tires grumbled around the last corner to Stork's.

* * *

At the time, it seemed brilliant. Even Ramirez, usually the toughest of our group, was impressed with Snuffles' stunt. We spent the first part of the night in the treehouse, making plans.

It never occurred to us things might not go our way.

The next morning, I woke up to someone banging on my bedroom window. I dragged myself out of bed, glancing at the clock as I slunk towards the sound: 11 o'clock.

I pulled up the old frame and leaned out, squinting into the crystal glare of the morning. They were all there, standing over their bikes in our side-yard.

"Get dressed and come out," Hub said.

"Why?" I asked. "What happened?"

"There's been another hit and run."

"Really? Where? Who?"

"We'll tell you on the way."

* * *

The police station was a good ten-minute ride from my house, taking the busiest roads. We took the side-roads, winding through the outskirts of Madras.

The wind whipped through my overshirt as I rode, cruising along the gravelly shoulder. It was early enough the breeze still had that summer sweetness to it, that would get baked out soon, leaving only breathtaking heat.

Snuff and Hub rode up ahead; Terry and Stork pressed up behind me. Ramirez cruised by my side. They all took turns filling me in.

"Lewis Bishop," Snuff said back to me. "Recognize that name?"

"No," I said.

"Wildfires' Short Stop," Ramirez said.

"Guess where they found him," Stork called up.

"Bear Drive?" I said.

"Damn right," Ramirez muttered.

"And do they have any idea---"

"None at all," Snuff cut me off. "Just like Coach."

"But Bishop's not dead," Stork said.

"They found him knocked clean out," said Ramirez. "News says they took him over to St. Charles. He's still sleeping."

"We figure after Mitch got our message," Hub said, "maybe he thought he knew who threw the ball. And got it wrong."

"But why Lewis?" I asked.

"Search me," said Hub.

This time Terry piped up. "So, the police still think it's just a hit and run?"

Snuff lifted both hands off his handlebars and turned back, shrugging. "Not after we tell them what we know."

* * *

Sheriff Alan Gloss pulled his glasses down and looked at us over the thin, wire rims. "Let me get this straight," he mumbled through yellowed front teeth, "you all are confessing to vandalizing a window with a baseball?"

The air conditioning rattled through the small vent near the ceiling of his office. Gloss had half-closed his blinds, and kept his lights off. The overhead fan slowly turned, churning the ice-cool air around in a frigid breeze. Still, beads of sweat broke across the huge man's meaty forehead as he spoke.

"Uh, no," said Snuffles.

"Then what exactly *are* you trying to tell me?"

This time Hub tried to recount the story. Then Stork. Each chose different starting places. By the time Terry got into the storytelling, Gloss was already patting the air with his heavy hands. "Hold up," he grumbled. "You're saying you saw Nancy and Gary Sleznik get into Gary's car. Then Gary got ran over. So, you went and threw a ball through Mitch's window?"

"Well, why d'you think she got in the car with Coach?" Ramirez said. "He was doin' her. That's why. That's motive, isn't it?"

We all went very quiet. Sheriff Gloss raised his eyebrows at Ramirez. Slowly, the overhead fan turned and turned and the air vent rattled.

Finally, Gloss let out a big sigh, pulling his glasses from his face and rubbing his eyes.

"Ok, boys," he said. "I'll look into it. I'll ask my deputies about Nancy and your coach, and maybe we'll go around to the Lavery place." Ramirez and Snuffles perked up in their seats. Hub opened his mouth to say something, but Sheriff Gloss cut him off. "But." He wagged his hot-dog finger at us and set his fat face in a mastiff grimace. "You guys are gonna sit your butts down at home…" He glanced at the baseball bulging from Ramirez's jacket pocket. "…or at the ballfield… and keep out of it. You all got that?"

"Yes, sir," we all said at once.

Sheriff Gloss growled and turned it into a sentence. "Or I'll see to it that Mitch presses charges for that window."

"Yes, sir."

"Now get out."

* * *

The sun was high and the air was thin as we unpacked our kit at Jackson Field. Hub pulled his favorite bat from where he'd bungee-corded it to the top-tube of his bike. Ramirez took the ball out of his pocket. Terry had the mitts.

Snuff made one or two half-hearted pitches to Ramirez, before sitting down in the shade of the big oak tree that overlooked the overflow parking.

"You think he believed us?" Snuff asked.

"Not a bit," Ramirez answered.

"So, what do we do?" asked Hub.

"We sit, don't we?" said Stork.

"Well…" Terry said, but stopped.

We all looked at the him. He was frowning, looking down at the crisp, packed dirt beneath the thin grass.

"'Well' what?" jabbed Ramirez.

"Well," Terry said again… "I usually go out with my mom shopping a few times a week. I drive the cart. We went yesterday, right?"

"Yeah," said Stork. "You saw Mark Gloss."

"Well, we usually go out today." Terry looked at his watch. "Right around now."

"So?" asked Hub.

"So, today is when Mrs. Lavery does her shopping, too," said Terry.

Stork cocked his head. "What, you mean every week?"

"Pretty much," said Terry.

Snuff jumped up, dragging a plume of dust with him that rose and filtered through the small ring of us under the tree. "So, if we go over to the store, now…"

"…We'd probably see Nancy," said Stork.

The dust hadn't even settled as we spun on our heels, grabbed bats and mitts and balls, and ran our bikes through the field towards the road.

* * *

"That's her," Terry said, peeking over the fresh-baked bread display.

Nancy Lavery was at the far side of the bakery department, where the wine aisles started, carefully reading the label on a bottle. She was slender, with chestnut hair and deep-tanned skin. She wore a sleeveless, loose-fitting, yellow dress that came down to her knees, belted at the waist. It looked like a toga, and Ramirez said as much, under his breath.

Snuffles snuck a look and dipped back below the bread, where we all crouched. "So, what now?" he asked, sliding his owl-glasses back up the bridge of his nose.

"If we're right," said Ramirez, "and Mitch killed Coach because he was doin' Mrs. Lavery, there's no way she doesn't know about it."

"You think?" asked Hub.

Ramirez nodded. "Sure," he said. "Best case, she suspects it. Worst case, she knows, or was involved."

An old lady, leaning against her cart like a walker, shuffled past us, giving us the stink-eye the whole way. We watched her disappear around the corner, into Meat.

"Whatever we do," said Hub, "it'd better be quick. Or somebody's gonna complain. We look super suspicious."

Stork sighed, suddenly, and stood. "Alright, Snuff," he said, straightening out his faded Maiden shirt. "My turn to do something stupid."

We watched as he walked briskly out of the department. A moment later he reappeared, down by the wine, driving an empty shopping cart. He moved it slowly towards Nancy Lavery, until it was parallel to hers. Then he just stood there.

I held my breath. I think we all did. The overhead music was playing some easy listening junk. Registers whirred and chirped in the distance, by the checkouts. A kid was crying somewhere, out across the aisles. But to me, it felt like we would have heard a pin drop if it fell anywhere around Bakery or Wine.

After a moment, Nancy lifted her head from the bottle and looked at Stork. She didn't say anything, just looked at him, frowning, confused.

Then he drove the cart into her. Straight into her.

Nancy stumbled backwards, and half-fell against a cake-display, without saying a word. She just hung there, against the display, looking at Stork, the bottle of wine still in her hand. Then she turned, slowly, and looked at us. All the color was drained from her freckled face, her lips were parted in a weird, toothy grimace.

The bottle slipped from her hand and broke on the floor. Then she did something I'd never seen an adult do. She ran. She turned on heels, pushed off from the display, and bolted down the wine aisle.

We all froze for a moment, before breaking from our cover like hounds after a fox. Terry slipped in the wine, and almost fell, but Snuff grabbed him by the collar and dragged him along.

We got to the front doors just in time to see the cherry-red sportscar peel out of the parking lot.

"Crap," said Terry. "What's that supposed to mean?"

"Means she knows," said Ramirez. "If she knows, she *doesn't* suspect. So… Worst case scenario, I think."

In the background, above the registers, and the kid screaming, an overhead page interrupted the music. "Clean up at Wine. Clean up at Wine."

* * *

"You think we're jumping to conclusions?" Stork asked.

After the debacle at the corner grocery, we'd all split up. Hub and Terry and Ramirez went off to do who-knew-what, and I and Snuff and Stork went back to the treehouse. Stork's mom made us sandwiches in the evening, and we took them up with some Pringles for dinner. Then, as dusk fell, Stork pulled an old mattress from a back shed and we dragged it up to the treehouse, and got some blankets, and a radio.

It was the witching-hour. The sun was well down; only the fuzzy zodiacal glow, leaping up into the night, lit the desert. Stork had found some Maiden on the radio. The thudding drums and wailing two- and three-part guitar lines crackled in the background as we lay on the mattress, talking.

"No," said Snuff. He was on his stomach, chin in his hands, looking out at the stars above Stork's house. "Maybe we're wrong on something, but…" he shook his head. "No way Mrs. Lavery would react like that if she wasn't involved."

"So, what then?" Stork asked. "She lures Coach, and kills him with her husband? Why?"

Snuff shrugged. "Maybe she didn't help. Maybe Mitch's threatening her. Maybe she's scared she'll be next. Who knows. Adults are weird."

"And what about Lewis?" Stork asked quietly, more to himself than us.

We'd found out earlier that day: Lewis Bishop was a comic nerd. His favorite series? Swamp Thing. Same comic we'd used to send our message to Mitch.

"Let's just hope he's alright," said Snuff.

Stork rolled over in the darkness and reached for the radio, but Snuffles put his hand out suddenly and grabbed Stork's shoulder. "Hey," Snuffles said, tugging at Stork and pointing out into the night.

We all looked. A car had pulled up in the street, with the lights off.

We could just see it under the zodiacal light. It cruised slowly down the street, and then stopped. After a moment, the door opened, and someone got out.

"Turn it down," Snuffles hissed. Stork snapped the radio off.

"You recognize the car?" Snuffles asked.

"No," said Stork. "Lavery's?"

"I don't think so," said Snuff. "At least, not the sports car, or the wagon."

"What's he doing?" muttered Stork.

The dark figured moved quickly across the field next to Stork's house. It couldn't have been more than forty feet away when it passed the treehouse. Even so, it was too dark to make out who it was.

The shadow crept up to the house and stopped under the second-floor window to Stork's bedroom. The window was open, just like most other bedroom windows in Madras that night, letting the cool evening breeze flush out the dry heat of the day. We watched as the figure paused, then threw something up into the window. After a moment, it turned, and jogged back to the car.

"Get the two-way," Snuff said.

Stork pulled a walkie-talkie from under the mattress and snapped it on, keeping the volume as low as possible. He hit the CALL button, and we waited.

The car sat silently at the end of the street.

"Hey, it's Stork," Stork whispered. "Over."

"Yo," said Ramirez. "Over."

"Hub here," another voice said. "I'm with Terry. Over."

Snuffles took the two-way. "How fast can you guys get over to Lavery's?"

"Why?" asked Hub. "What's up? Over."

"We're in Stork's treehouse. Somebody in a dark car just came and threw something into Stork's window. Over."

"No shit?" said Hub. "You think it's Lavery? Over."

"We couldn't see," said Snuff.

Ramirez radioed on. "I'm a half-hour away from Lavery. Over."

"We can make it in fifteen minutes," said Hub.

"Ok," Snuff said. "Jump on your bikes and get out there. Then hide. Don't let him see you. And take the radios. We'll tell you if the car leaves here before you get there."

"Over and out," said Hub.

* * *

In the next twenty minutes I thought I'd aged a year.

We lay, next to each other on the mattress, scooted back into the darkness of the treehouse. Far forward enough so we could see the shadow of the car, down the street, but far back enough so we couldn't be seen. Hopefully.

"If he catches us, here," Stork whispered, "we're sunk."

"He won't," said Snuffles.

The zodiacal light fell. The stars glittered in the darkness of the moonless night. After twenty minutes, we heard the soft hum of an engine. The car cruised down the street, lights still off. It slowed next to Stork's house, then sped up, and disappeared into the darkness. Then, about a mile down the road, we saw a pair of headlights flicker dimly to life.

"Heads up," Stork called into the radio. "The car just left."

"We're in place," came a hoarse, breathless reply. "Over."

"Ok. Stay quiet. Over."

"Hey," said Snuffles to Stork. "Go see what he threw into your room."

Stork shuffled out into the darkness. A light turned on in Stork's room. He waved to us from the lighted window, and disappeared back into the house. Moments later, we heard him running across the grass.

"Check it out!" Stork said as he climbed back up. He dropped a baseball onto the mattress. A note was tied to it: "Meet me at Jackson Field. Urgent. Benjamin."

"Who's 'Benjamin?'" I asked.

"Me," said Snuffles. "It's my name."

"*Benjamin?*" I asked again.

Before he could answer, the radio sizzled to life.

"He's here!" Terry snapped. "He just drove up, in some old refrigerator of a car from like the 60s or something. Drove it way back into their property and parked it under a wall-tent thing they've got there. That's why we didn't find it when we looked."

"When he goes back to the house," Stork said, "go and check the car."

"Will do. Over."

Again, we waited. About ten minutes later, Hub's voice came over the two-way. "We're at the car now," Hub said, "and guess what…Over."

"What?" Snuff asked. "Over."

"It's been washed."

* * *

Tuesday had been hot. Wednesday had been sweltering. By Thursday, we were so air-baked we barely noticed the sunburns. Friday, the heat cracked the dirt in the ballfields, chased the birds into the bramble thickets around the middle-school, and started a brush-fire out east of town.

And now it was Saturday. The day of the ballgame, in a cooked field so swept with dry dust we were afraid they'd cancel the game. But they didn't.

We sat in the dugouts, and watched the away team---The Wildfires--filter into their dugout across from the catcher's box. Dust picked up in little swirls, and carried itself on the breath of nearly imperceptible winds across the bases, salting the old bleachers, and everyone in them.

And there, in the Wildfires' dugout, was Mitch Lavery. He hung on the chainlink fence, glaring out across the diamond. Glaring at us. At Stork, and Hub, and Terry, and Ramirez, and Snuff, and me. His assistant organized the team, hung up the bats on the fence, tacked the lineup on the side of the dugout. But Mitch just stood there, looking at us.

After a few minutes of this, Ramirez stood up and leaned against the fence, too, just like Mitch was. But Ramirez hung by hooking just his middle fingers in the links. Mitch didn't really react. Just stayed locked in his cool stare on that hot, dusty day.

The game started like every other. The Wildfires went to bat at the top of the first inning. Ramirez was on the mound. He struck two out, but by then they had two points and three runners. The whole inning ended with them leading, 3-2.

We ran. We slid. We batted. We tried our damned hardest. We really did. Four innings in, the score was tied, 11-11. And all the time, Mitch stood there, hanging off the fence, head swaying back and forth tracking our movements, barely watching the game. And all the time, the dust billowed in swirls and plumes and little funnels across the field, blinding Ramirez at the mound, hiding the batter and his stance, confusing the infielders and distracting the catcher, soiling hot dogs on the stands, and filtering down to the bottom of warm sodas and cold coffees.

After pitching the top of the 5th inning, Ramirez came in from the mound, and slammed himself down on the wooden bench, soiled in sweat that had turned to silty mud across his forehead and neck. "Shit," he said, and snatched a bottle of Gatorade from his bag. He'd held onto the tie, and struck them out without any runners getting through. We still had a chance.

"Knock 'em out," he said, as I got up to bat.

I didn't. I got to third before they struck us out, and the tie carried over into the last inning.

I was benched that inning, me and a few other guys. Snuff, was infield. Right in the middle of the dust. Terry was at the mound, short and stocky, his eyes hard, locked onto the succession of batters The Wildfires were lining up.

The first swing was a hit, a groundball scooting to infield. Snuff caught it.

And that was when it happened.

I saw the umpire turn and walk to the fence. Wind whipped his grey dress pants. The crowd on the stands seemed to hush, seemed to lean all together, following the movement of something past the stands. We all craned our necks, but couldn't quite see.

Then I saw him. Sheriff Gloss. He sauntered into The Wildfires' dugout and went over to Mitch. Mitch turned, for the first time, and put that cold, hard glare onto Gloss instead of us. From where I sat, it looked like Gloss just smiled, but I couldn't be sure. There was dust in my eyes.

They talked for a good while. The longer they talked, the colder Mitch's stare seemed to get.

After a while, a little girl broke away from beside The Wildfire's dugout, and darted over to ours. She popped her head in, and started talking to her brother, who then turned and started talking to us.

Bishop woke up. Lewis bishop, the Wildfires' Short Stop. Apparently, he was going to be just fine, and, also apparently, he knew who hit him. It was Mitch.

I looked back at The Wildfires just in time to see Mitch grab a bat from the fence, and slam it into the side of Sheriff Gloss's head. The big man dropped to the ground in a heap, slopping over the bench and most of The Wildfires on his way down. Mitch turned and lit out across the diamond, just as the dust picked up in a great billow through the infield.

What happened next, happened fast. Mitch ran, each step kicking up dry silt into the air. And out there, at the edge of the infield, swallowed by the plume of dirt, I saw Snuffles lift his mitt, perch his leg up high, like the big-time pitchers do, and sling that damn ball.

The ball broke from the dust, cutting sharp through the air, and struck Mitch right on the side of his head.

Mitch dropped like sack of potatoes, and was instantly covered by the resulting cloud of dust.

* * *

We lost the game. We didn't really care, though. Mitch wasn't there to see it. They took him to the hospital. He stayed there until he was ready to transfer to jail, a few days later.

Turned out, Sheriff Gloss had taken our tip a lot more seriously than we'd thought. He and a deputy did some digging and found a surprising amount of circumstantial evidence against Mitch. Witnesses saw him driving Nancy's old Studebaker both the day Coach was killed and the day Lewis was struck. He'd washed all their cars the next morning---an excuse to try to clean the Studebaker, specifically.

The car was Nancy's from before they were even married. Mitch used that against her. Told her if anyone found out who hit Coach, she'd go to prison too. Apparently, Nancy's fear of prison was greater than sadness for her murdered lover, because she shut up tight after that.

Lewis Bishop made a full recovery with little more than a broken arm. I felt bad about that for years, but Bishop never seemed to mind.

And how did Mitch find out about Stork? About all of us? After we'd shown our hand to Nancy at the supermarket, she went right back to Mitch. Pretty pitiful, really.

And Snuffles? Well, they put him on the mound the very next season. After that throw, how could they not? And, of course, we never told his secret… We never told anyone how Snuff had closed his eyes when the dust hit him. How he threw the ball blind, and only looked to see where it went after Mitch had hit the ground. They didn't really need to know.

* * *

The bay glittered in the distance. For a moment, I couldn't even remember how long I'd been sitting there, in the little dry-docked runabout. But then I looked down at the hammer in my lap, and the tilt-tube, and the seized steering cable, and it all came back. It'd only been a few minutes.

The sticky wind swept through the yard, picking up the dust and swirling it towards the sky.

Thirty years ago, if you'd asked me where I'd be today, would I have said, "working in a marina for minimum wage"? Or would I have told you some story about Ramirez, Terry, Stork, Hub, and Snuff… and me?

On days like these, when the wind picks up under dry August skies, sometimes I can still see Snuff out there, standing in the dust, closing his eyes, getting ready to throw.

What I wouldn't give to see that ball fly, for real, just one last time.

Be Careful What You Wish For
Wendy Harrison

"You ain't never gonna make a living throwing that ball around," his father told Billy Thornton between his nightly shots of whiskey. Will Thornton was an alcoholic, no two ways about it, and a mean one at that.

"I will if I'm good enough. Sponsors. Clothing lines. Maybe even a sportscaster job." Billy wasn't sure why he let Will drag him into the same argument, night after night.

"You're crazy, boy. Even if you was the best in the world, no one cares about the shotput. I been tellin' you that for years."

When his father reached for his third drink during this nightly ritual, Billy knew it was time to go. The last time his father went after him with his belt, he was sixteen and two-hundred-fifty pounds of muscle. His father told everyone he had walked into a door to explain the black eye. He'd never tried it again, but Billy didn't trust him not to come after him if he were drunk enough.

The evening was cool and comfortable. Billy decided to leave his car at home and walk the two miles to Joe's Dive Bar to meet up with his friends. There would be no worries about getting caught driving under the influence. Things sometimes got out of hand on these Friday nights out. Billy was grateful the three of them had stayed close in the years after high school. They still had each other's backs, and their love of sports remained a common denominator.

When Billy reached the bar, he saw lights in the empty field across the road. A traveling carnival had arrived. When Billy joined his friends at their usual table, the sounds of a merry-go-round drifted through the bar's front door every time someone went in or out.

Be Careful What You Wish For

* * *

"I have an idea." Jake grinned a sloppy smile. He looked at his friends. "Hold your applause." He gulped the last of his glass of draft beer.

"We're in trouble now." Kenny was sitting across from him and kicked him under the table. "Never have ideas after your third beer."

Billy snorted. "Fourth or fifth, more likely, for Jake to have an idea." He shifted in his seat, trying to get his three hundred pounds and six-foot-six-inch frame distributed more comfortably in the hard wooden chair. He always made sure to get one without arms, knowing he wouldn't fit.

"First, another round?" Jake was slurring his words but so far, his sentences still made sense.

"How about if we hear your idea while you can still remember it," Kenny suggested.

"Okay. Here it is. Let's go see what trouble we can get into at the carnival. Maybe find us some good-looking women. Keep the party going."

Billy shook his head. "First off, I'm not sure us getting drunk on Friday night makes for a party. Second, did you forget you're getting married next month?" He paused. "What comes next? Oh, yeah, third, what makes you think a bunch of hot chicks would have any interest in us over-the-hill jocks?"

Jake raised his hand. "What'ya mean, over the hill? I'm in the best shape of my life. You're the one who's goin' downhill."

Billy pushed back from the table. "Oh yeah?"

Kenny sighed. "Listen, assholes. You make a scene here, and we're gonna be banned. Remember last time?"

"You're right." Billy turned toward Jake. "Love you, man."

"Love you too, asshole."

"Let's go to the carnival. Bet I'll whip your butts at the shooting galleries."

They each tossed money on the table and stumbled outside and across the road.

As they wandered through the crowd in search of the shooting games, Jake stopped them.

"Hey. Look at that." He pointed to a small tent across from the merry-go-round. A hand-painted sign said, "Your fortune told, tarot cards/palm reading. $25."

"You don't believe in that shit, do you?" Billy started to walk on.

"What're you, afraid?"

"Don't be stupid. I'm not afraid of nothin'."

Kenny sighed. "Chill. What's the worst that could happen?"

"Maybe I can find out if I should really be marrying Jenny." When they stared at Jake, he added, "Not that I need anyone to tell me I'm doing the right thing."

"Okay. Let's give it a try." Billy led the way to the open entrance into the tent.

Dark brocade drapes were hung on brass rings around the canvas walls. Easy to take down and move on, Billy thought. Smart. A table sat in the center of the tent with an empty folding chair on one side and a woman wrapped in shawls and veils on the other. A deck of cards sat face down in front of her.

"You wish a reading?"

Billy stuck his elbow into Jake's side. "This was your idea. You go first."

Jake started to shake his head, but Kenny joined in. "He's right, man, this was your idea."

Jake gave up and sat in the vacant chair.

"I am Madame Sylvia." The woman pointed to the cards. "Shall I read the tarot cards?"

"What? No crystal ball?"

Sylvia frowned. "That is for charlatans. I read the cards or your palm. Your choice."

Jake held up his hand. "Let's stick with this."

She pulled his hand down and studied his palm. "I see a long life ahead, with much success."

"Does that mean I'll get called up to the NFL?"

Billy groaned. Jake had thrown her a softball.

Sylvia's head tilted and then her eyes closed. "I see a large stadium in your future. And a football in your hand. The crowd is cheering. So are the cheerleaders. One of them is special."

Jake laughed. "Damn, woman, you're good. You're right. Jenny is special. So I should marry her?"

"Nothing can stop true love."

Billy grinned at the clever way Madame Sylvia failed to answer the question. Once Jake told her his football aspirations, she took a gamble that he would be interested in at least one of the cheerleaders.

Kenny had the lean look of a runner, so it wasn't hard for her to tell him of great success in races.

When it was Billy's turn, he wanted to refuse. He knew what his future held, and it wasn't winning any gold medals, no matter what she might claim to see in his palm. But he wasn't going to give his friends an opening to mock him.

He took Kenny's place and held out his hand. Madame Sylvia looked into his eyes and then down at his palm. She stared, motionless, until he said, "Hey. I'm still here. What do you see?"

She pushed his hand away. "I'm sorry. I can't do this. Please leave."

Billy thought she was joking. "What's the problem? Am I going on a long trip? Meeting the love of my life?"

The color was gone from her face, and Billy realized she was frightened.

"This isn't funny," Billy said. "Tell me what you saw." He was aware of his friends moving closer behind him, sensing something was wrong.

"There is something you want very much," she said. "You think you would do anything to get it."

Billy laughed. "You're right about that. I'd sell my soul to the Devil to win the Olympics someday."

"I'm sorry. I can't go on." She paused. "I can only tell you to be careful. Very careful. Stay away from the crossroads." She stood so quickly her chair tipped onto the floor as she moved past him and out of the tent.

"Damn, Billy. That was weird." Kenny patted his shoulder. "C'mon, dude. Let's go shoot some targets and forget about this."

It was midnight before they realized they were heading for major hangovers and should call it a night. Billy refused the offer for a ride from Kenny, who was the closest to sober of the three. He didn't mind walking the two miles back home. The fresh air might help sober him up. He knew his father would be passed out by the time he got there. He wouldn't have to worry about dealing with his anger over whatever imaginary sin he thought his son committed against him. For the hundredth time, Billy reminded himself he needed to find a place to live on his own with the money he'd been saving from his construction job.

When Billy came to the intersection of West Broadway and Polk, he remembered the warning of the palm reader. Was this considered a crossroad? He looked around and felt like an idiot. Did he really think a devil was waiting for him? As he started to turn left onto the cross street, a figure appeared in front of him.

"Hi, Billy. Were you looking for me?" The woman was beautiful, her clinging red dress leaving nothing to the imagination.

"Me? No. Just heading home. Who are you?"

"Call me Lucy. And I'll call you Billy. I'm here to take you up on your offer."

He tried to focus on her words and not her distracting appearance. "Offer? What offer?"

"Don't be coy. You know exactly what offer. Your soul for a gold Olympic medal. You know you meant it. I accept. We have a deal."

Billy closed his eyes, forcing them to stay shut. When he dared to open them, she was still there. "Is this some kind of joke? Who put you up to it? You're not the devil. You're a woman."

She smiled. "I'm whatever I want to be. Lucifer. Lucy. It doesn't matter. What does matter is that you live up to your end of the bargain."

"This is crazy. It must be the booze." He took a step to the side to get past her.

"You'll see," she said. "I'll be back to collect."

And she was gone, leaving Billy to convince himself he was imagining things as he made his way home.

* * *

On Sunday morning, Billy went to First Christian Church. Before his mother had escaped her abusive husband, she made Billy promise to continue to go to church. "God didn't protect me from your father," she said, "but maybe he'll watch out for you when I'm gone." He was fifteen, old enough to understand why she needed to leave and strong enough to protect himself. It was the last time he saw her, but he kept his promise, never missing a Sunday at church.

Billy no longer believed in a god that didn't care enough to save his mother from years of pain. He didn't believe in the devil either, but found some comfort in Father Xavier's sermons. They weren't preachy, he explained to his friends when they teased him about the way he spent Sunday mornings while they slept late. It was more like a conversation with a friend, he told them.

After church, Billy shook hands with the elderly priest on the church steps. "Can I talk to you, Father?"

"Of course. Just let me finish saying my goodbyes. Why don't you wait for me inside."

Billy walked down the aisle to a front pew and sat, trying to ignore the large depiction of Christ on the cross displayed behind the altar.

Billy jumped as the priest sat next to him.

"It's all right, son. It's just me." Father Xavier patted his hand. "What's on your mind?"

"Do you believe in the devil, Father?" Billy took a deep breath and told the story of the fortune teller and his encounter at the crossroads. When he finished, he was short of breath and felt as if he'd been running for miles. "I know how this sounds, but I swear, it was real."

Father Xavier sat quietly for a few minutes, and Billy began to feel foolish. He should've just let the whole thing go. The devil in a red dress? The priest was going to think he had lost it.

"Do *you* believe in the devil?"

"I'm not sure I even believe in God." Billy waited for the priest to be shocked and maybe angry.

"There are times when even I wrestle with my faith. What matters is how you live your life. And you, Billy, can be proud of how you've managed with the hand you were dealt. I suspect there may have been alcohol involved on Friday night. Yes?"

Billy nodded.

"The vision you had would be more troubling if the figure you saw had a tail and horns and a terrifying face. The beautiful Lucy sounds more like wishful thinking."

"I guess you're right. It does seem crazy. I swear I'm gonna stop drinking. It's what my coach has been sayin'. I think he's right."

After leaving the church, Billy headed to throwing practice at the high school track. He waved to his coach, who was standing near the shotput ring. Gary Stanford had coached him when he was a student at the school. Now retired, he was training some of his former students to help pass the time.

Billy pulled his equipment cart from the back of his car and dragged it across the parking lot to the ring.

Coach Stanford greeted him. "Warm up for ten minutes, and then we'll get started."

Billy completed the exercises designed to stretch his hips and legs. He felt looser than usual. "Guess it's the warmer weather," he said to the coach. "I feel good."

He emptied the cart, taking out three sixteen-pound shotputs and a one hundred-foot measuring tape. In the next competition, Billy would need to throw over sixty-six feet to be able to compete in the Olympic trials. A throw like that was six feet further than his best throw ever. The world record, at seventy-seven feet, was beyond his wildest dreams. Just getting to the trials would be the peak accomplishment of his years of training. Billy knew this probably was his last chance. Maybe it was time to pack it in, but he couldn't imagine his life without the shotput.

Billy stepped into the throwing ring. He tucked the ball into the right side of his neck and took a wide stance. Leaning over his bent right leg, he spun in a half circle, releasing the ball as he faced the field.

The coach walked out toward the shotput, trailing his tape measure. Billy usually could tell if a throw was good, and this one felt great. He began to walk downfield. His steps slowed as he realized how far away the coach was.

"How the hell did you do that?" His coach's voice was loud and tight with excitement. "Sixty-six feet. I don't get it."

Billy's first reaction was joyful. That would qualify him for the Olympic trials if he could throw that far at the next official track meet. As the coach hugged him, Billy saw a woman in a red dress standing back by the ring, smiling at him.

He turned his attention back to the coach. He realized he'd been asked a question. "Sorry? Could you repeat that?"

"Please tell me you could pass a drug test."

Billy didn't blame his coach for assuming he might be cheating. This kind of breakthrough was hard to believe. "Just gimmee the cup. You'll see. No steroids, no nothin', I swear."

The coach picked up the shotput. "Maybe we'd better weigh this. Just making sure it's regulation."

"I've been using that one for a long time, but do what you have to do."

They walked back to the ring. The coach reached into his large duffle bag and pulled out a scale. Placing it on a nearby wooden bench, he said, "Let's give this baby a look."

The two of them stared at the digital readout. "Yup. Sixteen pounds on the dot." The coach turned to Billy and held out his hand. "Guess all your hard work paid off. I'm proud of you, son."

Billy shook hands with the coach and hoped he didn't notice how much Billy's hand was trembling. Those words meant everything to him, but he knew they weren't earned. Father Xavier was wrong. There *was* a devil in a red dress, and she was going to steal his soul.

* * *

Billy's life was in turmoil. He felt empowered by the distances he was able to throw in practice, but the memory of Lucy mocked him as a fraud. He tried to convince himself he imagined the whole thing. Wasn't it possible he had improved because he pushed himself for years? The constant argument in his head was exhausting.

The morning of the next track meet came quickly. Coach Stanford greeted him with a hug, and Billy could see puzzled looks from his competitors. The coach usually saved his hugs for the winners among them.

Friends and family members sat on beach chairs outside the marked field with picnic baskets, there to enjoy the late spring weather. There were more spectators than usual this time. Today was the last qualifying event for the Olympic trials.

The lineup for the shotput competition was seeded. The man with the highest distance in earlier meets this year went first. Billy was, as always, in the lower half of the group. As he waited his turn, he could hear the sound of children in the playground across the road. He envied them their innocence and sense of joy in their games. It had been a long time since he had felt that way about his event. Maybe he should lose, ease up on his throws. Would that end the craziness? Would Lucy find a way to punish him? He wondered what would happen if he just walked out. He could find another focus for his life, couldn't he? But then his name was called.

Billy knew as soon as he released the shotput that his fate was sealed. Everyone grew silent. The spectators, who had been paying more attention to their lunch than to the games, realized something unusual was happening. All three officials had gathered at the far end of the field, taking turns measuring the distance of his throw. The other competitors stared at Billy. How had he set a new U.S. record?

He knew what would come next. They would re-weigh the shotput and then request a drug test. They wouldn't find anything to explain his extraordinary feat. He would always be tainted by their conviction that he must have cheated, even though they couldn't prove it.

He wouldn't have believed it either. Next up were the Olympic trials. How could he go on with this farce? He had to find a way to make it stop.

That evening, Billy returned to the crossroads. He wasn't surprised to see Lucy waiting for him.

"Nice throw. Wait 'til you see the one at the Olympics."

"No dice. It's over. You tricked me into this, and I'm not doing it. I was wrong. Winning this way isn't worth my soul."

"If you're sure, there is a way out," Lucy said and moved closer to him.

"Don't touch me." Billy was torn between his fear and the lust she aroused in him.

Lucy laughed, a sound that was more like a devil than a beautiful woman, deep and mocking. "Don't worry. You're not my type. But there is something I do want. If you get it for me, the deal will be off. No Olympic win. No lost soul."

"I'll do it." Billy thought he'd agree to anything she wanted, but he didn't expect what she said next.

"In the church, there's a large silver chalice. It's Father Xavier's most prized possession. I want it. He's been a thorn in my side for a long time. He needs to suffer."

"I can't." Billy was horrified. "It was a gift to him from the pope. He's an old man. It would break his heart."

"That's the offer. You have a week to bring it to me. If you don't, I'll be seeing you in hell when your life is over. Be here same time next week."

And she was gone.

* * *

Days passed. Billy skipped practice as he obsessed over Lucy's words. How could he betray Father Xavier? But wouldn't the priest want to help him save his soul? As he pondered the two questions, he convinced himself the old priest would understand and agree that Billy's soul was worth more than the chalice.

The night of the deadline, Billy drove to the church. He knew the front door was always unlocked. Father Xavier didn't want anyone to feel excluded if they needed the comfort of prayer any time of day or night.

The lights in the church were set to low. Billy made sure the door closed softly behind him and walked down the aisle. The chalice was kept in a cabinet under the altar. Unlike the front door, the cabinet was kept locked.

"I'm trusting," Father Xavier once told him, "but not stupid." Billy had laughed.

With the tools he brought with him, Billy forced the cabinet door open. The chalice glowed in the sudden light. He hesitated. Could he go through with this? He had to. Gently, he pulled the silver bowl toward him and slid it into his duffel bag. As he stood, he heard a voice behind him.

"Billy? What are you doing?"

He spun to face the priest, who had come up behind him.

"I'm so sorry, Father. I have no choice. I have to have the chalice."

The priest reached for the bag. "Give it to me, son, and we'll talk about it."

"I can't," Billy shouted and shoved the old man.

Father Xavier fell backward. Billy would never forget the sound as the priest's head crunched against the edge of the table behind the altar. Blood began to pool under his limp body. Billy knelt next to him and felt for a pulse, but he knew it was too late. He grabbed the bag and ran down the aisle to the door. He had to get to the crossroads before the deadline.

* * *

Lucy was waiting for him. "I was about to give up on you."

Billy held up the bag. "I did it. I got the chalice. Now it's your turn. You have to give me back my soul."

Lucy took the bag and opened it. The silver object gleamed in the streetlight. "It's the chalice, all right. But it's not what I wanted. I told you. I needed Father Xavier to suffer its loss. But he can't, now, can he? You sent him on his way to heaven. That wasn't our agreement."

Billy felt nauseous. "You can't do this. We had a deal."

She howled, a bone-chilling sound. "You killed a man. Not just a man. A man of God. You're going to hell. Nothing I can do to change that. But I'll tell you what. I'll still let you win the Olympics. It'll give you some memories to take with you through eternity."

* * *

Billy stood on the top podium in the Olympic Stadium in Paris. The American anthem played as he touched the gold medal hanging around his neck. The cameras closed in on his face as tears ran down his cheeks and he began to sob.

"Wow, look at that," the sportscaster told his audience. "I've been doing this a long time, and I've never seen anyone that emotional at winning gold. I'm sure this is a moment Billy Thornton will never forget."

The Center Is Your Friend
Kai Lovelace

I crack the window and light a cigarette while the radio crackles out *Rikki Don't Lose That Number* and the rain drums tiny fingernails on the rusted hood of my Camaro. Goddamn earworm.

The sign above the pool hall is missing a B and an R. *O'Dowd's -illiads & Lounge* glows orange neon, the only spot of color on the gray wash of drab downtown block, the one stretch of civilization in this economic cesspool. Chipped storefronts, filthy stoops, rats nosing in the gutters. The car is stuffy, it stinks of stale smoke, greasy fast food, a queasy note of cheap perfume I'd rather forget.

I check my watch—7:43. Where the hell is he?

Could go inside first, wait for him at the bar, but I don't like the idea of glancing over my shoulder every time the door squeals open. I need to get a look at him first, size him up when he thinks no one is watching. You can tell a lot about a person from the way they walk alone. Besides, I want to let him get into the groove first, feel nice and easy after a few beers before I make an appearance. We met in passing a couple times over the years, when I was in town visiting Harry, but I doubt he'd clock me on his own. I make it a point to remember names and faces.

The non-menthol cigarette tastes awful, like wet cardboard and gasoline, but my nerves are already quieting. A nip from the flask doesn't hurt either. Sweet burn swelling my chest. That's okay, Nathan, take your time.

I'll wait all night if I have to.

Comfortable in the center.

I'm patient because I can replay anything in my head, any time. Never remember what day of the week it is, but people, places, weather, those stick. Movies, TV shows, songs. Eidetic memory, a friend told me once. He's dead now. Blew his head off over a woman. Everyone was pissed at the time, or wailing and moaning, tearing their hair out. Why, they cried. Why the hell not, I say. You got a better reason?

Burke the Jerk is late. The rain's getting heavier. No sweat, I made it these three weeks since stumbling over Harry all twisted up at the bottom of the stairs like a pile of laundry, leaking booze and saliva and blood from his shaggy head. I'll make it a few more minutes.

In any case it gives me time to think.

I snap off the radio.

When I first encountered Nat Burke his beady eyes did a quick dance up and down before his laconic grin caught up, cloudy gray irises obscured by yellow-tinted aviators, and shook my hand too hard. He's one of those skinny, pigeon-toed guys who seems to dry out with age like a slab of jerky. No amount of beer guzzled over smoky green felt will thicken him like most of these louts you see haunting sports bars and betting parlors. On his deathbed he'll end up a desiccated husk in a loose flowing snap-button western shirt. I remember his hair too, not quite a mullet but almost, and a thick copper-hued handlebar mustache.

I thought he looked ridiculous, until I got a chance to see him shoot pool. Some people have an inner grace that overrides an initial physical impression, all the more admirable for the way it blindsides you. I sure as hell wouldn't have that confidence if I looked like a strung-out Woody Woodpecker, but then again I'm no prize myself.

The face in the rearview mirror looks, above all else, tired. The nose is okay, delicate bump adding a dignified element to an otherwise unremarkable visage. Hairline receding faster than the evacuation of Dunkirk. Thin lips, sloping shoulders. I've long since ceased to think of these disparate features as intrinsic to my personality, mainly because I'm so sick of looking at them. What a bum deal we wake up as the same person every day in this life. At least it doesn't last forever.

Or even very long, for some. Like Harry Condon.

The night he went to meet Burke we spoke on the phone, tossing around the idea of a visit. I had a weird feeling but chalked it up to paranoia. Harry was bouncing off the walls, talking about this mark he was going to squeeze, some joker down at the pool hall with a big mouth who agreed to lay down two hundred a rack, something only an amateur would do. I laughed when I realized who he meant, wished him good luck, but didn't want any part of it. The pathos gets to me sometimes, especially when the tears and begging starts. Harry used to leave them with enough at least to get smashed afterwards. What a sweetheart.

Anyway, I heard about it later. After the cops came for Harry and had a good chuckle about the whole thing. He reeked of Jim Beam so bad our eyes all started watering in the tight vestibule, also because of some other odors they tend to leave out of the movies. There's nothing dramatic or sexy about a dead body, just a sad sack of meat reminding everyone what this is all about and serving as a nice little preview of things to come.

His neck was broken. No sign of foul play. Square welt behind the ear where the lip of a step cracked him on the way down. They found his keys on the landing and figured he bent down to fish for them and lost his footing. I got the rest of the story later.

Things had been going okay until the skinny guy with a mullet, they said, turned it around and started sinking balls left and right. Harry got nervous, figured he was in too deep to cash out, talking about his old lady was going to kill him for this. Kept on taking shots, of both well-whiskey and missed corner pockets. The whole time this character Burke, a couple guys knew him from Randy's over in Wilmington, was cool as ice, sauntering around the table, staying calm and winding Harry up like a toy soldier. He never was the pool shark he claimed to be. The real ones tend to keep their mouths shut. Eventually the tears started, bargaining, pleading. Nat didn't leave him with enough to keep drinking, because he's not such a sweetheart.

Everyone else seemed to forget about it, raise a glass, pour one out, moment of silence, anyway what else is going on?

But not me. I remembered.

In fact, ever since they carted Harry away he's been on my mind like a tension headache, throbbing in and out. Or that mosquito bite in between your shoulder blades that keeps you up on a muggy night.

Known him since fifth grade, helped me dry out when I was circling the drain, lent me money, gave me a place to stay. Conscientious, you might say. Best of all he didn't talk much. Sure he had slip-ups as we all do, chinks in the armor. Of course someone smelled it, got inside and gummed up the works, now I'll never see him tug his left earlobe when he's thinking hard, never hear him bitch about some movie he'd seen being no good. It's tough to see your friends go, even as it becomes more common later in life. When some clown facilitates the process as part of his regular Saturday night routine, well that's unacceptable.

After my business wrapped up in Philadelphia I decided to swing by and deal with it.

So here I am, and the bastard's still MIA. 8:05. So much for his supposed punctuality, according to—

Hold on.

I squint through the lazy sweep of the windshield wipers.

It's him, skulking down the block under an umbrella big enough to hitch a ride to Cuba in a strong wind. Tight, uneasy steps for such a lithe frame. He scans the street before folding the umbrella and ducking into O'Dowd's, passing directly over me. I keep still and he's gone.

My newspaper is wet pulp by the time I'm inside but I'm not drenched. The weight in my windbreaker pocket slaps against my hip on the way upstairs but I try to ignore it. I may not even need it, depending on how things go. And what is the plan exactly? I stopped thinking that way a few years ago after something that happened in Pittsburgh on what was supposed to be a simple collection job. I'm strongly convinced that the blood never lies, instincts are always correct, and the intellect exists solely to fuck things up after the body's already decided what it wants to do.

The AC is chugging overtime and not making a dent in the humidity when I shoulder the door open, the bar to my left and two rows of pool tables stretching down on the right, walls knocked out to turn the whole second floor into a dimly lit, low-ceilinged room. Tuesday night so it's sparsely populated, like I'd planned, with a low susurration of subdued chatter, clinking glasses and cutlery, sharp clacks of colliding billiard balls.

The only pair of eyes that flicks up to register my presence are Aunt Grandma's behind the bar, thick bifocals flashing neon from Budweiser signs, buzzing nature scenes backlit by dim bulbs, logos, slogans, puns—Schlitz, Coors, Jameson. Detritus scoured from garage sales and antique shops, almost enough shit on the walls to distract from the stagnant atmosphere.

Burke is just moving away with his pint so I take my time approaching, keeping him in my peripheral as he reaches his table in the back corner and I settle at the bar.

Aunt Grandma knows something's up, that sixth sense from decades of wrangling dumbasses. Part therapist, part drug pusher, two hundred pounds of tough gristle in a fishing vest, plaid sleeves rolled up and black curly hair like a cheap wig. Once you get a glimpse of those cool green eyes an image flashes in your head—younger, thinner, happier, on the right side of hard years, marriages, careers. You struggle to connect points A and B, questions crowding your booze-addled mind to fill in the gaps. Then you realize you'd rather not know and take another sip, careful to duck out of the way of your reflection in the smudged mirror over her shoulders, worried you'll see the same dissipation there, the same unanswerable questions.

But she was always nice to me. Even now, when I hadn't seen her in years, she lights up and slaps a coaster down. Hasn't lost her edge, caught a whiff of something between me and the lanky guy swaggering down to his usual table, but still welcomes me like a pal. Can you ask for anything more in this world?

"How you doin,' Len? Been a few years." Her smoker's rasp has accumulated a few cartons of bass, a sprinkling of burst capillaries on the tip of her nose, but the impish grin has endured.

"I'm alright, thanks. Good to be back in town." The first words out of my mouth in hours feel stilted, amateur theater delivery from some hack who hasn't quite grasped the nature of his role.

"Whatcha been up to?"

"Bumming around the west coast."

The Center is Your Friend

"Sounds glamorous. You having your usual?"

"I'm surprised you remember."

She gives me a dry look and lumbers down to the rack of cheap well liquors, returning with a whisky sour complete with one of those sickly sweet bright red cherries.

"You seem awful distracted, Len."

For the first time a small lump forms in my throat. "What do you mean?"

Her smile fades and she adjusts her glasses. "Keep looking at that piece of work playing with himself down there. I'd hate for there to be some kind of problem tonight."

I sip my drink. "No trouble."

Her lips writhe in a distasteful smirk. "People been talking about you. How you dropped out of sight, the work you do now."

I'm sure they do, using all manner of kind words. Drifter, loser, drunk. Fine with me. I take another deeper sip, sucking down the watered-down liquor. "I do lots of different kinds of work now."

"I was sorry to hear about your friend." Our gazes are locked.

"So was I."

"Sounds like a terrible accident."

Somewhere inside me a door slams shut, a deadbolt slides home. "Maybe."

She heaves a sigh and appraises me. "You're what, forty? Forty-five?"

"Thirty-eight."

"Still got a lot of life in front of you."

I drain the glass like a life-saving antidote. "We'll see."

"Terrible thing to waste."

"Or to take."

After a beat she nods to herself. "You want another one?"

I shake my head. "I'm going to go say hi to somebody."

She flashes gritted teeth. "Good to see you, Len."

I push off from the bar, passing folks who appear to me as fuzzy blobs, inanimate obstacles. Some of them notice a vibe, step out of my way. They'll talk in the weeks to come, maybe even years. I was there, yeah. Saw the whole crazy thing. Why'd he do it? Who knows. I heard one thing, Jim told me something else.

Sometimes it's good to keep your ear to the ground, you might learn something. Like how Nat Burke was seen going home with Harry Condon that night, supporting the weeping man. How earlier he'd shaken him by his lapels in the corridor, slapped his face back and forth. Nobody saw him slink out of Harry's place later because it was past everyone's bedtime.

Could be true, could be horseshit. No one cared much afterwards either way.

Except me. So let them talk, if they're observant they'll recall how it started tonight, with a squat little guy stalking through the pool tables, gripping something in his pocket. Who would have thought.

Though it's heavy in my jacket, no one would mistake it for a gun. It doesn't swing the same way, throw off my stride, or appear with the same bulk. At first glance you might not even know what it was, white with a single red stripe, the orb decorated with small markings, labeled and measured in quadrants indicating target zones to aim your shot. I found it in Harry's nightstand, poking around after the cops left, traces of that awful reek mingling with must and mildew. Took even me a second to realize—his old practice ball. I remember him fooling around with it in the corner while the guys and I pursued more earthly delights at the bar, waiting for the shifts of cocktail waitresses to get off from Riverfront Casino. That was back when O'Dowd's had a shinier reputation, the block wasn't so rundown, and the bubbles in an amber ale didn't inspire weary dread from across the room. Good times. Maybe too good, which led straight to a series of rock bottoms, rebounds to white-knuckle sobriety, landing in my current limbo. I've managed to leave the hard stuff behind, but moderation is the best policy.

Harry's practice ball. Marked and scuffed, smeared with fingerprints. Not sure why he kept the damn thing, good luck maybe. So much for that.

When I first hefted it I was surprised at how dense it felt, how snugly it conformed to the contours of my palm. Six ounces, two and three-quarter inches around. Pretty innocuous, you'd think. But these things were made of tough lacquered resin, or possibly even hardwood if it was vintage enough. No give like a baseball or basketball. Hell, even football helmets are mainly protection from the other thugs running around the field.

No, a billiard ball is small, easy to handle, and can do a surprising amount of damage if it accidentally jumps.

Or comes down hard, say on a human skull.

Burke looks up and does a double take, brow furrowing as he tries to place me. I'm wading through mud, pushing past thick air, watching his mouth become a thin hard line as he straightens, the corners of his lips dancing, trying to decide whether to smile or frown.

What comes next, Leonard? You're off by a side rail with limited angles. I used to ask myself these types of questions, talk to myself so much in the third person I went half-crazy, split in two. That hasn't changed much, but the dialogue has stopped. Now I just watch from the corner of the room, see what the old boy is going to do, approaching with that worrisome hand in that pocket. Burke shoots quick nervous glances over my vinyl windbreaker shoulders, subconsciously grasping his cue like a lance.

A vivid picture comes to me, a road sign pointing to one possible exit for my life, coming up fast. Food, lodgings, courtesy of the state, indefinite stays and it won't cost you a penny, just the poor taxpayers. It'll be easy. Heft the ball, swing it around sideways, catch him in the temple. Hook one of those battered cowboy boots and bring him down, bounce that stubbled jaw off the edge of the table. Probably a gasp or two from the peanut gallery at that point. Aunt Grandma cursing to herself and waddling to the phone on the wall. Ten minutes response time for the local cops, give or take. What'll I do in that brief window? Keep swinging until there's not much face left? Toss the ball to leave a crimson streak on the felt like some macabre Christmas decoration? He should know what it's all about before he winks out. Or not. Maybe it doesn't matter, maybe it's not about him at all, or me, or even Harry Condon. Maybe it's just about what the blood wants.

It'll be fun to see how far it goes. Like breaking free from a cage, taking a leap and finding out where the pieces fall. I owe it to Harry, either to save myself or destroy myself, not sure which one.

"Holy shit, is that Len Starkey?"

I stop six feet away. Burke strides forward and claps me on the shoulder. Eager, forced, as if I'm expected. Behind him the billiard table glows under the lamp like a freshly cut lawn, the balls broken and scattered but nothing yet sunk.

"Great to see you, man," he says. "How the hell are you? Listen, I'm so fuckin' sorry about Harry, been meaning to talk to you about it."

He's close enough to breath fetid whisky and tobacco in my face. I shrug loose and step back. His Adam's apple bobs as he notices my concealed hand.

"Hey, Nat." I keep my voice even.

"Look, I understand you're probably upset with me. You know what, I feel pretty shitty about what happened."

"Do you."

"God yes," he chuckles. "I was shocked as the next guy. It was just some fun, who knew that would happen?"

My fingers ache gripping the ball. Why can't I do it? It's now or never. Exit's coming up, and beyond it just more road leading nowhere. Suddenly the place seems very quiet, everyone's attention like searchlights pinning me. Don't look at the eight ball, resting quiet and regal and full of potential as it stares down the spread, evenly distributed stripes and solids. Good break.

No, focus on what you came here to do.

Burke licks his lips and sighs. "Were you at the funeral?"

"No funeral. His mother had him cremated and that was it."

He shakes his head. "Hell of a thing. Guilt can really be a trip, huh?" I stare at him and he swallows, searching for more words. "You know I didn't really care about that debt, right?"

This is it, the moment's passing. Grab his throat. Wrench that pool cue out of his hands. The eight ball is just off center, could stand to be a little farther to the left. But there are interesting possibilities for opening shots.

The Center is Your Friend

The thing is, Burke's not like I remember him. I was expecting arrogance, rudeness, aggression. That ugly hollow face twisted in sadistic pleasure. For the first time my recollections seem off.

"You went home with Harry that night."

That does something. He raises his chin defensively.

"Who said that?"

"You followed him upstairs. Had to get your money."

This is more like it. His bony chest heaves. "What is this, Len? Am I being accused of something?"

"Must have been pissed when you realized you weren't getting it. Too much trouble to hound him for months after."

"You know," he scoffs, "I'm trying to be nice to you, I don't know what's going on here."

"Could have been an accident," I say, to myself more than anything, "could have been intentional. Result is the same."

"Fuck this," he hisses. "I'm out of here."

I feint left and block his path. He raises the cue and I slap it down hard. It clatters to the floor and he staggers back. I don't turn but I can feel people watching us. My hand emerges with the ball. Guess I'm taking the exit after all.

"Okay, okay," Burke whines, patting the air and smoothing down his hair, shifting and fidgeting like a speed freak. "You got a beef with me, anybody could understand that. But what you're saying is nuts, there's no fuckin' way I—look, let's talk, alright?"

"I bet Harry sounded just like this."

He rolls his eyes and crosses his arms, frowning deeply at the floor and tapping his foot. "What a fuckin' day, man. I don't believe it."

My palm is slick on the ball, fingers aching from the grip. Behind Burke I can see the red seven is ripe for a thirty degree bank shot and might even drop the four in the bargain. He notices my divided attention and tries a new tack.

"You want to play a quick one? Calm the nerves down? Then we can talk after."

"There's nothing to say." My heart isn't in it, though, and he puffs up his chest.

"C'mon, nobody wants a scene. Just a friendly game. You play?"

"I dabble," I shrug.

"I'll give you some tips. Bump up your average."

"Maybe one."

Ideas sparkle as Burke's face becomes animated, the old scheme percolating, and for a second the mask falls away and I perceive something serpentine, reptilian, a lust I recognize all too well. Even admire. Something Harry never had, God bless him.

"You know what," he says off-handedly, "let's make it interesting, huh? Give it some stakes."

"I like the sound of that."

I'm getting a more solid picture of this fool in front of me, starting to believe some of the things I've heard over the last month. Switchblade in his left boot. Snub-nosed .38 police special in his glove box. The butt of that kind of pistol makes a nice square welt just behind the ear, an easy target on someone bent down fishing for dropped keys. Do I know this for sure? No, how could I, I'm not the amazing Kreskin.

But I do just the same, deep down.

So what's it going to be—I don't deserve some righteous vengeance. Harry does, but he doesn't give a damn because he's dead. It's bullshit anyway, just a reason to beat and tear and kill like I've always wanted, a schoolyard bully eager for an excuse. I wonder if the story's even true, Harry set up for a big fall, or if he just got drunk and sloppy and lost fair and square.

The exit sign is shrinking in the rearview mirror and something deep inside me is hollering, throwing a tantrum. It's not too late, not too late, not—

Until it is.

The poor idiot has no idea how close he came, sauntering over to re-rack the balls, smug in the knowledge that he'll hustle me as easily as he hustled Harry into an early grave.

The Center is Your Friend

I peel off my jacket and drape it on a nearby stool. Burke instantly relaxes even more, shoulders bumping to the piped-in Motown.

So now comes the next question. How to play it. The cards have been so close to the vest for so many years it feels like stripping naked and strolling down mainstreet at noon. But I'm not out west anymore. The only thing to protect here is a reputation, a life I was ready to throw away a couple minutes ago, so how important can it really be.

Burke the Jerk breaks, whipping the cue back the way you're not supposed to. Hence the nickname. Also because he's a son of a bitch.

The balls disperse, caroming off each other and thumping the velvet edges. I'm flooded with calculations, considering angles, swimming in the sheer bliss of the game.

I give him the upper hand at first. Scratching a few times, swearing under my breath, hesitating over the next round before reluctantly accepting. I suggest we up the ante, much to his surprise, insisting that I feel a hot streak coming on. Beginner's luck, call it what you will. He asks if I'm sure, playing it cool but inside beaming like a birthday brat. Two rounds of drinks help the act. He doesn't have to know mine's ginger ale.

After the third game I push him a little, keeping it plausible. I'm as surprised as he is when my hook shot sinks the striped eleven. Ditto for the curving backspin I employ sporadically, letting a few more get close and venting my frustration when they miss. Never overplay your hand, that's rule number one.

He buys it. Not quite smart enough to judge himself objectively, a psychological blind spot I'm using as an inroad. Gotta love that Dunning-Kruger effect.

I won't pull out the big guns til the sixth or seventh round, soon as I can hook him with a big wager, the one he knows is sure to break the run of freak luck, the fluke that can't possibly be more than that. Around 1AM he'll be drunk, begging, maybe even crying a little. He'll put it together, word will get around, but it won't matter since I won't be in town long anyway. Then I'll decide how nice I want to be. Leave him enough to finish the bender, let him wake up in the morning. Or guide him to a similar fate as his last victim.

We'll just have to see.

I want to believe I'm a decent guy, like Harry, that I don't have more in common with this jittery beanpole across the table, that I'm not a coward who backed down from the only thing I've ever done without myself in mind. After a few more rounds I might be able to.

For now Nat's starting to get nervous, thrown for a loop after our initial meeting. Afraid for his life one minute, smooth operator the next, a sinking feeling that he's stumbled into quicksand muddled by booze, neon lights, the thickening crowd of day workers swarming in to drown their sorrows. After all, he's got a reputation too. Got to see things through.

So maybe it was a lie when I said I dabbled. Maybe I've been busy the last few years concentrating on one simple thing to anchor my excuse for a life, keeping a low profile. But it's not so simple, as it turns out. It's a whole universe of control, chaos, luck, skill. A perfect microcosm of the world, down to the fundamental precept that the center of the table is your greatest ally. The place of purest equilibrium, where the most options branch out before you to categorize, analyze, weigh. As much as possible you try to get back there, before you're stuck out on the edge, backed into impossible corners, hooked on a pocket. So close to the goal but so far.

Things make a little more sense now. This is my arena, the weapons of my vengeance a tad subtler than hard wood against soft flesh. I want to believe Harry would approve, so I do. Amazing what we convince ourselves of when we practice a little self-love. The rest happens naturally, so easy it's an anticlimax. Around 1 AM Nat is milked dry, hollow eyes, sunken chest heaving, gulping down his nausea. I walk him out, catching a dry glance from Aunt Grandma, a hint of relief.

I'm very careful guiding him down the stairs. Wouldn't want an accident.

Out on the street I drag him towards my car, the slim body oddly limp. With a pang of annoyance I let him fall, checking the empty street and fishing for my car keys. In my peripheral I see him digging in his boot—

scratching an itch, grabbing the bankroll to get this transaction over with, my senses dulled with victory, a shiver at how close I came to self-destruction. I'm halfway turned when the lancing agony pierces the soft part of my gut, blinding my world as it wrenches sideways, spilling crimson down my jeans. The handle of the knife is ivory, pale bone matching Nat's thin wrist, which I barely have time to grab and grind before he dents my forehead with the pistol butt. So I was right about the blade, but I guess he'd been too careful to leave the gun in the glove box.

I float down onto a feather bed, a sweet warmth of godly nectar spreading in my chest. Nat gropes for the cash roll in my inner pocket, slim fingers skittering like spider legs, then he's gone. Wet slaps on pavement receding into the tranquil night. I feel lighter without it. Suppose I'd have taken the exit if I knew how little road was left, but the gamble is part of the game. God it hurts, my ragged edges wailing, weeping blood, but already it's starting to dull.

Harry's going to give me hell when he hears about this.

I couldn't save him, or myself, but maybe there's a nice symmetry there. Did I let my guard down intentionally, using The Jerk to finish the job I almost started upstairs? He'll wonder about that, and I'll tell him sometimes you feel like beating a man to death and sometimes you just want to shoot some pool.

Sooner or later it'll be you, lying on glistening concrete, wedged between two parked sedans with mist tickling your numb face, coughing wet, bitter iron in your throat and bitter irony in the air. Or if you're on a comfy hospital bed surrounded by a doting wife, sons and daughters, solemn grand kids, content to go quietly into that good night cause it's all been a swell cabaret, good for you. Most of us don't have that luxury. Either way it's worth a chuckle, the whole jumbled mess. Pool takes it all and fits it into a neat package. It's an interesting game because it's a lot like life.

The center is your friend.

To Luisa, a good friend who loves to read & write mysteries as much as I do!
Diane

Golf Widow
Diane A. Hadac

"I'm going to play a quick nine, dear," said Ralph placidly, bending over his golf bag and reverently rearranging his clubs.

His wife Marie was scouring the kitchen sink. Her blue eyes blazed with frustration as she turned to look at him, cleaning sponge in hand. Ever since he'd retired, he golfed constantly.

"You promised to tour the museum's Egyptian exhibit with me today. It's leaving town next week, remember?" she reminded him irritably.

Ralph's round, cheerful, sunburned face assumed an apologetic expression. "I'm sorry, dear, but George called yesterday and asked if I could meet him at Eastern Acres to help correct his swing. It's just eight-thirty and since we're only playing nine holes, I'll be home by eleven. We'll spend the entire afternoon at the museum, I promise."

Marie knew that if she forced Ralph to cancel the outing, he'd grumble through the exhibit and spoil the day for her. "Well, go ahead, but you'd better be back before noon," she conceded with a rueful sigh.

He came over and kissed her cheek before shouldering his bag, saying happily, "You're so understanding, sweetheart."

The red pom-pom on his plaid cap bobbed jauntily as he ambled out the door. Marie felt like dashing up behind him and snipping it off. Lately, just hearing the word "golf" caused her teeth to grind. She had become that well-known cliché—the Golf Widow.

Marie sat down on a kitchen chair with a feeling of despair. Unlike some women, she'd welcomed her husband's retirement. They had planned to travel and explore the exciting foreign countries they'd read about over the years in the Travel Section of the Sunday newspaper. She had collected a folder full of clippings that highlighted celebrated attractions in each major European city. However, two years ago, Ralph had discovered golf—his office had initiated an after-work league—and their life hadn't been the same since. He did his best to encourage her to embrace the sport so they could play as a twosome.

Last year, for her birthday, Ralph had outfitted Marie with a set of clubs, a golf bag and shoes, and enough golf balls to last a lifetime. Occasionally, she'd accompany him to the driving range; but try as she might to enjoy the sport, it just didn't appeal to her. She had no desire to spend their so-called "Golden Years" on a golf course when they could be touring Europe instead.

Their basement was littered with clubs. Ralph had become adept at customizing his "sticks" and enjoyed commenting modestly to his cronies: "My set may look mismatched, but I build each club to my personal specifications." Over the past two years, he had tried explaining the intricacies of club assembly to Marie. Although she listened politely to his lectures emphasizing the importance of club weight and balance, in reality, her mind was a million miles away, focused on an exotic travel destination.

Sometimes, she thought wistfully of Halcyon Lake, the forest preserve running parallel to Eastern Acres, one of Ralph's favorite courses. Before golf came to occupy nearly ninety-nine percent of his leisure time, they would hike its well-marked trails. Now, if she could get him to go there at all, he headed for the fringe of trees marking the boundary between the two properties. Here, at the eighth green, he'd study the putting techniques of the various players and bore her to distraction with a lengthy commentary on their skill level.

Thinking of the "g" word again made her want to scream like a mad woman. "I simply must control myself and concentrate on something else," she murmured fretfully.

* * *

Ralph returned from his outing on time, as promised, and they spent the remainder of the day at the museum. He poked along dispiritedly, though, until they came to a section of the exhibit displaying recreational activities enjoyed by the ancient Egyptians. At this point, Ralph perked up, saying hopefully to Marie that maybe the pharaohs had played a sport similar to golf. Her icy stare discouraged him from pursuing that particular train of thought.

That evening, Ralph practiced his putting in the family room while Marie watched television. He always kept his putter and a few golf balls in a corner near the fireplace. It was difficult for Marie to concentrate on her program and ignore the persistent "tap" of the club as it struck the shiny white dimpled orbs and sent them rolling merrily back and forth across the slate blue carpeting. Finally, after about fifteen minutes of this activity, Marie switched off the TV, saying with exasperation, "Ralph, we have to talk."

Ralph dutifully joined her on the sofa, putter in hand, asking innocently, "What about, dear?"

She gave him a withering look, her voice rising with agitation. "Don't pretend you don't know! You can't possibly be that dense! Your constant preoccupation with golf is driving me crazy—it has to stop! We were supposed to go abroad after you retired, remember? Our thirty-fifth wedding anniversary is approaching in a few months, and our travel plans are nonexistent. I want to celebrate the occasion somewhere special."

Ralph's expression became sheepish, and he gazed contritely at the floor as he said, "I haven't forgotten our anniversary, dear; but I'm registered to play in a couple of tournaments this month. After they're over, I promise we'll take a nice, long trip." He put down his putter, reached over and embraced her fondly.

Heartened by the fact that she'd finally gotten her point across, the following morning, after Ralph left for his men's league, Marie stopped at a travel agency. She was happily poring over a brochure and had scores of others strewn across the coffee table when he returned. "Honey, listen to this!" she exclaimed excitedly, reading from a pamphlet: "'Unwind in the lush beauty of romantic Hawaii—your cozy private cottage nestles among towering palms and exotic flowering plants.' "Or, how does this sound? 'Escape to Bermuda—experience the gentility of Great Britain in a tropical paradise.'"

Marie failed to notice Ralph's enigmatic smile.

Her mood exuded indulgence—the colorful, engaging brochures had cast their spell. "How was your day, dear?" she inquired solicitously.

Ralph's smile faded. He exhaled forlornly, replied, "Not good," and proceeded to deliver a detailed account of his woeful performance on all eighteen holes. The glassy-eyed stare that had settled over his wife's face a quarter of the way through the narrative did nothing to stem its flow.

* * *

Several weeks later, Ralph breezed into the family room in a distinctly pleased manner and announced, "Sweetheart, I have a surprise for you!" Marie was sitting on the family room sofa reading a book. With a grin, he dropped a packet of paperwork into her lap.

"What's this?" She put down her book with a puzzled expression as she withdrew from the envelope several brochures and airline tickets to Edinburgh.

Ralph sat down next to her and wrapped an arm around her shoulders. "You said you wanted to spend our anniversary somewhere special, and I thought Scotland would be an ideal spot." His eyes glistened as he rhapsodized about the trip: "In addition to spectacular scenery, Scotland is where golf originated. You'll be able to walk eighteen holes with me on the oldest golf course in the world—the Old Course at St. Andrews. I'll show you how to extract an errant shot from the notoriously difficult Scottish sand traps, known as 'pot bunkers.' On the eleventh tee, we'll stand side by side gazing at the breathtaking view across the Eden Estuary. At the eighteenth fairway, we'll have our picture taken on the ancient Swilcan Bridge, just like the pros do." He rose and wagged an admonitory finger at her. "You'll be sorry you've never taken the game seriously when you experience the treeless windswept beauty of a true Links course. We'll take your golf clubs along, too. This trip may change your whole outlook on the game. See if you don't agree after you look through the brochures," he added earnestly as he retrieved his putter from beside the fireplace.

Marie stared at him in stunned silence. She didn't reply when he said, "I hope you don't mind, dear, but I want to play a quick nine by myself at Eastern Acres before dark. After all, I have to get my game 'up to par' before the trip." He chuckled at his own joke and winked at her before strolling away.

When Marie heard the garage door close, she tore the airline tickets and the brochures into tiny pieces and threw them into the wastebasket; then she went to the basement and coolly selected a club from one of Ralph's discarded sets. She fixed herself a cup of coffee and ate a powdered-sugar doughnut as she watched the early news. Later, she drove to Halcyon Lake, parked the car, and walked into the woods bordering Eastern Acres' eighth green, a short par three.

As twilight descended, a lone golfer appeared at the tee and hit his shot straight down the fairway where it bounced onto the green. There were no other golfers in sight. Marie left the woods and advanced toward him, club in hand.

"Sweetie," he remarked with surprise as she approached, "nice of you to join me, but you'll need more than a nine iron to play the last hole."

"That's what you think," she remarked placidly to herself.

As he lined up his putt, Marie took a powerful swing. Her style was not classic; but, nevertheless, the club met the base of Ralph's skull with a resounding crack. His body sprawled forward, hitting the ground with a thud.

Marie studied her husband's prone form dispassionately for a moment; then she calmly cleaned the weapon in a water hazard, dried it with his golf towel and placed it in his bag among the other clubs where it wouldn't attract attention—after all, everybody knew his set was mismatched.

"Maybe in the hereafter you'll discover whether or not the ancient

Golf Widow

Egyptians had recreation similar to golf," she reflected heartlessly as she tramped back through the woods to her car. Marie felt safe from suspicion. Usually the wife is the main suspect in a husband's murder investigation, but nobody knew she had gone to Eastern Acres, and the course was deserted except for Ralph.

Several hours later, she phoned the police station to say her husband hadn't returned home from his evening golf outing, and she wasn't able to reach him on his cell phone. She said she had tried calling the golf course, but the recording said it was closed. The officer who took her call explained that a person had to be missing twenty-four hours before a report could be filed.

Early the next morning her doorbell rang. Two officers were waiting respectfully on the porch when she opened the door. They asked to speak with her, and she led them to seats in the family room where they broke the news that Ralph's body had been discovered around six a.m. by an Eastern Acres greenskeeper.

Marie wore a suitably shocked expression. She wrung her hands fretfully and lamented, "I've always told my husband that it was unsafe to play alone in the evening, especially at Eastern Acres because it abuts a forest preserve. You never know if a lunatic is lurking in the woods."

Detective Stanton spoke first in a quiet, gentle manner. "Yes, ma'am. The course manager said your husband was an avid golfer who often frequented Eastern Acres for a nine-hole outing in the evening. He also said your husband followed the game's rules religiously—even during a casual round such as last night's. That information may be important."

Marie spoke absently. "It's true that Ralph loved the game and took it seriously, but I don't see how that could help the investigation."

"The point is this," explained Stanton. "Your husband's golf bag contained fifteen clubs; the extra stick being a nine iron. The course manager said the legal club limit in tournament play is fourteen, and he stated emphatically that your husband would never carry extra clubs, especially a nonessential nine iron, even during a practice round.

"Oh, really," said Marie, looking bewildered. She stammered, "I—I wouldn't know about that. I'm not familiar with the rules of the game."

Detective Barry spoke next. "The head angle on that particular club would make it an excellent weapon, Mrs. Anderson. Did anybody else, besides yourself, know that your husband would be at Eastern Acres last night?"

"I don't know," said Marie, "but my husband had no enemies. Some maniac must have attacked him, just as I always feared might happen." She reached out abstractedly to rearrange the travel brochures on the coffee table.

Stanton eyed the pamphlets. "Planning to take a trip?" he inquired.

Without looking up from her task, Marie said, "We would have been married thirty-five years in September, and we had planned to celebrate our anniversary in Scotland. My husband especially wanted to golf at St. Andrews."

"An ideal destination since your husband was such a keen player," said Stanton somberly.

"Yes," agreed Marie softly.

"Have you been to Eastern Acres recently, Mrs. Anderson?" queried Detective Barry.

Marie brushed a speck of dust from the tabletop, saying stiffly, "No. As I mentioned before, golf isn't my game."

Detective Stanton studied her speculatively for a moment, then said, "The course manager said the extra nine iron in your husband's bag was much lighter in weight than his other clubs. DNA evidence can possibly be recovered from the clubs' grips, showing who else may have handled them." He leaned slightly forward. "You see, Mrs. Anderson, I'm a golfer myself, and I know it would be highly unusual for a serious sportsman like your husband to play with unequally weighted clubs."

Marie looked at him mutely. She was already beginning to regret her long-standing disinterest in Ralph's pastime.

Par None
Wil A. Emerson

Marty Olson and Kevin Bryant sat at the club bar, each with a beer bottle in front of them, laughter in the background. Marty turned to the noise and grimaced. "Same group, same bull shit."

"Thursday night, last day to party before the tournament. You know, Marty, it's the routine."

Kevin, the club pro, had accepted Marty's invitation for an end of the day beer. Not a routine but the club pro, also its best salesman, knew it wasn't good for business to see a club member sitting alone. Good form was to be sociable with every member. In fact, the fellowship code as a member of Hope Valley Country Club included 'Camaraderie, Respect and Honesty'. All employees were expected to serve as an example. Kevin Bryant smiled as if he'd won the lottery when Olson extended the invitation. His good deed recorded for the week. No hounding from the management for at least a month.

Under his breath, Kevin said, "Take one for the team".

"More rain tomorrow and who gets the morning slots?" Marty Olson grabbed the beer bottle and swallowed hard. "Why is the club championship always held in the rainy season? Damn, can't you give us higher handicap guys a break?"

"I'll tell you what, Marty. If you win this weekend, I'll put you on the committee to select the dates and do the line-up. How about that?"

"Fat chance and you know it, but I'll take you up on it," Marty said with a snarl and then ordered another beer. Not one for Bryant. He knew Bryant was bull-shitting him again. Well, so what. Olson felt sure there would be a different winner this year. That is, if it all worked out as he planned.

As forewarned, the first round's tee time was eight-thirty. The sky as bleak as a Greyhound bus, not a wisp of golden light, but with no lightning predicted, the range master blew his whistle, and the first foursome rolled on to tee box number one. A three-par wonder that made a diehard look like a rookie. One-hundred and twelve yards out to hit the ridge, then a steep two-hundred-foot decline that took a mountain goat to traverse it with ease, then another one-twenty-five to the green. Simple enough if you were looking for a par on the first hole. For the hammers, those who had the muscle and guts, went for glory. They pulled back on those thousand-dollar titanium clubs and turned a golf ball into a bullet, shot over the huge rough on the left, over a thick patch of murky swamp and landed on the green. Birdie time. Marty Olson hated those guys with a vengeance. But laughed heartily when their balls fell into the thick sodden weeds. They ended up with the same one-over as he usually did.

No matter what happened at hole number one this year, the outcome would be different. Marty had worked hard, planned, plotted and set the stage for victory.

As Marty predicted, the tournament started under a bleak sky. Rain gear on but not sufficient to ward off a chill, neither Marty nor his teammates had parred number one. However, by the time he and his team, Rodney Fleetwood, Gary Schaffer, and Norm McCory, finished the sixth hole, the drizzle had turned into a slight mist and the sky had ripened to the color of an anemic blue bird. Hope hung in the air but the four men hadn't climbed out of their funk as yet.

Rodney Fleetwood said, "I'm putting money on Jordan falling flat on his face this year."

"Hope springs eternal," said Schaffer. "I don't want lightning to strike but if a tree came down, I know where I'd like it to land."

"Let the chips fall where they may, but if a hornet's nest happened to get disturbed, I sure wouldn't wait around looking for honey," McCory chimed in.

Marty broke out in a loud laugh, "Won't be anything sweet if that nest on eleven falls. Just a thousand nasty stings if you can't get away." Then he put his ball on the tee, eyed it a few seconds and swung like he'd been stung in the ass. As full of vigor as any serious golfer could muster. The four men watched as Marty's little white wonder flew skyward, took a dogleg to the left, rose higher over a cluster of maples and then plunked down in the middle of the fairway.

"I see a par coming up again," Fleetwood shouted.

"No, it's going to be a birdie. One way or the other," Marty chimed in.

The whir of the beverage cart came around for the second time and brought the foursome to a halt. Shelly, the attendant with a knack for knowing every member's name and always wearing a broad smile, offered Marty's team their second round of coffee laced with just a touch of Kahlua. "Ward off the chill. It's only a jigger," she said and twisted her shoulders as she giggled.

"Thanks, Shelly." Marty handed her a twenty-dollar bill.

"Oh, by the way, Harley Jordan and his buddies were the last to tee off. They finished number one with a terrific start. Three of the guys on the green with their first shot. Three birdies. Then one par."

"Tell me what I want to hear. Jordan ended up in the rough, skunked the ball in the gully to the left, landed in a pile of dog shit."

"Oh, Mr. Olson, you are so funny." But when she stepped on the gas pedal of the drink and snack cart, painted bright red like her fingernails, she wondered how Marty Olson knew Harley Jordan had dismayed his fellow golfers by not getting back on the fairway on his second shot. Worse, he was a stinking mess when he walked on the green. He might never recover from this embarrassment.

Fact was, in years past, Harley Jordan had been accused of hitting his ball into the rough just to prove he could lift it out and put it on the green to net a par. Two years in a row, he put it in the hole for a birdie on number one.

Those two years, when Harley bought beer for everyone back at the club house, Marty Olson had come in dead last. His goal as club champion would never be achieved if Jordan kept up his act. However, he didn't mind drinking the first round of beer after the tournament paid for by the club champion.

By the time Marty and his team started the twelfth hole, all four were feeling positive about their team's success. Their individual scores were equally impressive. A two-point range among them, one under par, two even and one over par. However, Marty didn't care what his teammates were doing. His game rocked. On par with the first nine and the holes ahead, on the back nine, were the ones he loved to play. He would easily birdie hole number twelve and if luck held solid, he'd eagle hole number fifteen. Year after year, he outshined the most aggressive players on those two holes. Almost as good as being club champion but not quite what he wanted as his legacy. Damn, he had to win this year.

What he counted on was hole number fifteen, par five, at four-hundred and twenty-five yards, being the worse shot of Harley Jordan's life. If Marty had his way, it would be Jordan's biggest failure. Marty would be in the club house by the time Jordan played the beastly hole. Water on each side of the long, winding fairway, with a shallow pond to the left of the green. The odds of any player making it onto the green in two was next to nothing. Marty's success had come with consistently playing three short shots, the last getting him on the green and then a birdie. He'd practiced that hole almost every day of the season. Why not? His house had a large deck overlooking fifteen and every morning, Marty got up early and played that very hole. Time and again, he knew it like the back of his hand.

Thing was, Marty usually grew tired by the sixteenth hole and really had to concentrate to keep in the game. For the last three years he'd been promoting a fifteen-hole championship. But that damn Kevin Bryant and his selected committee, Jordan included, wouldn't buy into it.

He was successful, however, in getting the groundskeeper to groom the fifteenth hole so it was less of a weed filled pond and more like a small pristine lagoon. If one had to look for a ball, at least he might be able to find it. The groundskeeper, Earl Shodley, thought it was an excellent idea and even said he'd talk to the owners, see if they would fall for it. Marty liked Earl and tipped him well for keeping number fifteen in pristine condition so Marty could enjoy his practice times and evenings on the deck, admiring the clear waters. Earl had become such an admirer of Marty Olson's that it wasn't difficult to convince him to add turtles in the pond to keep the algae from growing. Thing was, Marty knew that snapping turtles were the best kind to promote clarity and fewer weeds. Why not, Earl said to Mr. Olson, as he pocketed five new hundred-dollar bills.

On hole sixteen, the cart girl returned, "Good news, Mr. Olson, it's well past noon. Sun's out, nothing better than a gin and tonic with lots of ice. How about you boys, too?"

All four waited as the drinks were mixed. "Just as a favor for my favorite foursome, I've added double shots." With her finger to her lips, she said, "Shooo—keep it among friends." She giggled, started back to her little red cart but before she got in, she pulled Marty aside. "It's a crying shame, the Jordan foursome are in big trouble. Mr. Jordan didn't see a brown bundle on the cart path and ran over it. Somehow, some way, a hornet's nest fell from that old oak tree. The ranger, Charley Newsom, says he saw four kids with BeeBee guns. Wonders if they shot down the hornet's nest."

"Quite the eyes if they did," Marty said. "Of course, hope no harm came anyone's way."

"All four players are a sight to behold. Strawberries, hot and itchy, all over their faces and arms. But, my oh my, they are still playing."

Much to Marty's surprise the cart girl held out her hand. Marty obliged. Knew it was wise to keep the information flowing his way, and handed her a fifty-dollar bill. Shelly sped off, on to the next foursome.

On the finish of the eighteenth hole, the range master, Clinton Winters, pulled up to Marty's cart. He held up his hand for Schaffer and McCory to stay put, too. Dressed in the official Hope Valley Country Club's rangers' green and white golf shirt, with a designated 'master' gold crown on it, he said, "I want to make sure you four stay for the ceremonies," he said with a smile.

Marty took the invitation as a good sign. The scoreboard wasn't in sight but by all rights, Marty and his teammates should be in the run for first place. Marty, himself, was only three over par. If Jordan screwed up on every predictable hole, he'd be at the minimum of six over. Factor in the handicaps and Marty would be hugging that tall gold trophy. By nine p.m. it would be at his bedside table. Better to sleep beside a golf trophy than his last two wives.

"Gonna have a couple of drinks and wait for the other guys to come in." Marty smiled.

"Tables are set up in the banquet room. But, the manager closed the bar. Committee meeting before the buffet and award ceremony. No drinks served ahead of time. The general manager has something special for you in his office. Why not head over there." He pointed to the large mahogany double door that opened to the Hope Valley's offices.

"Strange," Marty said. He considered for a moment, "It's likely, though, they want the acceptance speech to be a short one. You know how Jordan blabbered on last year," as he and his buddies took the cobblestone path.

"Maybe we're being congratulated in private, maybe want us to be a little more gracious to the old rank and file. Those boys can grin and bare it, as far as I'm concerned." Fleetwood picked up his pace. "I've got something special to say to all of them."

When they approached the reception area, the cart girl and groundskeeper were sitting next to each other. Both waved, but it was the frightened look on the cart girl's face that made Marty's knees weak. Passing on scores to the other golfers? Maybe, though, she'd been reprimanded for not charging for double drinks.

Stubby, stalwart Arnold Gibbons, owner of the club with more enthusiasm for golf than anyone Marty had ever known but was the worst of all the club players, took a seat at the head of the table. "Never seen anything like this before. What an upset."

The foursome grinned. Marty said, "Golf is an unpredictable game, Mr. Gibbons. But it's always a thrill to play here, no matter the score. You know that better than anyone." Marty chuckled; his buddies did the same.

"Camaraderie, respect and honesty," Kevin, the pro said.

"Social decorum," said owner Gibbons.

Marty turned to his fellow golfers, "Let me speak for all of us. We are indeed proud to be members of Hope Valley. Yes, winning the championship this year means a lot to us. But in all honesty, it's being part of the community that counts the most."

Fleetwood, Schaffer, McCory nodded their heads in agreement.

"So, it was all teamwork, is that correct?" Kevin asked.

"No one person wins a tournament." Marty straightened his shoulders; a broad grin on his face. "We did our best. But, I must say I was rewarded by the golf god with two birdies and one eagle." He chuckled again.

Fleetwood startled. "Did I miss that eagle? I had three pars on the back nine."

McCory looked at Schaffer. "Not quite sure I saw either birdie, but my long drive on seventeen turned the tide for us. Indeed, it was my birdie."

Marty shuffled in his seat. "What does it matter. The final tally tells it all."

Gibbons and Bryant looked at each other.

"Camaraderie, respect and honesty. We can't dispute your record. The numbers have been posted. Just have a matter of deep concern to talk about. Seems like a couple of our employees have something to offer, too."

"No doubt their fine attendance to our needs contributed to our success," Marty said, another puff of pride in his chest.

Shelly started to sniffle. Earl pulled her to his side. "You did the right thing," he said.

"I had no idea." Then she sobbed.

"You did the right thing, Shelly," Gibbons said. "We'll discuss the extra drinks at another time. But, these incidents were not random acts of nature. You were wise in coming forward. Both of you," Gibbons nodded to Shelly and Earl.

"I've been a pro at this club for a long time. I must say your creativity was beyond belief, Marty. All for the club championship? A fifty-dollar trophy?"

"You only paid fifty dollars for the 'gold' plated trophy?" Marty grunted. "It's the honor that's important, though." Marty shuffled in his seat.

"No honor in setting traps, Marty," said Gibbons. "I agree. Quite creative." He eyed Shelly and Earl again.

"You rats. You turned us in. Didn't I pay you well enough." Marty stood, ready to barge the door.

Kevin Bryant barred the door. "Not quite yet."

"It was the turtles, Mr. Olson." She pointed a finger at Marty. "I swear, I almost died when my cart tipped over and slid into that pond. I screamed and screamed. Guess who came to my rescue. Harley Jordan. He ran into the pond, didn't blink an eye. Those fucking little snappers all around us and he didn't show a bit of fear. Why, Mr. Olson, they could have snapped off Mr. Jordan's…well…his fingers. He would'of never been able to…play…golf…again."

Then the groundskeeper scored a hole in one, "I never dreamed my Shelly would fall into the pond. Holy hell, it was a nightmare when I heard about it. Came running as fast as I could. Sorry, Mr. Olson, I'm as guilty as you are, but I believed you about the algae and that a clear pond would be better for everyone. Those snappers did their job, but I never intended to hurt anybody."

Gibbons said with a smile. "Marty, you'll get recognition all right. This will never happen at my club again. No public display of a trophy. Membership forfeited. You'll never play at Hope Valley again."

Fancy Car Lover
Ed Teja

Jimmy glanced around the garage. In three bays, greasy people in blue coveralls shuffled around doing greasy jobs underneath cars up on lifts.

It was nice to be there, seeing it, hearing the whine of the air gun.

Jimmy hated grease, but he loved cars, especially fancy ones, new ones. Their sleek lines and glossy paint, the smell of the interiors, made him feel good.

Not that he could afford one, but he could dream.

And sometimes do more than dream.

Two of the cars were just silver boxes, SUVs. But, in the last bay, sat a bright red Mercedes convertible to drool for, even sitting up on its perch having the brakes worked on.

"So what is it you want?" the pot-bellied man asked.

The man was Ernie, and he owned the garage. With a single, practiced look, he could tell Jimmy wasn't there to book a front-end alignment for his Ferrari.

"Looking for work," he said. "I just got out of the Army."

The man jerked his thumb toward the bays. "Full up. Even if you are a great mechanic."

His look suggested he seriously doubted that possibility.

"Not that. I'm no mechanic."

"Then I got nothing."

"My brother Tim said you sometimes had jobs for independent contractors... for the right person."

The man made a sour face. "You talking about Tim Willies?"

"Yeah."

"Then you are little Jimmy?"

"Not so little now." He was at least six inches taller than Ernie.

"Ain't Tim still doing time?"

"You know damn well he is doing a nickel for assault."

The man shook his head. "You got out of the Army or got kicked out?"

Jimmy shrugged. There was no point in lying. "I went in and they taught me how to fight and then kicked me out for using what they taught me. Go figure."

"I think the issue was probably it matters who you fight," Ernie said.

"Yeah, well, they coulda said that earlier."

The man nodded and put a hand on Jimmy's shoulder.

Jimmy tensed. He didn't like being touched. Not by a guy. The guy he beat up thought being an officer gave him the right to do what he wanted.

Well, he could, but such things had consequences.

But Ernie was just nudging him toward the back of the garage, away from prying ears. Or was it eyes? Jimmy wasn't sure.

"The Army figured me breaking an officer's arm was a bigger deal than doing it to another soldier."

"I heard that about the Army," Ernie said.

"Isn't America supposed to be where everyone is equal?"

"Yeah," Ernie said. "They say that. Go figure."

He stopped back by the sinks. Jimmy could smell the powerful odor of citrus from the shit they used to get grease off their hands.

"You know what kind of work your brother was doing?" the man asked.

Jimmy laughed. "Sure. Carjacking. He ripped them off and you piece and part them."

The man scowled. "What are you talking about?"

"Ain't that what it's called? Tim brings you a car and you break it down, ship the parts out."

The man glanced around. "Buddy, we don't spell shit out."

"Jimmy," Jimmy said. He hated the name Buddy. Jerks were called

Buddy.

"The way things work, I don't ask what the contractor does. I might mention a need for a car that ain't being used, some kind that people need parts for."

"You give him a list."

"Just some ideas. In case he runs across a car like it."

Jimmy didn't like the way the man pretended not to know how it worked. He didn't like the way the man hitched up his baggy polyester slacks, either. The guy had money and dressed like this.

Jimmy disliked him already, but he needed to break into the only line of work he knew of that actually paid good money.

"And Tim stole—"

The man put up a hand. "I don't know what your brother told you and I don't wanna hear it. All I know is that I would mention a few preferences for available vehicles and every so often he'd call and tell me he found one."

"And he brings it to you."

The man took out a pack of cigarettes and lit one. "Hell no!"

He didn't offer Jimmy a cigarette. Jimmy would have refused. He wasn't dumb enough to smoke, but still...

"Then what?" he asked.

"Tim would call a certain number and tell me what he had. If it was right, something I could use, then I'd send someone to meet him in a mall parking lot. My guy brings him some cash and picks up the car."

"Receiving stolen property."

Ernie put up his hands like he was surrendering to the cops on a television show. "I swear, I don't know that at all. See. I don't ask. I just buy cars to part out, that's it."

A cheap way to sleep at night.

Ernie shook his head.

"Honestly, Jimmy, I was shocked when I saw on the news that Tim was carjacking... using a gun to steal cars right from citizens on the street."

No doubt the news reports scared Ernie, but the man wasn't shocked any more than Jimmy. Not even surprised.

"Tim using a gun was stupid," Jimmy said. "It makes the consequences worse. But Tim ain't no fighter and he figured it made convincing the occupant of the vehicle more willing to go along with his request to borrow their car."

"Right. Convincing, until the occupant turned out to be an undercover cop."

"He was lucky the cop's bullet hit him in the shoulder," Jimmy said.

"That was a close call..." Ernie took a long drag of his smoke. He wasn't thinking about Tim's close call with death. More about his own ass. But Jimmy got that.

"I don't need that kind of attention," Ernie said.

"But with what the Army taught me, I don't need a gun."

"No?"

"All this time, Tim kept his mouth shut," Jimmy said. "He never gave them your name."

"I know," Ernie said.

"Tim said to tell you that hiring me would square you two. Totally square."

Ernie looked pleased. A weight lifted and all that. "He said that?"

"Why I'm here."

Tim had said nothing of the kind. But Ernie wouldn't know any of that. No way was this pig going to drop by the prison and visit with Tim. He stayed far, far away.

"And you can do this... acquisition work?"

"Acquisition?" That sounded nice.

"The job is acquiring vehicles."

"I worked with Tim awhile," Jimmy said. "When I was in high school."

But Tim cheated him out of his share and Jimmy enlisted, wanting to learn a new skill. Then Tim got busted.

"Now that I'm out, I want to apply my training. Tim taught me about the cars, and the Army trained me in the rest. So here I am."

Greedy Ernie considered the proposition, calculating. He didn't pay all that much for the cars considering what he got for the parts, and Jimmy would be taking the bigger risk.

With his plan, his combat-ready plan, Jimmy didn't figure the risk wasn't near what Tim dealt with.

At first, Ernie offered him less than he'd been paying Tim.

"No way," Jimmy said.

He didn't mind the guy trying to lowball him. That was business. But he called the man's bluff.

"Tim said your... what you call it?"

"Finder's fee."

"He told me it was about twice that."

"Did he now?"

Jimmy nodded. "And with the cost of living going up..." he'd heard about that on the news and it sounded like a reason to raise the finder's fee to a nicer figure.

Eventually, Ernie agreed, and when he finally shook the plump, not at all greasy hand, Jimmy figured he was starting out right.

Not that he trusted Ernie at all. The deal was cash on the barrelhead.

"Now, you can't ever come here again," Ernie said.

He tore a corner off a three-year-old calendar featuring a naked girl who looked bored and pulled a cheap ballpoint out of his pocket. The pen skipped badly, and it took three tries before he managed to scribble a legible number on the paper and put it in Jimmy's hand.

"You and me don't fucking know each other at all," he said. "Got it? You came in here this once. You was looking for work and I sent you on your way."

"You gave me the bum's rush," Jimmy said.

"Whatever. Buy yourself a cheap burner phone and call this number today. I'll text you info on what I need. You happen to find something you think fits the bill, you text. I want it, I tell you where to meet my guys."

Fancy Car Lover

"I need fifty bucks," Jimmy said.

"For what?"

"A phone. I don't figure I should be totally out of pocket for a business expense."

"If I'm seen handing you cash..."

"You are helping an out-of-work vet," Jimmy said. "You are a fucking patriotic citizen thanking me for my service."

Ernie groaned like a stuck pig, but he dug a fat billfold out of his back pocket and pulled out a ten and two twenties. "I'm thanking you for doing what, a year in the Army?"

"Six months," Jimmy said. "That was plenty."

* * *

Going to work for Ernie was important, but actually Jimmy's second job.

His combat-ready plan, the one he'd worked out sitting in jail, awaiting his court-martial, also required him getting a part-time job working for a pool cleaning service.

He picked a big one. He knew they stayed profitable by hiring illegal immigrants to work the motels, hotels, and places like that. These people were no trouble, mostly hard-working men and women, trying to build a future.

For the upmarket homes in upmarket suburbs, where a brown face was automatically grounds for suspicion, they employed otherwise unemployable white men—an assortment of shell-shocked vets, guys with criminal records the company could ignore, and guys trying to scrape together enough to move on.

For quality control, each team had a supervisor. "We got us a zero-tolerance policy about stealing from clients," the ex-marine who ran Jimmy's team told him. Knowing that his labor pool would not be all that intimidated by termination, he also suggested that retribution for doing anything to upset clients would be serious. And physical.

He even pointed out, accurately, that guys like them would not be missed.

That didn't bother Jimmy. He didn't want to lift the silverware, he wanted to observe rich neighborhoods without attracting attention.

The job was perfect. Each week they did a different section of a subdivision or group of McMansions. It didn't take long to see that rich people, especially those with really nice, shiny new cars, tended to create rituals around them.

Rituals were great... made the marks predictable.

Jimmy's crew only worked three days a week... Monday through Wednesday. Thirty hours a week. No way was the company getting stuck with paying benefits.

That was fine, too.

Every Wednesday, his team cleaned a big-ass pool on Ash Street in Lovely Vista Acres. Directly across the street, visible by looking over the low fence that surrounded the pool, lived a dapper young man who drove a shiny blue, brand new Camaro LT1.

He arrived home late every Wednesday afternoon, pulled into his driveway, and got out of the car with it still running. Then he stared at it, and let out a sigh before using the remote to turn it off and lock it.

Then he went inside.

After cleaning that pool, the crew moved down the street to another one. About the time they were finishing, right at six, the man walked out to his car and drove off again.

And Jimmy watched. Then, on two successive Wednesdays, after work, Jimmy drove his ancient Nissan to a mall outside the subdivision.

Jimmy parked his ratty Nissan among other cars and then he walked to the house where the Camaro lived, staying off the sidewalks, and slipping through the shadows between darkened homes.

Leaning against a fake adobe wall of the house across the street, he waited.

Both nights, right at nine, the man drove into his driveway and repeated his ritual.

Jimmy noted two other new cars in the neighborhood, as well as the location of several doorbell and surveillance cameras.

The subdivision was filled with them, but most were pointed at access points for the house. No one wanted alerts going off every time a jogger ran by.

New Camaros were on Ernie's list. Very high on the list.

The next Wednesday, he took a deep breath as they wrapped up cleaning the second pool and saw his man driving off right on schedule.

The stars, the ones that mattered, were aligned just right. His cell phone app told him it would be a quarter moon, 70 degrees, and clear—a perfect night for boosting cars.

In the pool van on the way back to the company office, he sent Ernie a text with just the make, model, and the word "tonight."

The response came immediately. "Let me know when you've got it."

"Hot date?" a guy named Billie asked.

"Very," he said, rubbing his hands together.

Tonight he'd put the skills, the training the Army had provided him to work.

"Your tax dollars at work," he said to himself.

Walmart conveniently stayed open 24/7 and people parked there all night. Again, he parked the Nissan among the employee's cars.

At the edge of the parking light, out of the light, he put on a pair of thin leather gloves, a black tee shirt, jeans, and a green ski mask.

Walmart had been out of black ones.

The familiar route threaded him between silent houses (barring the occasional television blaring out and a rather interesting fight a couple were having) and took him, not to his lookout spot, but into a shadow alongside the house that the Camaro belonged to.

Belonged to for the moment, anyway.

He lurked right around the corner from the garage door, steps away from where the car would stop.

When the lovely car slipped into the driveway and stopped, he waited until the driver's door opened.

As the man stepped out and closed the door, walking toward the house, stopped to turn and admire his possession, Jimmy came up behind him.

The man was on the smallish side and since Jimmy didn't put a high value on subtlety, his tactic was to grab the man by an arm and spin him around, slamming him face-first into the garage wall, right next to the garage door.

Without a sound beyond the air whooshing out of him, the dapper young man dropped into a heap. Out cold.

"Sweet," Jimmy said. The plan was working.

Jimmy picked up the key fob, put it in his pocket, then fished out the man's wallet and pocketed that.

Taking spot ties out of his pocket, he secured the man's wrists and ankles, then scooped him up and carried him to the back of the car. Opening what passed for a trunk, he jammed the man inside and used his weight to shut it.

It was a very tight fit and Jimmy wasn't entirely sure that forcing the trunk closed hadn't broken the man's arm.

Then he got into the car and slowly drove away.

Far away.

The night air was stimulating and the whirr of the powerful engine excited him, tearing up into the hills overlooking the town.

A lovely night for a drive.

The rush of being behind the wheel of this beautiful machine, feeling the power waiting for him to unleash, if he chose to, thrilled him. Knowing that for a time this brand new Camaro LT1, this stolen Camaro LT1, was his to use as he pleased... and he'd be paid for it.

He drove out to the old highway and stopped on a steep hill, pulling into a deserted pull off where a sign encouraged truckers to check their brakes.

No one was taking advantage of that opportunity, so he opened the trunk and pulled out the owner and carried him to the side of the road.

"You should be okay here," he said, tossing him on the dirt.

He took out the man's wallet and stripped out a hundred in cash. Sweet.

He glanced at the driver's license before putting it back and tossing the wallet on top of the man.

"Well, Roger, I'm sure someone will find you in the morning. You'll be fine."

The man's arm sat at a really bad, unnatural angle. Before he could check it, out of the corner of his eye, he caught sight of a dog-sized something scurrying past in the dark.

"Sorry about the arm," he said. "And I hope the coyotes don't eat you."

He had nothing against the guy, after all.

Getting back in the car, he texted Ernie.

The rest was even easier. He drove to a mall where one of Ernie's guys handed him an envelope in return for the car key and waited for him to count it while his partner drove off in the lovely blue Camaro.

Then Jimmy went inside the mall to get a coffee.

Inside, he chatted up a friendly cashier name Kathy and found out that she was getting off soon. He invited her out for a drink.

They had a couple and wound up at her place.

In the morning, he got Kathy to take him back to his Nissan.

All in all, a good night.

Stealing too many cars in the same subdivision seemed like a bad idea, so although it was more work and required patience, Jimmy used his Mondays, cleaning pools in a neighborhood across town, to find another car.

He found one and repeated his successful strategy. You didn't fuck with a good thing.

It wasn't until his third score, back in the first neighborhood, that he had to adapt.

First, the guy didn't stand around admiring his car. He used an automatic door opener and drove straight in.

That didn't matter. Stealth training taught him how to follow the car right in.

When the car door opened, he was there as the guy got out. The wall inside the garage proved just as good as the wall outside—when he slammed the guy face-first into the concrete block, the result was the same.

More or less.

But this guy was bigger and stronger than the first two. Making him lose consciousness took a little more effort.

And a pipe wrench.

When he dragged his bound victim to the trunk, he opened it and stared.

"Fuck!" he said.

There was no way this guy would fit inside.

He'd never paid attention to how tiny they made the trunks these days. This guy, someone his own size, shit he'd have to chop him into little pieces to get him in there.

He didn't want to kill him and chopping up a body was messy and took time.

Taking the money from his wallet and leaving him bound in the garage was a better option for all concerned—for him, Ernie, and the guy lying on the ground.

And that's what he did.

The Ferrari F8 was amazing.

Jimmy was starting to think he'd want his own supercar one day, if he could find one with a decent trunk. Roaring the down the freeway, knowing he didn't have to drop off a passenger this time, he accelerated amd let himself enjoy the way the G-forces pushed him back into the plush seats.

Finally, he pulled off the freeway and into a motel parking lot.

After he texted Ernie, he texted Kathy about where to meet him when she got off.

When he met Ernie's guys, they gave him a message.

"The cars you are getting are too exotic," they said.

"Like leopards and shit?"

They didn't know either. "Ernie said he needs cars that are

expensive, but that the companies sell a shitload of. Otherwise, stuff sits around until he can find a market."

That disappointed him. "So he doesn't want this one?"

A bald guy handed him the envelope. "He wants it, dumb fuck, or we wouldn't have come."

"Just none of these fancy cars from now on," the other guy said, walking to the Ferrari.

"More top-end BMWs and Toyotas and shit," the bald guy said.

That was disappointing.

When they got to Kathy's place, she was talking about a news story.

"Did you see about that home invasion?" she asked. "It was in that fancy subdivision where you clean pools."

"No. I hope it didn't happen while we were there."

So they sat on her couch and she found a news summary online with the story. It was the house where Jimmy acquired the Ferrari.

"That wasn't a home invasion," Jimmy said, pointing at the television. "How can they call it that? He didn't invade the guy's home."

"Sure he did. The guy got mugged getting out of his car--"

"In his garage," Jimmy said. "Not in his house. It ain't the same thing."

"It would be to me."

"Well..."

"At least he wasn't hurt."

He wanted to explain that he tried not to hurt people. But that would open a hell of a can of worms.

"Wow!" she said. "Look at that car."

He looked and saw her going gaga over a picture they showed of the guy's car. The one he'd stolen. It looked even better on the screen... more exotic.

"What a sexy car."

"It's a Ferrari F8," he said.

She gave him a funny, pouty, curious look and the rest just popped out. He couldn't resist.

"Fucker drives like a dream. You can hardly get out of second gear in this town."

"You drove one?" she asked.

On a roll now, Jimmy pointed at the screen.

"That one," he said. He was bragging now, wanting to impress her.

"No shit?" Then it dawned on her. "You are the fucking car thief?"

Happily, that idea didn't seem to upset her. Excited her, more like.

He grinned. "Seems so."

Then she had to hear the story, all about how he stole cars to order and turned them the same day. Him beating the guy up didn't seem to bother her. In fact, that seemed to turn her on as much as the car.

"I love fancy cars," she said.

"Yeah, they are cool," Jimmy said. He squirmed. It was easy to see where this conversation was going, and it made him uneasy.

"I want to sit in one of those," she said.

"I could take you to a dealership," he suggested.

She sneered. "How about, the next time you grab a nice one, you take me for a ride before you sell it?"

He pretended not to get it. "A ride?"

"Pick me up and we could take it up in the hills," she said. She leaned close to him, nibbled on his ear. It felt good.

"It would be wild to fuck in the back seat," she said.

"Most of these don't have a back seat," he said.

She shrugged. "Anywhere in the car," she said. "Hell, we park at a lookout point and do it on the hood."

That did sound cool.

"You work Wednesdays," he said.

"You could boost one on a Thursday or a Friday," she said. "It's not like you make a reservation. I don't work on Thursday or Friday."

It was possible, and if it really turned her on...

"You couldn't call in sick for a ride in a car like that?" he asked.

"I guess so," she said. "But we'd have to make it a good ride, not just around the block or something.

The idea of sharing the excitement, the idea of being up in the hills with a girl all eager to get laid in a stolen supercar, made it even better.

It was a week before he found another car he thought Ernie would like. A Corvette. With no back seat.

This owner was forceful in his argument about keeping his car for himself. By the time Jimmy was done negotiating with him, the guy was pretty busted up.

Jimmy left him in a dumpster behind his apartment building.

Kathy adored the car and begged until he let her drive it. She was the one that found a quiet place up on the hills where she could realize the last part of her fantasy.

When they parked, she stripped naked and went at him like a crazy woman.

After he took her home, he took the car to Ernie's guys, then went back to her place.

"We gotta do that again," she said. "And know the car I want you to steal next," she said.

"What kind of car?" he asked.

"A Maserati," she said.

"Isn't that some kind of SUV?"

She laughed and grabbed her phone and found a picture. "This one. It's an MC20. A two-seater coup."

"Wow," he said.

"The damn thing sells for over two hundred grand."

"And you know where we can find one?"

She nodded. "I had to go talk to my ex's lawyer last week, and that's what she drove up in."

"Ernie won't want one. Not a big enough market for parts."

"The hell with Ernie," she said. "I want to drive it. We can push it off a cliff after if you got no use for it. But I bet, with your connections, you could find a buyer that would give us ten grand for it, no questions asked."

The 'us' kind of stuck in his brain. Kathy was dealing herself into his gig.

"You know where she lives?"

She smiled. "I followed her home. Nice fucking house, too. Up in the hills. Once we bust the gate, no one can see from the road."

He nodded, noticing that 'us' again, but getting caught up in the adventure.

"Understand… sometimes when I take a car, the owner resists. Now I don't try to hurt them, but it does happen."

"The guy you left on the truck pullout got his arm gnawed off by animals," she said.

He'd told her about that one back when it seemed to excite her.

"It happens."

"So, right? If we grab her fancy fucking car and she gets in our way, you do what you have to do."

"Maybe her husband tries to stop us."

Now he was doing it. Stop us?

"Bitch lives alone. I checked."

Jimmy saw the intense look on her face. "This is more than just a joy ride and humping in a stupidly expensive car, ain't it?"

She grinned and slipped her hand into his lap. "That isn't enough for you?"

"Sure, but I like to know the… what you call it… the list of things."

"The agenda."

"Yeah. I like knowing your agenda."

"Okay, then I want the thrill of stealing the car, driving, having incredible sex in a stolen vehicle, and yes, revenge. She fucked me over in the divorce."

"How?"

"You don't need to know that."

"You want to help steal the car, right?"

She grinned. "Damn right. I want to be the one who drives it out of her yard." She was all over him now. "Just thinking about doing it, watching you deal with anyone who tries to stop us—it gets me wet,

Jimmy. Really wet."

It was an unfair argument, really, using pussy to get what she wanted, but on the other hand, Kathy was wild in bed.

*　*　*

Jimmy insisted that he take the time to scout the house and check out the things Kathy had told him, but three days later, they were ready to go.

Jimmy managed to climb the fence around the big house and then open the gate and let Kathy in. Being a gentleman.

"She isn't here," Kathy said.

"I called her office and made a late appointment with her under a phony name."

"What for?"

"To make sure we got here while she was there," he said.

Kathy scowled. "And that's because…"

"We will be waiting for her."

"So we go in the house?"

He saw it in her eyes. She was thinking about taking and breaking shit.

"No. We wait out here. I want to grab the car as she gets out of it."

"Why?" she asked.

"It's how I do it. My style."

"Fine," she said.

It was an hour before the car, a bright red Maserati convertible, purred up the gate. The automated system identified her car, and the gate whirred open.

The car came to a stop in front of the house, the door opened smoothly, and the woman stuck out two lovely long legs.

As she stood, Jimmy decided he liked the package that emerged—a bright red dress that accented a trim figure, red heels, blonde hair cut short…

Another time…

As she got her purse and headed for the front door of the house,

Kathy and Jimmy emerged from the doorway, intercepting her. She tried to open her purse.

Jimmy saw her tense to scream and punched her in the face, smearing red lipstick over his knuckles.

She was out.

"Nice," Kathy said. "I read the owner's manual. There's a trick to opening the back."

"Why do that?" Jimmy said.

He had bent down to secure her ankles and then pulled her wrists behind her back.

"For her," she said.

"We can toss her in the bushes," Jimmy said.

"She might have company coming over. They'd find her. She's not here… it buys us time."

That made enough sense that Jimmy went along with it. Although the storage space behind the front seats was small, and it took effort, they crammed the senseless woman into it.

Kathy picked up a plush coat from the passenger seat and started stuffing it in, too.

"Cramped in there," he said as he watched her lower the hatch that closed it off.

"She'll live."

Jimmy doubted it. But then he was seeing a new side of Kathy.

"You sure about that?"

Kathy shrugged and gleefully held up the key fob. "Time to go for a ride."

On the way around to the driver's seat, she scooped up the woman's purse and brought it with her, sliding into the driver's seat.

With her hands on the wheel, Kathy's face began to glow. She looked sexy as hell as they left the driveway to the sound of the automatic gate closing.

She had her route all planned and soon they were on a stretch of open road heading south.

"Where are we going?" he asked.

"It's a surprise," she said.

The road was quite empty and an hour later she pulled off at what used to be a truck weighing station. The station itself was boarded up, and tall weeds poked up through the asphalt.

Kathy was undoing his pants before the engine stopped ticking over. Soon they had the passenger door up all the way and he was screwing her from behind.

It was great.

Then she decided they should strip naked.

As he stepped to the side of the car, Kathy picked up the purse and opened it.

"Bet she's got a wad of cash," she said.

Then she reached inside and pulled out a 38 revolver. It was a little one, a snub nose, but when she pointed it at him, it looked just as scary as a bigger gun.

"What's going on?" he said.

"Well, what happened is, I decided I didn't like being a cashier. And now I know I can play this game better than you."

"Except for beating people up to get the car."

She grinned. "You don't think I can find guys willing to do that part?"

He was sure she could.

"Who you going to sell them to?"

She laughed. "I found someone on the dark web willing to pay a good price. I'm not dumb enough to settle for handouts from guys like Ernie. I got offered twenty grand to deliver this one."

"That's a good deal. Ernie would give me five, tops."

"See?"

"So why not let me be your partner?"

She waved the gun. "I'm better off leaving you. They'll catch your dumb ass and pin this theft on you."

"I guess they would."

"Toss your clothes in the car," she said.

"Why?"

"So it will take you a while to get help and even longer to convince them you aren't a pervert."

"This isn't nice of you."

She laughed. "Nope."

When she drove off, leaving him standing there, naked, heading south, he was sure she was still laughing.

Pleased with herself.

* * *

It was an hour before a Highway Patrol car came by and Jimmy waved them down.

"My boss and I stopped to help a woman who flagged us down," he told them. "She pulled a gun and left me here with no clothes."

"And your boss?"

"The woman stuffed her in that little compartment behind the seats and drove off."

"What kind of car?" the officer asked as he called it in.

"A Maserati." He gave them the license number.

"Shit. That's a sweet car."

"Looks nice. I never got a chance to drive it."

* * *

He was at the police station in borrowed coveralls when word came that they had caught Kathy.

"Your boss was in the back, dead," they told him.

With Kathy shrieking hysterical-sounding accusations about Jimmy, they logged in his wallet and phone and gave them back to him, along with his clothes.

He gave them Kathy's address as his residence and they said he could go home if he promised to come in the next day and make a full statement.

When the cop at the desk offered, he turned down a ride home.

"I'll have a friend pick me up," he said.

In the parking lot, he found a Cadillac XT4 that was unlocked, hotwired it, and drove back to town.

On the way, he texted Ernie.

The response was a protest. "In the middle of the day?"

"This work has office hours?"

It didn't.

He thought about telling Ernie that this was the last one, that he would be relocating. But Ernie would probably stiff him, have his guys beat him and take the car.

Pass on that.

As he made his way to the meeting place, he turned on the news. Apparently, the police had decided that the similarities in the car thefts suggested Kathy had masterminded them all. She likely had a partner, but just hired muscle.

Jimmy switched off the radio and thought about Kathy. She'd gotten to be a criminal mastermind real fast. Most people took years to get there.

He didn't need to be a mastermind. He had a nice stash of cash now and when it ran short, well, when he started up again, he'd do it different. Having a woman in on it was good, but this time he'd start by finding one who got turned on by fancy cars and knew that people like them had to steal them to get the pleasure.

And he'd make sure. Talk it through. Setting it up right from the beginning, maybe he could make the relationship work. Then they could indulge their love of stealing fancy cars. He'd try harder not to hurt anyone.

But it happened.

Ballbreaker
Harris Coverley

I'd thought ever so briefly of trying to go professional when I was eighteen. That was back in sixth form. Instead, went on to uni, time served, got out with the old BA, not that it did me much fucking good. Went on into the labour market, went from shit job to shit job, but I kept playing and playing, as much as I could in the old pub, the good old Warlock, or the 'Lock as we called it, down near Letby centre.

Kind table, well, one you could *know*. Only maybe this stain or that one. Well-balanced except for perhaps the left corner at the head of the table (that was the end facing the toilets and across from the jukebox on the wall). Fifty pence a play. Line 'em up on the edge. That's mine, this is yours. Don't take no shit. Code of honour. All that crap.

I remember the whole night, the whole day well, even after a decade: it'd been a shite shift at The Kirk Arms. A carvery from the steam trays, as anyone will tell you, is fucking disgusting. Why does anyone subject themselves to that? Meat that's mostly fat. Potatoes like sea mines and twice as dense. Gravy like pond scum and twice as rank. Peas like bullets and twice as deadly. Carrots spray-painted orange. Two year olds screaming like there's a fucking earthquake going on. But that's what you have to put up with when you're the poor wanker who carves the meat—the shitty, rubbery, bouncing, sweaty meat that looks like it's always about to bite back. Even now I'm disgusted with myself; I really am. Stinking, stinking, stinking…and the beer there reeked too.

Anyway: I got off at eight and the match had started at that time, so I came right over to 'Lock and got there at ten past, ready to take over from Teg. Screwed my Guinness cue together. (You'd never think a Guinness brand cue would be any good would you? But I tell you now:

it was best cue I ever had. But people kept saying I needed to re-tip the thing, over and over, even though I thought it played fine, perfect I'd say, but me I followed their bastard advice, thinking it might improve my game, and the dumb fucker I took it to sawed the fucking end right off and then bent the fucking thing when he put it in a vice at an angle for the glue to dry through the night. New tip didn't even fucking stay on; fell right off onto the floor. I cried when I saw what he'd done—cracked his front window with the fat end of the cue as well. Still got it though; can't bear to part from it. Just goes to show: people are fucking stupid and you should ignore them if things are fine.)

There was me, Teg, Chrissy, Smokes, Old John, and Kipps. That was the Warlock pool league team. It was where and how I'd cut my teeth. It was Chrissy who'd trained me, well, *re-trained* me really. Week after week of him beating my arse. And then, through patience and practice, month after month of *me* beating *his* arse. Of course he'd tell it differently. He's full of shit, but I love the fat git.

Anyway, I got there, and the challengers were from The Bell Tower. Not too bad a crew really. They were all right.

Kipps had to leave well before the game was over, work in the morning at six, sorry bastard. It was actually just as he went through the door that the one man plague entered. In fact, I think Kipps held the door for him as he left, not that he thanked him.

He swaggered in with his purple tracksuit, three gold chains swinging from his neck, sides shaved and the hair on the crown curling and stuck high like the wacky one from that *Seinfeld* show. What got me though were the mirrored shades. Almost put me off my shot.

Now, management had banned tracksuits to try and keep a basic standard of class in 'Lock (they were also the people most likely to pull a knife or whatever), but a moment's chat with the assistant manager and an exchange of a couple notes excused him from that rule (I'm going here by what Old Kevin at the bar told me).

I saw that he ordered a drink, a bottle of Bud, the worst thing in stock, Yankee piss-water, and came and sat by us, not saying anything, just observing. We should've dealt with him in retrospect there and then, but that wouldn't have been too friendly would it?

Anyway, the match went on, and by half nine we had *thinly* beaten The Bell Tower crew. Like I said, good team really. We shook hands, and as standard courtesy they would convey to the fellas at The Opal Ring over in Havely Hill (you know, that bit just next to Rose Hill) that they had to come to *us* the following the Tuesday for the next match.

We toasted our victory with a fresh round, and as we were taking our triumphant glug the tracksuit approached us, clapping slow and noxious.

"Good game boys," he said.

We looked at each other: *Cockney*. Rarely a good sign if ever.

I took the lead.

"Thanks man," I said, nodding my pint of pale towards him. "Years of practice and a concentrated team effort."

He grinned at me and shook his head.

"Not just that son," he said, licking his top teeth. "It's *you*. You're the key."

Chrissy laughed. "*I* trained him y'know…"

I elbowed him in his upper tattoo, but only lightly. "You gave me a bloody *refresher* at best."

We had a *faux* fist fight for a few seconds before it petered out and I said to the intruder, "I don't know about rankings, but it's a group effort each time."

The Cockney grinned tighter and introduced himself: his name was Jason Hyde, born and raised in Tower Hamlets. He had moved up to Manchester for his "line of work". When we asked him what it was, he gave us a load of vague shit that made plain that what he did was trouble. Again: we should've tossed his arse out then and there, but…

"How do you join the league?" he asked.

We looked at each other.

"Well", I said, "it's more of a *native* thing."

"What?" he asked, crooking his thin little head.

"Locals only mon," grinned Smokes at my side.

Hyde pointed at Smokes. "Then how do *you* count?"

Smokes looked like he was ready to lump him one, but I jumped in. "*Naturalisation* they call it…been here for thirty-odd years now. He counts."

That just about cooled it.

The table had been granted to some civilians having a night out (they knew to put a twenty pence piece on the rim just above the coin slot to reserve it) so we sat in the far corner. We let this Hyde join us, well, because—I guess we were just *curious*. Who really *was* this prick anyway?

As we wound down for a time, I recall Hyde asked Smokes why he was called "Smokes".

"It's what I do," he replied, eyeing his beerline in a pint of dark bitter.

"But *what* do you smoke?" he asked.

"What the fuck do *you* think?" Smokes smiled at him, and we actually had a good laugh on that.

Hyde kept asking questions, and he asked me about the wildest thing that I'd ever seen happened in the 'Lock.

I looked at the others, thought for a moment, and I told him the following story, or something like it:

* * *

Up until a year ago, 'Lock used to do a pub quiz on Monday. There were various sects of varying quality as quizers, but in terms of pub quiz etiquette, the Poon Tang Clan were the very worst. They sat around the corner, over there. Every time they won—which was fairly often—and the result was announced over the mic, they would all stand up whooping, unzip their trousers, and slap their dicks on their table in semi-unison, chanting their team name. The barmaid would return their quiz sheet, laughing like it was nothing, telling them, "Come on, come on now, put 'em away, you'll get us shut down again…"

When our own team, the Foxy Stoats, made up of me, Chrissy, Kipps, Mark, and Sally, and occasionally others (or maybe we formed a supergroup once in a while) happened to win they'd make a scene, accusing us of cheating, spraying beer into the air. They'd come up to us, their cocks out, and slap them on our table, going: "OI! OI! OI! OI! OI! OI! OI! OI! OI! OI!" And the barmaid would return our quiz sheet, chuckling as always, saying, "Come on, come on, be good sports now…"

"OI! OI! OI!"

The sight of those pale peach members hitting the wood before our eyes was bad enough, but since we shared the crisps and peanuts and pretzel chunks on our table by opening the packets fully as a spread so anyone could take from wherever they were sat, we were anxious not get any penile sweat or loose smegma in our hard-bought pub snacks.

One time when this was happening we'd got a 55 out of 62, our highest ever score, so I was particularly pissed off at their usual stink-making.

Gary, their de facto leader, I found especially obnoxious, so as he slid out his limp grey sausage skin of a lady-poker and smacked it down, I took a drink of my ale and then slammed the pint glass on his glans.

He yelped and swung his right arm at me. I ducked and bent the edge of the glass into his shaft as he whimpered.

The other Poon Tangers were too horrified to do anything, while the rest of the Foxy Stoats and at least half of the pub hooted and cheered.

Gary got his hands around my neck, squeezing, but I just twisted the glass tighter into him.

My demand was clear: "I don't want any more dickmeat on this corner table you greasy motherfucker!"

"What's going on here?!" cried the barmaid as she returned our sheet.

"We're sick of it," said Kipps. "He's just giving him a lesson!"

"Release him or you're barred!" she shouted at me.

"Release this cocksucker?" I grunted as Gary's hands tightened about my throat. "He's the cunt with his lil' shrimper slapping against the table!"

"YOU BASTARD!" he screamed, and he finally got my windpipe to collapse. At this I released his todger, but not before dragging the glass against his glans, scraping his Jap's eye—or, to use the correct medical term, urethral meatus.

Free from my pint he fell to the floor in agony, whereupon on pure impulse I kicked him in his still exposed parts.

"Hope you've learnt your fuckin' lesson you fuckin' perverted son-of-a-bitch!"

Bob, Gary's second in the Clan, slapped the back of my head, so I threw the rest of my pint in his face. He swung for me, catching my ear, but I got him in the guts with my right fist. Another Poon Tanger grabbed my shoulders from behind and pulled me back, the chair tipping. On the floor blows thundered down, but I slid my chair into his shins and he dropped, his jaw a perfect target for my knee.

I got back up as the barmaid stood between the two teams as a breakwater, an impenetrable force.

"I'm not 'avin' this shit!" she shouted, all red-faced and bouncing.

She pointed her finger at me: "You! Out! NOW!"

"I'm the one who's barred?!" I asked. "Are you fuckin' nuts?!"

"I'm not arguing with you—OUT!"

Her pointing finger went from me to the front entrance. The pub was silent. Not even the pool table balls clacked.

I looked at the entrance, then her, and said, "When, if I'm barred, I might as well be barred for the right reasons."

I reached out and grabbed her large, milky-pale breasts, barely covered by her summer dress.

"I've got a case of the *mammary madness*!" I yelled. Men cheered, women screamed, and the barmaid slapped me across the cheek with added fingernails, not that I blame her really.

She then grabbed me by the scruff of the neck, hauled me out the front singlehanded, and tossed me onto the pavement.

The manager eventually let me back in after a month and a sincere enough sounding apology, written in ink, but from then until they stopped the quiz, the Poon Tang Clan no longer slapped their dicks on any tables. In fact, we didn't see any male genitalia at all. And every time Gary walks past me, even now when he's in, I'm sure to cough and softly bang my pint glass on the beermat once, twice, maybe three times, just to remind him that I don't want any pricks or their natural excretions near my crisps or peanuts ever again.

* * *

Hyde hung on every word. After I was done he finished off his bottle and went to the toilet, at which point Chrissy, silent throughout my recounting, leaned over to me and said, "I've never heard such shite in all my life."

I lifted my glass to him. "Bullshit to a bullshitter."

"This guy's bad news…I don't think we should fuck with him."

"He's a fuckin' dummy…but even then, I wanna know what he *really* wants."

"You think he wants something?"

"Maybe…just maybe…"

Morgan Freeman voice everybody: *He* did *want something…*

When Hyde came back to us, Teg and Old John had reclaimed the table for a friendly knockabout and it was then about ten-thirty or so.

The pub was now half empty but they'd still keep serving until a quarter-to-midnight or thereabouts.

Hyde sat back down and eyed me.

"Yeah?" I asked, holding a fresh pint, now Jaipur IPA, at 5.9% the strongest they had on draft.

"How many you had this evening?" he asked, shit-eating smirk unblemished.

"What are you my fucking mother?" I laughed. "Or is this a roundabout marriage proposal? Getting to know my habits and chastising me in advance?"

He gritted his teeth. It was a mix of amusement and frustration I could see.

"You're a funny geezer," he said, sliding his shades off and folding them into an inner pocket. His eyes were small, holes in an oily face. I realised how young he was, younger than me in fact—and I was then the youngest on the team—but he was also already so worn and weathered. I didn't like this guy. Right then and there he weirded me out afresh.

"I have a proposition…" he began.

With Chrissy and Smokes listening, he laid it out: he had been watching me and he liked the way I played. He himself had played the game ever since he was a "nipper", down in the backstreets of Whitechapel and wherever else 'round there. (I think I passed through there once when I was in London. It was shit, naturally.) He was always looking for a new challenger. But he had to keep raising the stakes, higher and higher. He only played "amateurs", because they were open to higher risks.

"What higher risks?" I asked.

The answer turned my fucking stomach.

In his line of work—some right nasty shit it would appear—he had accumulated a *load* of disposable income, and that meant a high wager. He had done this bet four times beforehand—he had won it twice, lost it twice, a perfect balance.

It was this: he'd put up a five grand bet, but the loser, inevitably a broke fucker on the arse-end of society, had to sacrifice not only his left index finger, but the *knuckle* above it too. It would completely ruin the way the guy held his cue, and he'd either have to give up the game or adopt a new style. It would also be a fucking ugly thing to live with, fuck up his sex life, and so on—but the core point was it'd fuck with his pool game.

Mortified, to use a more high society type of word, ain't enough to describe how I felt.

"No fucking way bruv," I said, trying to laugh it off, shaking my head, tapping my hand on the table. "I've kinda grown fond of the little appendage…"

He ignored the scowls of the others and smiled, "Not even with *ten grand* on the line."

At this I paused. That was almost everything I'd made last year. I had fuck all in savings then. At twenty-four I still lived with mum and that agreement was going south to say the least. I hadn't had a holiday since I was seventeen, and I had always had a desire to go to New Zealand, probably because the place was so bloody far south and isolated from the rest of the world. They have some nice-looking birds, *avians* that is, down there.

"Let me think," I said.

Chrissy grabbed my shoulder.

"Christ dude! You can't be fuckin' serious?"

"Hold on a minute, hold on…"

"Fuck me…"

The gang listened in as we talked it over: I said fifteen grand on the table. He said he wasn't going to be bargained with on the wager. I lowered it to twelve grand. He agreed.

I asked him how he would do the deed if he had to, and he nipped out to his car and returned two minutes later with a pair of secateurs. Two cuts would do it: one below the knuckle to server the bone, one beside it to cut it from the flesh. Sharp fuckers they were—said he had a whetstone just for the purpose.

He brought the cash in too: the briefest glimpse of a dense forest of thick wads. He returned the cash to his car, but kept the secateurs on him in his inner pocket. I could see the bulge on the handles making a pair of V'ed fingers at me.

He asked me if I was a man of my word, and I said I was. (But I forgot to ask him the same, which was really, *really* fucking stupid of me.)

We agreed also on a neutral observer, a ref who knew the game: Theo Blanchard had just come in, half-steamed from a session elsewhere, most likely at the Wetherspoons by the bus station. We didn't like each other, but I knew he wouldn't fuck me on this 'cause I'd fuck him easily enough. He did it for two free pints and a small debt he owed me being cancelled.

Hyde paid the fifty pence for the game when we were ready.

"Jesus," Blanchard said to me as we set up. "Who the fuck is this guy?"

Chrissy interrupted us: "Do you know what the fuck you're doing?"

"Come on," I said. "Have some faith."

"*Faith*? Are you outta your fuckin' mind?"

"Look: straight, I think he's fulla shit."

"And the cash?"

"We've seen the cash…"

"And the cutters?"

"Just for show."

But what if I was wrong? I asked myself. I didn't want to know.

The table was set: red and yellow in the rack, lined, eight-ball in the centre on the dot.

In front of everyone, me and Hyde agreed on holding to league rules. Tough, but not Draconian.

Blanchard flipped a coin and Hyde called heads.

He got it.

In league rules you can start anywhere behind the line. Hyde put the white on the far right side of the table's head, about two inches from the line. Using his own cue he'd brought in—a cute number with a racing car stripe on the length, ash build I think—he cracked it and broke the triangle on the side of the second row, that's the two balls behind the head. There was not much movement overall, but the force went through it, and the left-hand-most ball rolled from its place and into the corner pocket.

"Hyde's yellow," said Blanchard. "You're red."

"I know how it's played!" I snapped, and the fellas looked at me. They all knew I was thinking I'd fucked myself already.

Hyde tapped the triangle again from the side, but it was a tactical move: he'd jammed the white into the balls and made a decent shot nigh-on impossible.

I considered it for a good minute. I responded with essentially the same shot, jamming it further in. It was really a test: I wanted to see what he'd do.

He responded with a big blow. He broke the balls apart and across the table, potting nothing.

He can *be reckless*, I thought. *That could be useful.*

However, after that, we were both pretty surgical, barely acknowledging the other's existence.

Pool is a chase done without you hardly moving. Potting too many of your own balls may move you ahead in raw numbers, but it opens up space for your opponent to have a big run of pots, and then you've either equalled up or he's ahead of you even. Shit, some games he's won after your own streak otherwise cleared the table.

I'm not gonna to lie: the cunt was pretty bloody good.

Halfway through the game I had the same red going around the table a good twenty times, belaying his shot for like six or seven minutes, over and over, the red ball blocking, within an inch, half-an-inch, long, short. From the corner of my eye I could see the Cockney bastard getting antsy, but he played it cool, the white returning always to prime position within an inch or more, until at last he had just enough room to break the deadlock.

At one point I got careless and knocked one of his yellows with my cue, moving it by about two inches. I looked apologetically at Blanchard, but he was bound by the rules to let Hyde have two shots as recompense. It would've fucked me if on his second shot he'd not fallen short. His run would've been unstoppable.

As the match went on the crowd grew. Usually by the time it was half-eleven a lad would come from behind the bar and tell us that it was to be the "last game", but the staff and the manager were watching close with the rest of them.

The team was on edge. Not one eye left the green.

At last, at ten-to-midnight, we were at an end: he'd potted all his balls and I had one red left. He'd tried to bounce the black across the green into the left-hand side pocket, but he'd missed by an inch or so, and it had careened towards the right-hand corner pocket at the foot of the table.

By the time it stopped a good six inches away the crowd, and myself, could breathe again.

I had to make my shot count. I could feel my left index finger and adjoining knuckle already aching.

I angled up. The room was quiet, the jukebox knocked off.

I could feel my chest going in and out.

The Guinness cue slid forward in a jab.

The white fired up and left. It knocked the last red hard—it was off! It bounced off the side of the left hand corner pocket at the head of the table and ended up lazing just behind the line, almost at the middle.

A big grin was on the bastard's face against a sea of soured lips.

He leant over with his fancy schoolboy cue. He was going to make a big show with the cue rest taken off the wall rack—but that was his mistake.

He'd let showmanship and his ego take him, too cocky the wanker. If only he'd taken his time…

He aimed.

He fired.

The white went from the near-centre of the table with ferocity to the black almost at the table's end.

It tapped hard on the edge—but he was off by millimetres!

It bounced from the edge of the right-hand side pocket and after knocking from side to side ended up about five inches from the hole.

Warburtons could've sliced the atmosphere and sold it as a breakfast food.

This was my last and only chance.

The white had landed back towards the very centre of the table. My red was stuck in table's head quarter.

It was as awkward as it could get.

Should I go left or right?

Left or right?

Left or right?
I flipped a coin in my head: I'd go left.
I'd do it with force and put a spin on it, let the white drift back to middle of the table.
I refused the rest. I leant over. I let the good cue rest on my knuckle, pulsing with its own self-knowing fear.
The cue came back and forward, back and forward, back and forward…*what was I doing?*
I needed to go!
Go!
FIRE!
It struck.
The white fired.
It hit the red with gusto, with explosion.
It was off!
Way off!
It hit the head cushion, bounced to the side, and shot down the table towards the black on the opposing side.
The crowd gasped.
Getting the black down before the red would be the end—automatic loss.
Fucked.
But that was only for second—it sped past it by less than two inches! Down, down, down…slower, slower, slower…and gently, no, *meekly* and without bravado, into the left-hand corner pocket.
A collective relieved exhale came so strongly as to nearly cause a gale.
The white had followed after it, and was in the foot end's quarter, near the middle.
Now it really was it: either I got the black down now or that would be the end.
Hyde was watching me. I knew that even as I ignored him. Watching, waiting for the next fuck up. This is a game of fuck ups and waiting for the fuck ups. It's only a matter of time.

I leant down and washed the whole room from my mind. Nothing else mattered but that black ball.

It only needed a tap. Sharp, but little.

I aimed.

I breathed in.

I rocked.

I breathed out.

I thought of nothing.

I held.

I bit my lower lip.

I fired.

The white ball rolled, not slid.

It tapped the black like you'd tap a guy on the shoulder.

The black rolled over to the pocket, inch by gut-turning inch.

It approached cautiously, as though apprehensive, and, with an insulting reluctance, as though it believed my shot had not been good enough for it, dropped over the edge and into darkness.

I ignored the cheers and the fist pumps as I kept my eyes on the white to the very last stop—potting the white on the black would also be an automatic loss.

However, the white tapped off the head of the table and dawdled over to the cushion on the left-hand side, equal between the corner and side pockets.

When it was completely still I could rest.

I had won.

Blanchard had known what I was doing and had waited for the same thing. He then came over and lifted my arm as though it had been a prize fight in Las Vegas.

"Winner!" he cried over a round of applause. "All rules followed! Game over! Elvis has left the building!"

I pulled my arm from him.

"Don't be a dickhead!" I said, but I said it with a smile.

Hyde stood there on the other side, arms folded. He clearly wasn't happy, but what man would be with twelve grand down the shitter?

I went over to him, hand out for a shake.

"Good game!" I said, and waited for his hand.

He looked at my open palm as though it was caked in horse semen.

"You won on bullshit shots," he said, leaning his head down so I could see those beady eyes over the lenses.

I had to laugh as others sneered.

"Oh fuck off mate…"

I withdrew the hand.

"Whatever man…where's my money?"

"What money?"

With that the place became as cold as the centre of a high street bakery's Cornish pasty (*you know* which chain I mean).

"You fuckin' what?" I said. A rage was swelling.

"He's pulling a fast one," Chrissy said behind me, and the rest of the team grunted and swore in displeasure.

"Look 'ere matey," Blanchard interjected, definitely drunk at this point but without losing that much of his senses. "I watched the whole game, know the rules, and nothing under-the-table happened, and not any of these 'bullshit shots' either, which I don't even know what the fuck those are…"

Before he could finish rambling, Hyde brought the secateurs out of his inner pocket and slashed across Blanchard's face. Blanchard had enough about him to throw himself back, and Hyde was *just* able to get him across the tip of the nose with the blade. About a millimetre deep for less than a centimetre across the skin, it bled profusely enough but ultimately left next-to-no scar.

Hyde managed to somehow flee out the front door in the commotion and get to his car, but we fixed that fucker's wagon as they say.

We did some digging over the next fortnight. Found out who he worked for: some Geordie wide boy who was expanding through the Scawn Valley.

We even managed to find where he liked to hang out, a place called *Kim Singer's* towards the city.

We all went out there one Saturday, including Blanchard, and waited till about two in the morning a short way from his car.

He came out alone, silver tracksuit now, black trim, but the same stupid mirrored sunglasses. He looked like a fucking chrome dildo with legs.

We grabbed him and dragged him behind the skips, but not before gagging him.

My Nan had a great selection of secateurs. She kept them in a plastic bucket in a kitchen cupboard near the backdoor. I'd selected one that I thought would do the job nicely, and in the end it did. Smokes was on hand with a big lighter to cauterise the wound—spewed like a motherfucker, half a pint I'm sure—and when the bleeding stopped Blanchard called the game finally and conclusively over, but not before him and me had given Hyde a good tenderising while Chrissy and Tegs held him down. A team loyal to the very last throw.

We never got punished by him or his mates for what we did. I later heard the Geordie boy had grown tired of his shit and sent him back down south in his incomplete state.

Shame we never got the money. Still not been to New Zealand. Might never get there at this rate short of going on a game show like *Pinball Wizards* and winning big.

Still got that finger and knuckle mind. Put it in one of those pickling jars. You can buy them pre-filled from the supermarket y'know. It went black in there after a while, and you can't really see it anymore, but you can still feel it knocking against the glass when you tip it about…sorta like a pool ball from cushion to cushion…tap…tap…*tap*…

The Usual Unusual Suspects

Arthur Vidro is a newspaper columnist and freelance editor, who has sold mystery fiction to *Ellery Queen's Mystery Magazine, Mystery Magazine, Woman's World,* and the Malice Domestic anthologies *Mystery Most Theatrical* and *Mystery Most Traditional.* He publishes and edits the thrice-yearly journal *Old-Time Detection.*

Dave Dempster is a retired lawyer, who practised in Scotland and Western Australia — and who has now settled in the UK — Norwich, in Norfolk — enjoying his new-found hobby of writing creative short fiction.

Diana Parrilla is a versatile writer. With a degree in economics and mastery in Japanese, she shares her passion for anime and games on her YouTube channel and social networks, where she goes by the handle buffyta17. Her publications span various horror and speculative fiction genres.

John M. Floyd is the author of more than a thousand short stories in publications like *AHMM, EQMM, Strand Magazine, Best American Mystery Stories, Best Mystery Stories of the Year,* and *Best Crime Stories of the Year* (UK). A former Air Force captain and IBM systems engineer, John is also an Edgar nominee, a Shamus Award winner, a six-time Derringer Award winner, and the author of nine books.

Jesse Aaron served as a police officer in New York City and Connecticut for over five years and also worked in the field of private security/investigations. His first novel, *Shafer City Stories* is available on Amazon.com (https://www.amazon.com/Shafer-City-Stories-Tales-NYPD-Harlem/dp/1518853137/). Jesse's short story *The Leaky Faucet* was featured in *Crimeucopia—It's Always Raining in Noir City* and *The Gathering Puddle* in *Crimeucopia — One More Thing To Worry About*. Jesse has two more short stories on the way to publication and is currently at work on his upcoming serial killer thriller *Harlem Hipster Homicides*. Jesse's style is dark and gritty, and his stories focus on the underside of the police and private detective worlds. Jesse has a love of all things Noir, Science Fiction, and Fantasy.

John B. Elliott has worked as a typesetter, pressman, bartender, social worker, biologist and teacher. He has a passion for the natural world, especially deserts and mountains; has had play productions, notably one about Federico Garcia Lorca, and published fiction in, or upcoming in, *Calliope, Sonoran Horror, Open Ceilings, Lifespan Anthologies Loss and Older, and Crimeucopia*, as well as poetry in *The Comstock Review, Southwestern American Literature, Poetry Quarterly, Borderlands: Texas Poetry Review, Tanka Journal, The Fourth River,* and three anthologies.

William Kitcher's stories, plays, and comedy sketches have been published, produced, and/or broadcast in Australia, Belgium, Bosnia and Herzegovina, Canada, Czechia, England, Germany, Guernsey, Holland, India, Ireland, Nigeria, Singapore, South Africa, Sweden, the U.S., and Wales. His stories have appeared in Shotgun Honey, Guilty, New Contrast, Spinozablue, Granfalloon, Horror Sleaze Trash, Mystery Magazine, Punk Noir Magazine, Yellow Mama, and many other journals. His comic noir novel, *Farewell And Goodbye, My Maltese Sleep*, the second funniest novel ever written, was published in 2023 by Close To The Bone Publishing, and is available on Amazon.

J. F. Benedetto is an active member of the *Mystery Writers of America* and has had work published in numerous anthologies and short story collections in both Australia and the United States — the most recent being in the *Colp: Desert/Dessert* short story collection. His 1901 period piece, *The Canadian: Death in the Chinese Darkness*, appears in *Crimeucopia — Through The Past Darkly*.

The Usual Unusual Suspects

Nikki Knight is the pen name of **Kathleen Marple Kalb** who describes herself as an Author/Anchor/Mom…but not necessarily in that order. An award-winning weekend anchor at New York's 1010 WINS Radio, she writes short stories and novels including the *Old Stuff*, and (as Nikki Knight) *Vermont Radio Mysteries*. Her stories have been in *Crimeucopia, Alfred Hitchcock's Mystery Magazine,* and other major publications, and she has been short-listed for Derringer and Black Orchid Novella Awards. She, her husband, and son live in a Connecticut house owned by their cat.

Mark James McDonough is an avid motorcycle enthusiast. He doesn't own one or know how to ride them but he likes to sneak into people's driveways and sit on them. His *Like A Brother* appears in *Crimeucopia — Crank It Up!*

Paul R. Paradise is the author of the *Brian Gilmore* detective series. The first is *Truth Is Always Changing*, a finalist in the Killer Nashville Claymore Competition (Best Investigator category). Mr. Paradise is an expert on the crime called trademark or product counterfeiting which the FBI calls the 'business crime of the 21st Century.' He's written numerous articles and a best-selling non-fiction book, and his *The Knockoff King* appears in *Crimeucopia — the I's Have It.*

Robert Petyo is a Derringer award finalist whose recent work has appeared in *Flash Bang Mysteries, The Black Beacon Book of Mystery, Asinine Assassins, Now There Was a Story, Whodunit, Mickey Finn 21st Century Noir,* and *Stonewall Detectives*. He has also appeared in various *Crimeucopias* including *We're All Animals Under the Skin, Careless Love, Strictly Off The Record, Boomshakalaking!* and *Crank It Up!*
He writes primarily mysteries, but also SF, fantasy and horror and an occasional mainstream piece. He lives in Northeastern Pennsylvania, is happily married, and has now retired from the Postal Service, which allows him more time to read and write. Unfortunately, there never seems to be enough time to read and write.

S. B. Watson lives in Keizer, Oregon, USA — and has had numerous pieces published in *Spinetingler Magazine, The Dark City Mystery Magazine, Mystery Magazine, Mystery Tribune,* and *Punk Noir Magazine.* His *Crimeucopia* appearances so far have been in the historical *Through The Past Darkly* and *Great Googly Moo!*

Wendy Harrison is a retired prosecutor who turned to short mystery fiction during the pandemic. Her stories have been published in numerous anthologies including *Peace, Love & Crime, Autumn Noir, Crimeucopia (Tales from the Back Porch-*and*-One More Thing to worry About), The Big Fang, Gargoylicon,* and *Death of a Bad Neighbour* as well as in *Shotgun Honey.* When Hurricane Ian destroyed her home in Florida, she moved to Washington State, as far from Florida as she could get.

Kai Lovelace is a freelance musician & writer based in Manhattan.
His *Only a Story* appears in *Crimeucopia — Through The Past Darkly*, and when not writing fiction he heads up The Lovelace band — a shifting ensemble specializing in jazz, blues, funk, bossa nova & lounge music — along with other music projects. Find out more by visiting:
https://www.klovelacemusic.com/music

Diane A. Hadac is an Active Member of the Mystery Writers of America and a former advertising copywriter. She's also a fan of Golden Age cozy mysteries, admiring the skill and time-consuming effort required to construct them. Her credits include, *The Secret*, Mystery Magazine, March 2022; *Kegler Killer,* Black Coffee Anthology, 2016; *The First White House Costume Ball and Other Trumpery,* We've Been Trumped! Anthology, 2016; *Golf Widow,* 3rd Place Winner, Arizona Mystery Writers Short Story Competition, 2014; *Arthur's Indiscretion*, (under Philomena Benedetto), Strand Magazine First Issue, 1998.

Wil A. Emerson has been on the writing path for approximately 15 years. While not fresh out of college to write the Best Seller, she spent her early years as a Registered Nurse. Now on the fringe of being overlooked due to the inconvenient late start, she's successfully published in anthologies and has one novel under her belt. *Taking Rosie's Arm*, a Five Star, Thorndike publication, recounts the story of an elderly woman who befriends a troubled, but determined young girl. Writer, artist, traveler, cook: soup's on.

Wil's recent work is mainly mystery and women's fiction, and she has appeared in the following *Crimeucopia* anthologies: *Careless Love*, with her piece, *The Driver* — followed by the 'second installment' *The Road to Reconciliation* in *Crimeucopia — Crank It Up!* Her latest, Cracker Jacks and Granny Cases

Also a struggling artist, her art can be viewed on her website. *www.wilemerson.com*

Ed Teja is a lifelong storyteller, as well as a martial artist, former Caribbean boat bum, blues musician, and magazine editor. His stories blend and crisscross crime and speculative fiction and the strange situations and people often come from his somewhat surreal life. Ed's *Crimeucopia* debut is in *Crank It Up!*

For more information and news, go to www.edteja.com

Harris Coverley has more than ninety short stories published or forthcoming in *Penumbra, Hypnos, JOURN-E,* and *The Black Beacon Book of Horror* (Black Beacon Books), amongst many other places. A former *Rhysling* nominee, he has also had over two hundred poems published in journals around the world, and his *If You Can Smell it, You're Probably Already in It* appears in *Crimeucopia — Rule Britannia, Britannia Waves the Rules*. He lives in Manchester, England.

Don't You Never Look Inside the Mojo Bag...
...'Cos it got the juju! An' that is hot stuff...

However, it's true to say that all the wordsmiths contained within the covers of this Crimeucopia, have been looking inside all sorts of Mojo bags, and are more than willing to recount what it is they've seen.

So sit back, relax, and let:

Anthony Kane Evans, Carlos Ramet, Tristan J. Deehan, Christopher Deliso, Tucker Struyk, Ed Teja, Gene Kendall, Hal Dygert, Ian Blackwell, L.C. Adams, Patrick Ambrose, Kamal Mouhoune, Rand Gaynor, Rob Loughran,
and *Edward St. Boniface*

take you on guided tours around their worlds—going from Cosy Country to Noir Central, and back again, provided you booked a return ticket that is.

Because we hope that, whenever and wherever these authors take you, you'll find something that you immediately like, as well as something that takes you out of your GPS and Timezone monitored comfort zones—and puts you into a completely new one.

Because, in the Random Shuffle spirit of our Murderous Ink Press motto:
You never know what you like until you read it.

Paperback ISBN: 9781909498648 — eBook ISBN: 9781909498655

CRIMEUCOPIA
Chicka-Chicka Boomba!

FEATURING:
Nina Mansfield
Vera Brook
donalee Moulton
Jill Hand
Stormy White
N. M. Cedeño
Maroula Blades
Mary Jo Rabe
Denise Johnson
Christina Hoag
Marie Anderson
Heather C. Morris
Wendy Harrison
Ruth Morgan
Diane Arrelle
Issy Jinarmo
Lyn Fraser
Kimberly Scott
and
Carol Goodman Kaufman

It would be hard to pinpoint exactly when Crimeucopia moved from being a 'scratch project title' and became a masthead—but it seemed to match our idea of presenting as wide a spectrum of Crime fiction genres as we could.

From there it was probably *Fate* which brought together the Aly Fell base artwork, and the 16 contributors who went on to become the initial Countesses of Crime, and appeared in Crimeucopia—The Lady Thrillers.

4 years down the proverbial publishing line, we felt it was time to celebrate the anniversary with another all-women anthology—and let these 19 Countesses of Crime tell it like it is, was, or could have been....

Because, in the eclectic, off-centred spirit of our Murderous Ink Press motto: You never know what you like until you read it.

Paperback Edition ISBN: 9781909498662 — eBook Edition ISBN: 9781909498679

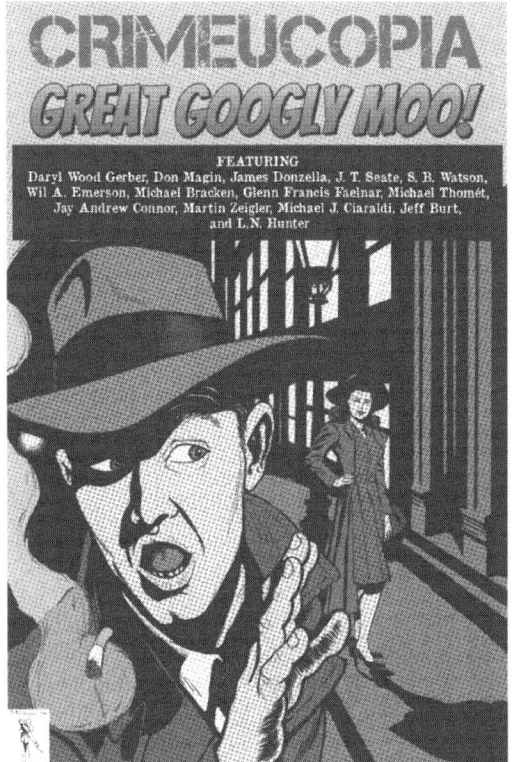

I Remember the Dame Well...

Mainly as she had a laugh that reminded me of two cheese graters energetically fornicating in an iron bathtub. I looked out the open window at the Johnson Memorial, standing upright and resolute in the persistent rain. The clock on it said it was 3:15 in the a.m. and I figured, what-the-Hell, it was time to review the 14 case files scattered across my desk.

I glanced back out across the skyline and wondered: *Why is it* always *raining in Noir City?* I got up and moved over to the chess board. I hadn't see the cat in several hours, so I rearranged the pieces a little to give myself a bit of an advantage...

As with all of these anthologies, we hope you'll detect something that you immediately like, as well as something that takes you out of your investigative comfort zone — and puts you into a completely new one.

Because, in the spirit of our Murderous Ink Press motto:

You never know what you like until you discover it.

Paperback ISBN: 9781909498624 eBook ISBN: 9781909498631

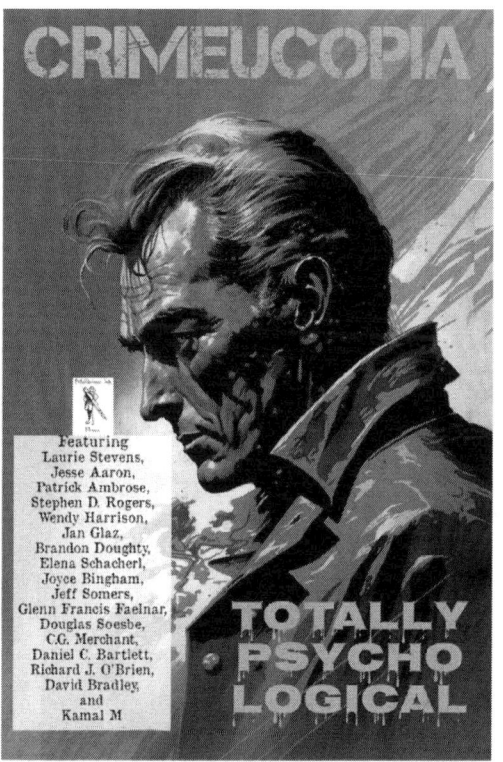

Totally — **adverb:** completely; absolutely. Used to emphasize a clause or statement. "He/She is totally bat-shit crazy!"

Psycho — **noun:** an unstable and aggressive person. "Don't you know? My ex is a total psycho!" — **adjective:** exhibiting unstable and aggressive behaviour "There's some kind of psycho nut job on the loose out there!"

Logical — **adjective:** characterised by or capable of clear, sound reasoning. "His/Her logical mind? Are you nuts or something?"

But are all psychos 'nut jobs'?

Laurie Stevens, Jesse Aaron, Patrick Ambrose, Stephen D. Rogers, Wendy Harrison, Jan Glaz, Brandon Doughty, Elena Schacherl, Joyce Bingham, Jeff Somers, Glenn Francis Faelnar, Douglas Soesbe, C.G. Merchant, Daniel C. Bartlett, Richard J. O'Brien, David Bradley, and Kamal M present 17 cases for the defence.

Paperback 9781909498563 eBook 9781909498570

Made in the USA
Monee, IL
12 September 2025